TULUM TAKEDOWN

A
WHEELS UP
YUCATÁN THRILLER
BOOK 2

TULUM TAKEDOWN

A
WHEELS UP
YUCATÁN THRILLER
BOOK 2

JEANINE KITCHEL

To request permission to reproduce selections from this book, contact Jeanine Kitchel at info@jeaninekitchel.com

Published by Jeanine Kitchel

ISBN: 978-0-578-63014-4 (paperback)
ISBN: 978-0-578-63013-7 (ebook)
Library of Congress Control Number: 2020901693

Jill Wyatt Logan's artwork *Palm Boat with Blue Shadows* has been adapted for the front cover, jilllogan.com
Cover graphic design by Damonza.com
Interior book design by ebooklaunch.com

Printed and bound in the USA

First edition

Author website: www.jeaninekitchel.com

Disclaimer: This is a work of fiction. All of the names, characters, organizations, places, incidents, events, and dialogue in this novel are either products of the author's imagination or are used fictitiously. Any resemblance to actual events, locales, or persons, living or dead, is entirely coincidental.

This book is dedicated to the journalists of Mexico, who put their lives at risk every time they add a byline to a story.

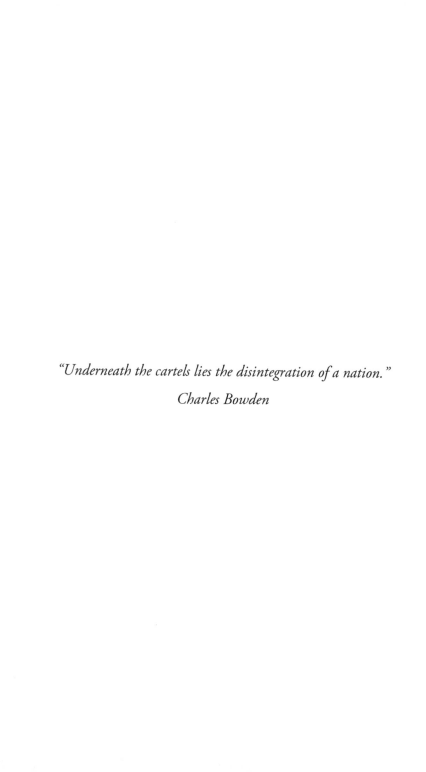

"Underneath the cartels lies the disintegration of a nation."
Charles Bowden

CHAPTER 1

Mexico City (CDMX)
Present Day

L ayla stared at the menacing inch-high headlines in the *Mexico City News* that shouted, "We Do Not Want More Deaths." Beneath the lead, the sub-heading read, "An Open Letter to the Cartels." It was signed by the publisher and a list of staff reporters.

Holed up in a Mexico City hotel, hiding out after assassinating Guatemalan capo Don Guillermo in the Yucatán, Layla's nerves were already shattered. Couldn't she go one single day without hearing that word—cartels? Whoever heard of an open letter to the cartels? All this before her morning coffee. Where was room service? Was this a five-star hotel or some knock-off wannabe?

She marched to the phone, rang room service, and demanded the order she'd placed the previous evening. Pronto! A short robe swung just above her knees as she flipped dark hair over one shoulder before plunking down on the sofa in her suite at the Hotel Excelencia. She leaned back, leaving the paper untouched, still unready to digest the diatribe against those to whom she owed her allegiance. Like her imprisoned drug-lord uncle, El Patrón.

It was bad enough being without Carlos, her body-guard and lover, dead in a plane crash in the Yucatán during a mucked-up coke deal she'd entered into with dealer Clay Lasalle. Less than a week ago in the dead of night, she and Clay had escaped to Mexico City hours after Guillermo's murder. Every single day she woke from nightmares to the gut-wrenching reality that she'd shot and killed the Guatemalan kingpin. Asleep or awake, the memory haunted her.

Especially since El Zoyo, El Patrón's first lieutenant and lifelong friend, had been Don Guillermo's business associate and—apparently—his accomplice, in a shady deal to reap big bucks from trafficking young girls as sex slaves. By keeping the unsanctioned dealings secret, Zoyo retained all his sex trade profits and discredited her uncle.

The Culiacan Cartel—actually all Mexican cartels—had been in an uproar ever since the severe message Layla'd sent by killing Guillermo. Her *take no prisoners* attitude had placed a proverbial notch on her belt, proving a young señorita could kill like a man. Of course Zoyo—after being grilled over the phone by Patrón, and in person by her brother Martín, along with others from the inner circle—had scoffed off all wrong-doing. He also denied stealing two tons of coke Layla and Clay were flying in when their plane, after being denied a landing at Cancun International, crashed in the jungle. The contraband had mysteriously disappeared.

For the time being, a dangerous game of "he said, she said" was being played, and Zoyo had as many believers on his side as she did on hers. If she didn't tread carefully, she could end up in a ditch with two bullets to the head.

Layla sighed and glanced out the hotel window overlooking the treetops of a lush city park. Martín's choice in hotels, the Excelencia, was perfect. Located in an upscale neighborhood where sophisticated lodging, pricey restaurants, and trendy boutiques were the norm, it was a safe place to catch her breath. Not too showy, no penthouse this time. She needed to stay under the radar to see if they could coax Zoyo to reveal his true colors.

She felt nervous without Carlos or Clay. Clay had stayed around for a while after their stealthy getaway, but business dealings called him back to Canada where he was putting together a deal to make up for what they'd lost after the crash. Now with him gone, she was beginning to miss his company.

Jitters or not, she best get used to it. She had to rebuild what was left of her life, lover or no. And it would be up to Martín, her last surviving sibling, to handle details with Patrón, their uncle, as he ran the country's most powerful cartel from behind prison walls, while she sat on the sidelines.

"Lay low for now, hermana," Martín had insisted the day after she departed from the Yucatán.

"But I feel useless," Layla said. "I'm not pulling my weight."

"Zoyo's already come out swinging and Guillermo's not even in the ground. He's extremely pissed that you're contradicting him. He's dangerous. And don't forget, you're coming off life's two curses—death and destruction."

Truer words were never spoken. Carlos was dead and she'd murdered Guillermo. Out of six players—if one included the poor sex-trafficked child Lupita, killed by Guillermo—she and Clay were the last narcos standing.

The plane crash took the life of the co-pilot, and their pilot, Donavon, was murdered by Guillermo's death squad days later.

She gazed at the newspaper, her only connection to the outside world. Any internet surfing would need to be done from an anonymous computer café. She could take no chance of being located by the triangulation of Google or the long arms of El Zoyo. Layla paged quickly through section one to see if there was any news of the Yucatán killing. Nothing. Politics and the upcoming elections, a visit from Brazil's foreign ambassador, rising oil prices. She flipped back to the front page, ready to digest the bizarre announcement from the newspaper's publisher.

Her focus shifted again to the plea: "To Those in Charge: You are, at present, the de facto authorities in this city because the legal institutions have not been able to keep our colleagues from dying. We do not want more deaths. We do not want more injuries. Tell us, then, what do you expect of us as a medium? This is not a surrender ..."

A knock at the door made her jump. She regained her composure, walked over, and peeked through the eyehole. "Hola?"

"Room service."

She appraised the microscopic scene. An indigenous young man stood waiting with a room service cart. Hijole! Being without a bodyguard had given her a bad case of nerves.

"Ándale," Layla said, swinging open the door. Once the attendant entered, she quickly shut the door behind him.

"Buenos dias, señora," the man said. A smile lit his face on meeting the dark-haired Latina, who moved across the room with the calm assurance of a woman who knew she was beautiful. "Your order."

"Gracias. Place it over there," Layla said, pointing to an arty glass and granite block table.

The server did the narca's bidding, lifted the silver compartments off the plates, and began to arrange the food and silver coffee pot in a welcoming display.

Layla picked up the paper and pointed at the headlines. "What is this?"

The server looked first at Layla's disturbed expression. Her striking face had turned apprehensive as she swept her dark hair off her brow. He next turned his eyes to the headlines.

"Can you read?" Layla demanded, hand on her hip.

He nodded, slowly acknowledging the meaning that was written clear as the ink on the page in front of him.

"What does it mean?" Her charcoal eyes bored into him without a glimmer of kindness. They were nearly eye to eye.

He shot a glance at Layla, then became preoccupied with his shoes. "Cartels."

"Of course it's the cartels!" Layla snorted. "But what have they done to cause this reaction from the *Mexico City News*?"

"You don't know?"

"If I knew I wouldn't be asking you!"

"The cartels murdered another journalist yesterday. Alfredo 'Fredo' Martinez. He was very popular, the father of Mexican news, El Viejo."

"What happened?"

"He was leaving the office when they fired at him, about fifteen shots. Two bystanders got hit, too."

She shook her head. "What had he written?"

"Oh, he was always going after them. About corruption, payoffs, money laundering ..."

"Okay." She cut him off and went for her purse, pulling out a fifty peso note. "Thank you," she said, handing him the tip and motioning to the door with a disdainful wave.

After he left she sat at the table, pausing to look at the paper. She knew the Culiacan Cartel wasn't responsible. Mexico City wasn't their territory. New Guaymas Generation? Well, this wasn't her concern.

She dove into her breakfast, savoring the fruit while appreciating the jolt of hot coffee. Time to shower. She'd let the water wash away her fears before she got on with the day. Her plan included a haircut along with shopping and finding an internet café.

After showering, Layla unfolded the newspaper that lay on the couch. She shook her head as she re-read the troubling message. Sides had been drawn. Everything was out in the open. A new play in an old game.

᠊᠊᠊

Her phone rang just as she was heading for the door.

She grabbed it and heard a rough bark. "Layla! It's Martín. You gotta leave Mexico City. Zoyo knows you're there."

"How?"

"Not sure, but," he paused before saying, "José is dead."

A sob escaped. She pictured José and Alfonso, her getaway guys in Merida. "What happened?" She quickly moved to the sofa and sank into it.

"He and Alfonso were doing a regular run, a pick-up from Guadalajara plaza. After leaving they were ambushed. Could have been New Guaymas, but not sure. Alfonso took a hit in the arm but he'll be okay. He jumped from the car when they started taking fire, rode it out in a ditch on the side of the road. Broke a leg, too. They never came back to look for him. Just lucky. José was driving and they pursued him. He didn't have a chance."

First Carlos, now José? "Oh, Martín! No!" Her shoulders folded in as she began to cry.

He waited a moment before he spoke. "Hermana, I'm sorry, so sorry."

"Oh, Martín." Her voice was raspy. She was having trouble speaking. "What is going on? Why are people dying all around us?"

Martín didn't immediately answer. They both knew the stakes. People in their line of work, especially the lower ranks, rarely lasted five years. Alfonso and José, until now, had beaten the odds. As her uncle said, someone always wants what you have. They will make your life miserable if you're a rival, especially a successful one.

"Patrón's in prison. Things are changing," Martín said.

The two of them were vulnerable and so were the people who worked for them. Rivals wanted in on the lucrative trade routes to the United States her uncle had carved out over twenty years ago. With Patrón behind bars, they looked like an easy target, and with de facto head Layla on the run and afraid to show her pretty face, even more so.

"He was a good man, José," her brother continued.

"The best." She thought back to their time in the Yucatán, planning the attack on Guillermo. How ready and able both he and Alfonso had been. "How's Alfonso taking it?"

"He feels guilty as hell."

"He couldn't have stopped an ambush."

"You know Alfonso usually drives," Martín said. "He was riding shotgun. Not up to par."

She well remembered their getaway, Alfonso driving, pushing at breakneck speed for the Merida-Cancun highway. Alfonso was always at the wheel.

"Chinga, Martín. How's his arm?"

"Doing okay. He'll make it. Lucky it's not his shooting arm. The leg thing's tricky, but he's tough, even though he doesn't look it with that round baby face. Once he stops hobbling around we'll get him set up with you. Now, about you leaving. Where to?"

"Hmm. Listen, I was just heading out the door. I'm going to get a haircut to change my look, buy some clothes, get a new burner. It's a big city, Martín."

"It's not safe to stay there or come back to Sinaloa. Not yet," her brother warned.

"Let me think about it. I'll get back to you soon, okay?"

"Okay. Ciao, hermana," Martín said, signing off.

CHAPTER 2

A short while later Layla found herself on the upscale streets of one of Mexico City's finest neighborhoods. She located a beauty salon and an hour later, her hair fell in a long shag just above the shoulders. She walked through the neighborhood, crammed with small boutiques, perfumeries, and eclectic shops. For a full transformation she needed a change from the clothes she'd been wearing since the crash. She walked in one designer shop and out another. Before she knew it, she had accumulated some shopping bags, and was dressed in a navy pencil skirt with a soft, cream-colored voile blouse. On passing a store window she appraised her haircut in the reflection. In a matter of hours she had remade herself. She could be any other wealthy Mexico City matron, out for a day of shopping. Even her own image of herself as a narca had vanished. Time for a glass of wine and a mid-day meal in one of the city's better restaurants—a good place to contemplate her next landing spot. She wandered into the lobby of an old established standard.

"Table for one?" an elegant maître d' who could have passed for a male model asked, as she walked up to the dais where he stood next to a credenza.

"Please."

He led her to a corner table, handing over a menu with a flourish. The lunch crowd was leaving and it appeared she would have the dining room to herself with the exception of a well-dressed woman a table away. Too close for comfort, but that's how it always was. The waiter came. She ordered lunch and a glass of white wine. He soon returned with her beverage. Though the woman at the next table was staring at her, Layla pretended not to notice. She first conspicuously swirled the wine, and next stuck her nose in the glass as she'd been taught by her uncle.

"Excuse me, señora?"

"Yes?" Layla gave a stiff response. Couldn't she even have lunch without being pestered? The woman looked harmless, but she could do without the inconvenience of small talk.

"Your bracelets. Beautiful. May I take a closer look?"

Layla stared hard at the woman. No one spoke to anyone here.

She regained her composure. "Of course," she said and jangled them a bit.

"Oh, sorry," the interloper said, picking up on Layla's vibe. "Am I disturbing you?"

Layla gave a tight smile. "No. It's fine."

The woman materialized next to her, pulled out a chair and took a seat. The nerve!

"They're gorgeous! Where did you get them?"

"At a boutique down the street."

"I love bracelets. These," she said, touching her arm, "were a gift from an artist friend."

Layla commented on the style. "Very nice. That blue is different."

10

"It's the artist's trademark. She's going through a color phase. Everything is cobalt."

"Hmm. I don't know much about art."

"She has an opening tonight. I'm sure she wouldn't mind another guest. It's around the corner. Galeria La Musa."

"I'm here on business and have meetings that run into the evening, but thank you. Oh, here comes lunch. I'm famished," she said.

"Of course. Well, sorry to disturb you but I had to ask about your bracelets. By the way, my name is Yolanda."

"Layla, and the pleasure is mine."

As the waiter moved closer, her neighbor departed to her table. "Think about the opening," Yolanda said over her shoulder.

"Gracias," Layla said, doling out another small smile as she remembered her manners. And lunch was served.

ﭪﭪﭪ

After lunch Layla wandered aimlessly through neighborhood parks before taking a taxi to an electronics store where she picked up a new burner. Back at the hotel, she turned on the TV and immersed herself in mindless game shows to take her mind off Martín's call pressing for a sudden change to her living arrangements. It was only eight and she was far from tired and a little bored. She remembered the woman in the restaurant describing the gallery exhibition and stood up to admire her new haircut in the mirror. Maybe she'd step out. She was going stir crazy. How many telenovelas could a person watch? Time to change the channel.

ﭪﭪﭪ

Layla's taxi dropped her in front of Galeria La Musa. No doubt an event was happening. Sky-high windows were aglow in soft-colored LEDs exposing silhouettes of muses and fairies, heads cocked towards the heavens. She paid the taxista and stepped onto the curb.

Her Gucci sheath, black brushed silk with a light gold weave running throughout, felt and looked as expensive as it was. The low-cut bodice revealed just enough cleavage to give pause to anyone looking her way. With her well-proportioned five-foot-six figure and a casual air of entitlement, Layla exuded sexy charm; she could wear jeans and a T-shirt and still look chic.

At the entrance a doorman dressed in a cobalt blue uniform with epaulets at the shoulders opened the wide mahogany door that was covered in carved flowers, stems brushed with gold leaf. Up a short stairway, a grand entry was sprinkled with event-goers, champagne glasses in hand. Layla surveyed the crowd, all as well dressed as she.

Layla welcomed the anonymity of CDMX, one of the world's largest cities. Yes, she loved Culiacan, her hometown, headquarters to the Culiacan Cartel and rumored to be the wealthiest city in Mexico, but it couldn't compare to Mexico City's vibe with its cosmopolitan edge, intellectual flair, architectural beauty and art.

At the top of the next set of stairs stood another uniformed cadet, a leggy twenty- something with black hair pulled back into a sleek ponytail. She also wore cobalt blue and held a silver tray in a white-gloved hand, the other positioned behind her back. She offered Layla champagne.

With glass in hand, Layla freely wandered the gallery and gazed at walls hung with artwork, mostly oils in vibrant colors, mural-like compositions in the style of Rivera or

Orozco—brash and brilliant. The dramatically oversized paintings gave her pause, and as a neophyte to the art scene, she curiously watched art-goers discuss the paintings on display. Layla moved to the next room and noticed it was painted entirely in cobalt blue. Hadn't the woman she'd met earlier mentioned something about the artist's color obsession?

She felt a slight tug on her elbow. She turned and faced Yolanda.

"So glad you decided to come! Have you seen the jewelry exhibit?"

"No," Layla said with a slight shake of her head, still adjusting to her haircut. "I just arrived. Quite a showplace."

"I thought you'd like it. Come join me. I was talking to some friends."

Layla followed Yolanda to a mixed group of men and women who were listening intently to a petite, dynamic woman standing dead center. Layla faded back as she eavesdropped on the conversation.

"He was coming out of the office, another long work day," the animated woman, who was dressed in a gray linen pant suit, said. "They mowed him down like a dog in the street."

That got Layla's attention. Were they talking about the journalist?

"What had he done?" one of the men asked.

"Oh, please, Javier! What hadn't he done or written about those savages? He never let it rest. Do you know how many death threats he'd had over the years? Six! Can you imagine living your life, going to work, not knowing if you'd make it out of the building alive? Even inside isn't safe! Remember Monterrey!"

Everyone nodded. Who could forget the cartel's boldness when they'd stormed past a security guard at *El Universal de Monterrey*, killing the guard, receptionist, and two journalists, over an ambiguous news story. One person survived by hiding under a desk.

"Whose idea was it to run it?"

"Augusto's of course," the speaker said. "As publisher, he calls the shots. I think it was clever. What else can be done, except to try to appease them? The police and government are no help."

Again, everyone nodded, no doubt thinking their own thoughts on the death and destruction that had come not only to those involved in cartel business, but to those who merely put pen to paper and wrote about it. Now journalists were as at risk as the poor musicians who wrote the narco-corrido songs lauding the lives and exploits of the despots. If a cartel capo didn't like a song composed about him, he killed the singer. Musicians' deaths were collateral damage in a country ravaged by drug-related violence.

"It's easy to kill a journalist in Mexico," the reporter said, her shiny hair pulled back in a sophisticated chignon. Her charisma was palpable and her appealing face came alive with the anger that burned inside her. "They killed a hundred and twenty-five of us since 2000—that are known. Twenty-five have disappeared. How many federal investigations? Eight! Convictions—one. It's laughable. At times the government puts out a statement hours after a journalist is found dead, that the killing had nothing to do with their work, before the investigation even begins."

"Can't someone do something?" a fellow party-goer asked.

"Hmmph. Who? The president? He's too busy coiffing his hair for his next TV close-up."

Someone snickered.

"Veracruz, Sinaloa, Guerrero, Monterrey, Quintana Roo, Tamaulipas. Mexico is the most dangerous country in the western hemisphere to be a journalist. And if we're not threatened by cartels, we're stalked by the government. They're the worst. Crime and corruption—destroying the country's freedom of press. No one is brought to justice. We're living in a moment when it's dangerous to tell the truth."

Layla, standing a slight distance from the crowd, nudged Yolanda. "Who is she?"

Yolanda leaned in. "Alma Reyes. The only woman reporter for the *News*. She was kidnapped out of her apartment last year, with her bodyguard. Men pretending to be federal agents closed off an entire city block searching for her in a manhunt, going from apartment to apartment. They put her in a car trunk. She survived, but her bodyguard was murdered."

Layla digested the info and pivoted. "I think I read her this morning. The elections?"

"Yes, she writes politics but that's not what got her noticed."

"What does she write?"

"Now, about corruption of officials in Cancun and the sex industry."

"But we're in Mexico City," Layla said.

Yolanda gave her a look just short of an eye roll. "Corruption has long arms."

"Oh," Alma continued, "and we're not allowed to use certain words, like shootout, kidnapping, or execution. But look at us. We're nerdy and near-sighted. We wear glasses, not holsters. How can we compete with assault rifles and snipers? We already censor seventy percent of what we write—to stay alive! We're no match."

"Go get 'em, Alma!" someone from the circle said loudly.

Another guest chimed in. "You give us someone to believe in. You're very brave."

Alma sighed and gazed at the group surrounding her. She smiled wanly and, in a voice just above a whisper, said, "If you'll excuse me, I need to find the ladies' room."

Her departure was swift, and the group began to disperse. Layla touched Yolanda's arm.

"I'm stunned," she said. "How can it be, corruption at the highest levels?"

"She was targeted by the chief of police of the government," Yolanda lowered her voice to a whisper. "They're in bed with the Culiacan Cartel."

At hearing the name of her organization, Layla stifled a shudder and wondered if coming to the opening had been such a good idea. She nearly ran the other way rather than stay to hear what Yolanda was about to reveal.

"She says the man who runs the cartel is nearly illiterate, but he's a strategic genius and with the backing of the government, they've given him protection to fight off other cartels to assure his success. In exchange, he gives them a percent of the operation." She paused before whispering, "Even the president. He was bought off for a hundred million. Dollars, not pesos. It's no wonder they want her dead."

Layla stared at Yolanda, barely comprehending what the outside world said about who she was related to, worked for, and fully supported.

Stalling for time, Layla blurted out, "But how can that be?"

"If Alma wrote it, it's true," Yolanda said. "She has no reason to lie. That's why everyone loves her. She reports the news, and the news here is ugly, horrible. It's worse in Tamaulipas. They sent a severed head in an ice cooler and left it in the newspaper parking lot as a warning. For reporters, it's become a choice—silence or death."

Layla gave a brief nod as she choked down a burp. Somehow she suppressed the impulse to hurl the contents of the lunch she'd digested hours earlier. "I need to find the ladies' room."

"It's through that door," Yolanda said, pointing the way. "Past the bar."

Layla adjusted the tie on her dress and tried to compose herself as she headed to the restroom. Walking past the bar, she saw Alma Reyes standing alone looking lost in thought, her eyes focused on a half-empty glass of something amber and toxic.

Taking a detour before the ladies' room, Layla walked up beside her. "Excuse me."

Alma looked warily at Layla. "Do I know you?"

"Oh, no, sorry, you don't. Layla. I overheard what you were saying about the paper and your friend's death. I'm so sorry."

Suspicious, Alma looked Layla over and clearly gave her a pass. "Thank you," she said, the whiff of a grudge still underlying her tone. "Sometimes I can't help myself."

"Of course. What the paper did was a bold move."

17

"It's our last gasp," she muttered, more to her glass than to the woman beside her.

"Pardon me?"

"Our last chance. We already censor ourselves—and still they come for us. We can't take more chances on losing lives. With Alfredo gone, we're down to six. Nothing for a paper our size."

"Do you have bodyguards?" Layla asked.

"Of course," Alma said dismissively. She nodded to the short bulky man with Aztec features standing in a corner near the restroom doorway.

"Good. He looks like he can keep you safe," Layla said, realizing he could have been her getaway guy José's double.

The reporter let out another heavy sigh. "But he couldn't save my niece."

"What?"

"He couldn't save Silvia," she stammered. "My niece. She's gone missing . Sometimes they come after the people you love if you're too well protected."

"Who?"

"The cartels. Who else? The police won't even begin to look for her until tomorrow, after she's been missing forty-eight hours. She hasn't called, and that's not like her."

"Where could she have gone?"

"Tulum. She has a new boyfriend, not a very nice boyfriend in my opinion, but a good-looking talker. Attorney," she said, swirling the ice in her glass.

"What's happening in Tulum?"

"He has business in Cancun and took her with him. They went there a few weeks ago. Afterwards he said they'd do a Tulum vacation for beach time. I don't trust him."

"Surely you can get through on his cell," Layla said.

"No answer on either his or hers. I'm afraid," Alma said. She started to shake as if a chill breeze had just blown through the room. "I'm afraid of what might have happened to her."

She was falling apart. Having been there herself, Layla recognized the symptoms. "Excuse me. This may sound forward because I've just met you, but I might be able to help if the police won't. I know someone who does private investigations. He's good."

Where did that come from? She didn't know this woman. What part of her uncle's stern warning on assisting others, "Stick your neck out for no one," had she not understood?

The reporter glanced up from her drink and verbalized Layla's thoughts, like she'd stepped inside her mind. The shaking was gone, replaced by a chip on the shoulder. "Why would you help me? I don't know you."

That gave Layla pause. When even the recipient of a good deed is skeptical about your aims, maybe it's time to back off. Why *was* she going out on a limb for this woman? Was she starstruck? Or feeling guilty about poor dead Lupita from Guatemala, attempting to right that wrong by helping someone else save *their* lost girl? Dammit! Without Carlos she was a ship without a rudder. If he'd been around she wouldn't even be at this crazy reception. Hold it. No feeling sorry for past events that were impossible to reverse. She had to get her shit together. A little late now—the horse was out of the barn.

"But everyone feels they know you, because of the work you do," she heard herself say from some far-off place. "I feel I know you."

She did. It wasn't a lie. Layla felt an odd connection with the reporter even though they'd just met. Maybe she *was* losing it. Alma gave the hint of a sarcastic smile. With journalism, everyone was either your fast friend or worst enemy. The reporter went into the zone for a long moment. Layla could almost hear her mind working as she pondered the situation, trying to not look discouraged when opportunity might be knocking.

"Okay, okay. If I don't hear anything from the police by tomorrow we can meet. Call me." She scribbled a number on a cocktail napkin and handed it to Layla.

"Gracias. Maybe I can help," Layla said as she took the napkin and glanced at the number. "Hasta mañana."

Alma nodded, picked up her slim purse, and pushed away from the bar, a defeated warrior. She walked towards the main gallery. Layla watched her leave, bodyguard trailing behind.

CHAPTER 3

The next day Layla called Alma around noon. The reporter picked up on the third ring.

"Layla, from last night. We were talking at the bar."

"Si, si. Como esta?" she asked in a brisk tone.

"I meant what I said, about knowing a private investigator who may be able to help you."

Alma let out a sigh, then it was back to business. "Oh, forgive me. I shouldn't have been so direct. I think the alcohol was talking. I appreciate your call, but I must get back to work."

"Wait, wait!" Layla said. "I can help you. Let's at least meet and discuss the situation."

There was a pause. For a moment Layla thought she'd lost the connection. "Hola. Hola?"

Finally, she heard, "How can you help me?" The tone was one of distrust, resignation. "Today the police said they'll open an investigation, but everyone knows their shameful record for solving kidnapping cases. How can anyone help me?"

"Alma, I know people. Believe me, I have contacts and they're not in the government, so no worries there." That was an understatement.

"Who do you know?" Alma asked.

"I'd rather not say over the phone, but if you want to meet, I can lay it out for you."

The thought, the hope, had been dangled before her like a fishing line with fresh bait. The clock was ticking. With kidnapping, every hour, every minute, counted.

"Okay. My apartment, five p.m. My bodyguard will meet you in the lobby." She gave Layla the address.

"Gracias, hasta luego."

೫ ௫ ௫

The taxi dropped Layla in front of a baroque colonial building in a neighborhood not far from the hotel. She called from the street. Alma picked up on the first ring.

"It's Layla."

"I'll send Ricardo down."

In a few minutes the bodyguard from the previous evening lumbered into the lobby.

"Ándale," he said, ushering her in. "Ricardo."

He led her to an antique elevator. They rode up to the fifth floor in silence. The doors opened onto a hallway with parquet floors and avocado green walls. He motioned for Layla to exit, and they walked to the end of the hall, a corner apartment. He knocked quickly, three times.

A few moments later Alma Reyes opened the door. She was casually dressed in jeans and a loose salmon colored tunic over a V-neck T-shirt. On her feet she wore tan leather sandals with thin straps. She looked both alert and relaxed, different than her persona from the previous evening. She appeared smaller, more delicate.

"How nice that you have come," she said with real meaning. "I appreciate it."

Layla smiled. "I'm here to help if I can."

"Let's sit in the sala. Thank you, Ricardo," she said with a nod at the bodyguard. He faded into the background.

"Here, the sofa is comfortable. Can I offer you something to drink? Wine, water, coke?"

"Coke."

She came back with two refrescos, setting one in front of Layla on a wide mahogany coffee table after she cleared a stack of papers next to a laptop.

"How unusual. I meet a stranger at a gallery who may be able to mysteriously help me materialize my missing niece." Alma's tone was candid, if a bit wary.

"I call it serendipity. There really is no such thing as coincidence, right?"

"Hmm. A philosopher."

Layla was dressed casually, but not in simple street clothes. She too wore designer jeans, but her mauve Valentino blouse screamed fashionista as did an Armani jacket in dark purple.

Suspicion crept into the reporter's tone. "So who are you?"

"I work with my uncle's organization throughout Mexico. He's incapacitated at the moment, can't get around very well, and though I've usually managed the accounting, at present I'm busy handling his position. It's a role I'm not very familiar with. He works in chemicals. He's freelance and can get whatever's needed for big pharma—here, the EU or in the US—through suppliers he's groomed for decades. Tosca Industries."

She recited the name of a shell company they'd set up in the Cayman Islands, to launder money and look officially legal.

"Never heard of it."

"Most people haven't, because unlike pharma and chemical companies, he's merely a supplier."

"Hmm. Well, welcome to DF. Where do you live?"

"Guadalajara," Layla lied.

"How do you know people who are private investigators? That seems very underground."

"I don't have to tell you how Mexico works. Everything is done on age-old promises and handshakes. Sometimes they've gone on for generations. My uncle has always been good at working with people, bringing them together, and he never lets go of a contact once he's worked with them," she explained. Truer words were never spoken.

"It's a two-way street. Even though he's been in the business a while, sometimes chasing down hard-to-find chemicals is tough, so he hires people to sniff out the best locations and prices."

"Then they're not really investigators," Alma said.

"Not precisely, but they're ready and willing to do whatever it takes to get the necessary results," Layla said, looking directly into Alma's eyes. She could stare down a tiger.

Alma shrugged. "A little unconventional, but as you say, it's Mexico." She trailed off, allowing the subject to drop. "How would you go about finding my niece?"

"To start, I'd need to know everything you can tell me—her full name, where she lives. I'll pass this on to my colleague."

"She was staying with me."

Layla raised an eyebrow. "You're very close then."

"Like sisters. She's only twenty-one, my older sister's youngest. I feel devastated and … guilty. She wanted to go into broadcasting. I have contacts. She lived with her mother in Cuernavaca, but it was simpler being here in the heart of the city, not an hour's drive away, for interviews or jobs. I suggested she move in. I have an extra room and it made sense. Or did, until now." Alma frowned and became preoccupied with her refresco.

"Who is the man she's been seeing?"

"Francisco Ramirez. From here. He works at MBC as a finance attorney in their commercial loans department. And my niece's full name is Silvia Ortega Castillo."

"Can I see her room?"

Glad for the distraction, Alma nodded. "Certainly. Follow me."

They walked down the hallway to what looked like an office, but with a hideaway bed.

"It was my office until Silvia came to stay. I'm always at work anyway." She shrugged.

"Did she use the dresser drawer for her clothes?"

"Of course. Do you want to look through them?"

"I think it's a good idea—I may find something."

Layla pulled open the top drawer and saw it was an underwear drawer. The second drawer held tops and shorts, and the bottom was filled with pants and jeans.

"How about the closet?" Layla asked.

She spied a hook on the closet wall towards the back, next to a clothing rack with dresses and skirts. A leather handbag hung on it. "Can I take a look?"

Alma nodded. Layla pulled open the leather drawstrings. Inside she found a coin purse, a napkin, and a matchbook.

"What airline did she fly on?" Layla asked as she rifled through the rest of the purse, finding nothing more of interest.

"Aero Mexico. They were supposed to arrive there two days ago. Day three now."

"Were they staying in Cancun?"

"The first few nights, yes. It was sketchy when they'd head to Tulum. He had meetings."

Layla laid out the items from the purse on the hideaway bed and sat down to sort it out. Finding only a handful of pesos in the coin purse, she turned over the halfway crumpled napkin, the same kind Alma had written her number on the night before.

"This number look familiar to you?"

"Of course not. No one remembers numbers any more with cell phones. Do you?"

Layla shook her head and handed it to Alma. "Any idea of the prefix?"

Alma had a look. "Could be Quintana Roo."

"Home to Tulum. Maybe a hotel number?"

"Seems she'd do a search for hotels online, unless her boyfriend made arrangements."

"True. Has she been there before?"

"Who hasn't been to Cancun?" Alma asked. Realizing her flip response, she softened her tone before continuing. "Yes, we were even there together a couple of years ago. Me, her mother, and Silvia."

"Did you meet anyone when you were there?"

"Well, we did meet up with one of Silvia's friends. Right after graduation, her friend moved to Cancun. She met us in the hotel zone and we all went to the Tulum pyramids for the day. Silvia and her friend stayed over for an extra beach day and spent the night at Analisa y José's. She caught the bus back a day later and her friend stayed on in Tulum."

"Do you remember the friend's name? Is she still there?" Layla asked.

"Are you sure you're not the private investigator?" Alma joked. "You're good."

"In business these days, you have to know what questions to ask," was Layla's dry response. "And time isn't on our side.

"Look at this matchbook," Layla continued. "Azul? With a number written on the back?"

"Oh yes. It's a hip eco-lodge, hard to get reservations. Silvia and her friend went there for drinks. It's very popular. You wait in line at the bar at sunset, to take a selfie in a big hammock overlooking the ocean. She and Francisco stayed there too, a few weeks ago."

"What's her friend's name?" Layla asked again.

Alma paused and considered. "Gabriella."

"If she's still there, she may know where Silvia is. In case she tried to get in touch."

Alma grimaced and looked away from the bed. "It's not much to go on, is it?"

Layla steered the reporter clear of emotions trying to erupt. "Tell me about the boyfriend. You said you didn't like him. Why not?"

"Just a hunch, but he may be laundering money for the cartels."

There was that word again. Layla arched an eyebrow. "What gives you that idea?"

"I've written articles on how the cartels launder cash." Alma continued, "He works for MBC. They've been cooperating with the federales for a long time, but no one has nailed them yet."

"Not new news."

"Someone has to be their laundrymen," Alma said. "How else does that money get into the system? It's not hard to find a corrupt banker, and it's gone global now. But back to Francisco, he isn't only handsome—I'll send you his company website photo—he has money to throw around. A lot of money. My niece is young. She's impressed by that."

"Makes sense." Layla turned the Azul matchbook over in her hand. "Let me copy this number, and this one," she pointed at the cocktail napkin. "I'll make a couple of calls. Do you have a photo of your niece?"

Alma bit her lip. "Hmm. Let me check my phone." She scrolled through the photos. "Here, taken a while back, but it's a good likeness."

She leaned over Layla's shoulder with Silvia's picture, a smiling twenty-one year-old, ready to take on the world. Dark hair parted in the middle, bright sparkling eyes, dimpled cheeks.

"Pretty. Can you send that to my email?" Layla asked. She reached into her purse, still on her shoulder, grabbed a pen and paper, and wrote it down.

She looked at her watch. "It's six. I'm sure you've had a long day. I'll leave and get back to you tomorrow. You heard nothing today from the police?"

Alma gave her a sour look. "No, I'd have told you."

Layla pushed herself up from the bed, and Alma, still standing, looked at her. "What do you think?"

"Tulum's small, a pueblo. People still know their neighbors, what they're doing. I'll call and tell you what I've found out if anything. I'll be leaving for Cancun soon."

"How do I pay you? A retainer?"

"No need. I was planning on taking some time off anyway. I'll only be asking a few questions and seeing if my associates can find anything out for us."

As they prepared to exit the room, Alma touched Layla's arm. "Excuse me, but I have to ask. Why are you helping me? This has nothing to do with you, someone from Guadalajara, a businessperson with—I'm sure—much more pressing issues. Why?"

A flush of emotion caused Layla's cheeks to redden. She felt short of breath, as though two large hands had grabbed her lungs and squeezed, siphoning out all the air. Lupita, a voice whispered in her head. Lupita.

She looked away before facing Alma, tried to stabilize, waiting until she could speak without unleashing an emotional tidal wave. "Let's just say I've been in a similar situation. Not exactly the same, but not so different."

"What happened?" Alma demanded.

"I'd rather not go into it, but it was a young girl I felt very ... close to. She was put in a brutal situation, and even though I tried to help her, I ..." She stumbled for words, finding it hard to admit what she would state now as fact. "I failed."

Why could she not stop thinking of Lupita?

As Layla's face drained of color, Alma said, "I'm so sorry."

Unwilling to show weakness, Layla loudly cleared her throat, a clumsy attempt to throw Alma off track. Reconsidering, she spoke from the heart. "Sometimes do you think life gives you second chances?" she asked, rubbing her index and middle finger back and forth across her forehead as though grappling for the answer to an impossible physics problem.

Ever the realist, Alma's response was composed. "Maybe. Maybe someone somewhere's keeping score. Let's hope so."

Caught off guard by her unexpected emotions, Layla summoned a smile and pulled herself together. Where was this sensitivity coming from? "We'll talk soon."

"Gracias," Alma said as she ushered Layla through the door and into the sala. "Buenos noches. Ricardo will escort you out."

She opened the door and promptly closed it as Layla departed. Layla heard the deadbolt click as she followed the bodyguard back down the hallway.

CHAPTER 4

L ayla awoke in Hotel Excelencia with Silvia on her mind. She stretched, got up and reached for her phone. First call would be to Clay Lasalle. It had been a week since he left.

"Clay?"

"Layla? What a surprise!" The Canadian dealer didn't bother to hide his pleasure.

"How's the reboot going up there? You making progress?"

"Yes, I put together another deal. Trying to locate a pilot …"

There was a moment of silence. No doubt Clay also flashed on the two brothers, pilot and co-pilot, who'd been killed in their coke deal gone bad in the Yucatán.

"How's that working out?" Layla asked.

"Maybe got someone lined up. So, to what do I owe this call?"

"I'm heading to Tulum for a week or so. Wondered if you'd like to join me?"

"Tulum? Any special occasion?"

"Nothing like that," Layla said, the tone of her voice indicating this was no drug deal. "A change of pace … and going to do a favor for a new friend. Help her find her niece."

"Um, say what? As in how?"

"She's gone missing," Layla said.

"Now you're a detective? You switching sides on me?"

"No, well…err… I met this reporter and I just connected with her. Do you ever get those feelings about people? Don't answer." They both laughed.

"I met her at a gallery opening, of all things, and she was talking to a group of friends. I listened in and learned that not only had she herself escaped after being kidnapped, most likely by New Guaymas, but they or someone kidnapped her niece, because since she has a bodyguard, they can't get to her," Layla said.

"Whoa. What can you do about that?"

"I talked to Martín. It's time to leave DF," she said, without divulging that Mexico City was now dangerous. "Think Tulum's the spot. Take some beach time. He told me earlier we have a contact in Cancun that I didn't know about. I'll meet him and see if he can assist. Check around a bit. This woman is special, Clay. She has this passion—for life, for her writing, and especially for her young niece …"

Clay was quiet for a moment. Lupita's presence was strong—another girl gone missing. "Layla, you sure about this? Are you chasing redemption because of Lupita?"

"Clay." Hesitation tinged with displeasure preceded a lengthy pause. Finally, she spat out, "No, it's just something I gotta do. For personal reasons. Everything's not about Lupita."

"Aah, Layla." He paused again. "You know best." For a moment there was merely air on the line, a silent vacuum as they both avoided the elephant in the room. "Back to Tulum. I can't tell if you're a born-risk taker or if it's boredom. You know you're tempting me. It's still cold up here in Vancouver. Now that I have a new deal going, I got cabin fever as we Canucks say. Maybe beach time would be good, after all we've been through."

The conversation went quiet again as they silently weighed in on recent events that had created major havoc for them as well as for a multitude of others.

"Just tell me where and when," Clay continued. "I'll meet you there."

元 囶 囶

Layla's next call was to Martín. "Hola. I figured out my next spot. But first, how serious is the threat from Zoyo?"

"Not sure, but we can't take chances. I talked to Patrón yesterday on his secure line at the prison. Seems Zoyo is throwing a lot of shade your way, saying you're all over the map with the accusations. You know, about the sex trafficking. He's still denying it."

"Of course he'd say that." The very thought of the slime trying to lie his way out of it rankled her. "What's Patrón think?"

"He's worried for your safety. He believes you and he's wary of Zoyo, but what can he do when he's behind bars?"

She nodded absent-mindedly. "True. He's vulnerable. Did you get to any of the inmates?"

"Everything's set up. He has cover while he's inside. Ten men—solid—who'll give their lives to protect him."

"Ojalá," she said with a sigh, though she knew as well as the inmates did what price would be paid if they didn't protect him—their families would be murdered across generations. When you worked with the cartels, the cards were never stacked in your favor.

"And the warden?"

"In our pocket along with a number of guards."

"You've got it under control. Is it hard to handle everything, Martín, with me missing?"

"No, chica. Patrón's just a phone call away, and over the years I picked up as much about the business as you and Reynoldo did."

The mention of their dead brother—the one who should be running the cartel with their uncle behind bars but who had been killed in an ambush—brought another conversation lull.

"All three of us learned a lot," Martín continued easily. "Patrón was a good teacher. So where to?"

"Think I'll take some beach time in Tulum," Layla said.

"Tulum? Is that too close to the whole Guillermo mess? Don't want you jumping from the frying pan into the fire."

"I don't think so. The Riviera Maya is a world away from Merida. Plus I'm anonymous there. It's not Sinaloa. I met a woman here and she has a niece …" She let the sentence dangle. Why was she keeping things from her brother?

His voice took a steely turn. "It's not wise to mix with people you don't know," Martín said. It could have been a tape recording of her dead bodyguard. Carlos had told her time and again to be more cautious now that she was sitting head of the Culiacan Cartel. "Are you sure you're okay with Carlos gone? You going loco?"

"No, no." Just chasing my demons.

"Okay. Gotta ask the big questions. Go, but be careful. You're without a bodyguard. Are you leaving soon?"

"Tomorrow. Do we still have that contact?"

"You mean Jaime? Yeah," Martín said.

"In case I need something."

"I'll get you his number. And listen, Layla. Promise me you'll be careful?"

"Clay might meet up with me." There. She'd blurted it out.

"Hijole, Layla. You don't need a bodyguard. You need a babysitter."

"What?" she demanded, waiting for his response, a hardness in her tone. "Nothing wrong with it. Cut that shit out! You and Reynoldo always taunted me. Screw that! I'm thirty-five and if he was still alive, everything would be different!"

"Listen," Martín cajoled, trying to lighten things up. "Reynoldo's dead and I gotta be both brothers to you now. Can't you see me as Reynoldo?"

She let out the breath she'd been holding in and laughed. Martín's quiet resolve was as far off from her dead brother's swagger as a fox from a rabbit. "Shut up! Stop making me laugh!"

"It's just ... oh, shit. It'll take your mind off things. I'm worried about you with Carlos gone. But Clay, that'll be good. Listen, I'll be in touch and let you know when Alfonso's ready to travel. Get out of there, keep me up on your whereabouts."

"Thanks, Martín," she said, feeling guilty she'd been less than honest with her last surviving sibling. "Ciao."

CHAPTER 5

The burner phone's ring jangled in her ear. What time was it? She checked the clock. Seven. Her flight left at eleven. Still plenty of time to dress and get to the airport.

"Bueno."

"Get going, get going now!" her brother's voice barked.

She sat straight up in bed. "What?"

"You heard me! They've located you. I don't know how, but move it! Avoid the elevator and all open areas."

She threw the phone across the bed, thankful she'd showered and packed the night before. Clothes, clothes, where were her clothes? Coffee was a far-off dream. And safety? Well, maybe that, too.

After throwing water on her face, she scrambled into a travel outfit, still maintaining the Mexico City matron look. She forced herself to remain cool-headed. Being a jumble of nerves would help nothing. It was times like these she missed Carlos, who had been calmness personified. In ten minutes flat she was ready to depart. She edged to the door and warily put eye to keyhole, staring at the microscopic scene down the hallway. She froze. Two bulky, dark-suited men were getting out of the elevator—definitely not hotel employees.

Also exiting the elevator was the room service guy, pushing a lumbering silver cart her way. She stood beside the door, back against the wall, and forced herself to breathe. Four breaths in, four breaths out.

A moment later there was a knock at the door. Damn! Though afraid to open it, necessity made her stare through the keyhole. The kid from room service. She was relieved to see the two suited men had moved towards the far end of the hall. As they became smaller and smaller in her microscopic view, one shot an insignificant backwards glance at the service attendant. She swung the door open and motioned the youth inside before he could announce himself.

"Hurry, hurry," she whispered. "Get in here."

Surprised by her panicky request, he pushed the cart quickly into the suite while she stood behind the door.

"What are you doing here?" she asked.

"Management wanted to make up for yesterday's delay. We're comping you a full breakfast, with coffee."

"Hijole. Those men in the elevator with you ... " she stammered.

He stared at her, wide-eyed. "Yes?"

"Did they say anything?" she asked.

He shook his head. "No."

"I need your help. Pronto."

"Si, señora. Would you like your breakfast on the table?"

"No! Not that! I need to get out of here. Those are bad men—they're after me. They want to hurt me."

He watched her shudder. "But why would they want to hurt you?"

"Don't ask. Will you help me?"

Her testiness from the previous day had been replaced by sheer terror. "Of course. How?"

"The cart. Undo the cart. Put the breakfast there. Fast! Do you have another tablecloth?"

"Yes, we always come prepared for accidents," he said.

"Well, this could be an accident waiting to happen—to me!"

He cringed and pushed the cart to the granite block table. He placed all silver platters on top, leaving the lids in place.

"Now, get me that extra tablecloth and I'll grab my valise and purse," Layla said as she ran from the room.

She returned immediately. "This," she said, placing the valise on top of the cart and covering it with a silver tray and the extra cloth, "will fit here. I'll ride underneath, and you make sure there is no way you can see me. Got it?"

"Señora, you're scaring me. Are you sure you are in danger?"

Her eyes were wide with fear. "Do you remember what I asked you about yesterday?"

His face turned the color of the cloth he'd just retrieved. "Yes."

"Well, I *am*. In danger. Those men are looking for me, but you are going to save me. You will calmly push the cart with me in it out the door. Ready?"

She climbed underneath the five-foot-long service cart. From her subterranean roost she asked, "Are the tablecloths arranged so I can't be seen? What's your name?"

"Manuel."

"Manuel, am I covered?"

Painstakingly he layered the tablecloths, overlapping them, taking special care so there would be no exposure of his cargo. She watched his progress, peeking between the tablecloth folds, and could see him circling the cart. She felt the cart shift as he checked that the tray was firmly in place over her valise.

"You're good," he said. "When do we leave?"

"Check through the eyehole. Where are those men?" Layla asked.

He did her bidding. It took a few seconds before he responded.

"They're at the far end of the hall, talking," he said.

"Just standing there?"

"Yes."

"Okay. Time to leave. Act normal."

꧁꧂꧂

Before moving to the door, Manuel blessed himself. He edged it open, using the service cart for a doorstop, same as he'd done hundreds of times in the past. He chose not to glance towards the far end of the hall. With his stowaway beneath, the cart was heavy, but he put real effort into making it look exactly the same as when he had pushed the cart out of the elevator earlier.

The cart was in the hallway—step one complete. Manuel left it sitting alone while he closed Layla's door, ready for the next leg of their journey. For the first time in memory, the length of hall from Layla's door to the elevators resembled that of a futbol field. Manuel pushed the cart, humming softly in between chanting a stream of prayers to Saint Jude, patron saint of hopeless causes.

Eventually, the lumbering cart reached the elevator. Manuel faced away from the dark-suited men as he pushed

39

the button, calmed by the fact that he heard no noise coming from their direction. Although the intruders paid him no mind, the elevator's response was painfully slow. He was on his fourth recitation of the Twenty-Third Psalm before it arrived.

The familiar ding sounded like music from celestials on high. He dared not look towards the men and willed himself to act normally—just another day in room service at the Hotel Excelencia. But now he was hauling a beautiful Mexicana in the bottom of his cart who was hiding from suspicious meddlers who looked a whole lot like cartel guys.

𝌆 𝌆 𝌆

They arrived at the kitchen after an achingly long trip with the elevator stopping multiple times. Layla made not a peep, and even though she thought she remembered the number of hotel floors, without coffee and an unseemly wake-up call, she was numb to timing. Finally, they reached the ground floor, evidenced by Manuel pushing the cart out of the elevator and the familiar sounds of a working kitchen.

Layla tried to remain composed in spite of the fact that her body had been crammed for fifteen minutes like a crab in its shell. In a stage whisper she called out, "Manuel?"

"Si," he answered.

"Is there a place in the kitchen where I can get out without being seen?"

"Si, señora. Do not worry."

She tried to calm herself, realizing the kid had a head on his shoulders. Plus, thanks to her, he now had skin in the game. If anyone saw her exit his room service cart, who knew what repercussions might come.

She heard him push open the kitchen doors; loud noises surfaced. The cart glided through a medley of tantalizing smells, past sinks with running water and the clanging of pots and pans. Further and further they went into the beating heart of every restaurant, its kitchen. At last he slowed down and paused to open a door. He pushed the cart into a room; it came to a stop.

He spoke softly, "Señora, we are here. Safe."

"Are you sure?" Layla whispered.

"Si, si. It's time to get out."

After a crazy journey of being lodged in a space with her knees shoved to her ears, it took Layla a few moments to be rid of her quarters. She first stuck out a leg, sat on the cart's bottom rung, and pushed out the other leg, glad she'd decided on a pant suit for travel. She grabbed at the top of the cart, while Manuel extended a hand towards hers and gave a pull. She stood. Looking around, she realized they were in a roomy bodega with shelves stocked high with folded linens. Several stuffed hampers, filled with soiled uniforms, awaited laundry service.

"Manuel," she whispered, giving his hand a squeeze. "Gracias."

"Señora, it is okay, but you must leave quickly. Let me get your valise."

Her purse was on her shoulder; she reached inside and pulled out a stack of pesos. "Here," she said, stuffing them into his hand. "I can't thank you enough. Where's the outside door?"

"It's close," he said, as he peeked into the hall. "All clear. You'll exit into an alley. Walk three hundred meters and you'll be at a main avenida where you can catch a taxi."

"Oh, gracias, gracias. What will you tell your jefe if anyone asks?"

"Don't worry, I have it figured out."

Although far from religious, Layla felt a conversion coming on. "Vaya con Dios, Manuel," she said.

She shook his hand and he checked again to see if all was clear. He gave a nod. "To you as well, señora. Á Dios."

And she was gone.

CHAPTER 6

To say Tulum had changed since Layla had last been there was an understatement. How many years had it been? Five, six? She'd been in Cancun with Clay just two weeks earlier and was surprised by the growth and flash, but nothing prepared her for the transformation of Tulum.

It had once been a two-lane road passing through the center of town with a median for parking in the middle, lined with funky hostels, low-key restaurants, and fruit stands. Now tourists swarmed the streets and some of the shops looked downright posh. The road had widened, too, and it was asphalt, no longer hardened gravel. Even the palapas and smooth wall concrete buildings seemed brighter, as if a fresh coat of paint had been applied to the entire pueblo. Tulum—previous outlier and one-time hippie paradise—had a distinctly upscale vibe. Not quite Playa del Carmen, but close. She'd read New York models and artists along with the international crowd—rock musicians, tech billionaires, movie stars —had embraced it. Change was happening and it smelled like money.

After a little internet surfing, Layla had decided to stay at Analisa y José's. Since it was May, low season was upon them and hotels offered rock bottom discounts for longer stays. Analisa y José's was where Silvia and her friend Gabriella had stayed too, when they'd visited Tulum two years earlier. That trail was ice-cold but could be worth checking out.

Layla rode in the taxi she'd picked up from Cancun International. Tulum beach road was at a standstill. What began as a haven for small B and B's and funky restaurants years earlier had grown into wall-to-wall businesses, hotels bordering beach on one side, and shops creeping into the jungle on the other. A carnival-style atmosphere complete with prayer flags and quirky signs was lacking one thing only—barkers. Her destination was at the end of the line.

"Is this normal for weekends?" she asked the taxista.

"Not just weekends. Every day now."

She watched a steady stream of tourists, locals, and shopkeepers wander in and out of standstill traffic. What happened? It used to be a blend of backpacker campgrounds and locals renting out hammocks. About half way down the road she was taken aback by a stretch of chain link fence several lots long, an ugly mark on an otherwise stunning landscape.

"What's that?"

"Oh, problems. They closed fourteen hotels a year ago. Ownership battles."

"Over what?"

"Titles," the driver said, apparently in no hurry to disclose more.

Layla knew when to not pursue a subject and gazed at the man-made ugliness. She'd find out the reason later. At the south end of the sequestered property they passed armed guards, a cross between federales and hired security. She couldn't figure out who they represented, but obviously the cordoned lots were off-limits. On the fence, 'No Pasa' signs were posted every few meters. The effect was like a blemish on a Hollywood starlet's gorgeous face. No matter how hard you tried, you couldn't look away.

After passing Playamar on the beach where she spent vacation time several years earlier, the road wars lessened. Eventually she saw a wooden sign, Analisa y José's, and massive stone walls that surrounded her destination. The once low-key jungle-style entrance had been replaced by an elegant display of Maya stone and art.

"Señor, this is so different from what I remember."

"Aah, si," he said reluctantly. "The two sisters, hurricanes Emily and Wilma, in 2005. They totally changed the land."

"How do you mean?"

"Everything, *everything* on the beach disappeared in the first storm, and Wilma flattened what was left— concrete buildings, walls, houses. Including titles, fidi comisos, leases. It was a clean landscape, ripe and ready to be plucked, or skinned I should say."

"Surely someone must have held clear title," Layla insisted. This was a recurring problem not only in Quintana Roo, home to the Riviera Maya, but in any growing part of Mexico. Add ocean and beach and it upped the ante.

He turned to face her, sitting in the back seat of his Tsuru cab. Though his look was passive she could feel intense emotion when he spoke. "Por supuesto. Como siempre, los politicos and los cartels." As always, the politicians and the cartels.

"No one did anything about it? They stole the land?" she demanded. It was easy to get worked up about crooked land deals, the one thing her cartel wasn't involved in.

"What can be done when they rule with not one fist but two? The government," he said, holding out his left clenched fist, "and the other, los pistolas." He held up his right, simulating Father Hidalgo's call to arms for the War of Independence.

She shivered in the cab's back seat in spite of the stifling heat. When he voiced his opinion on cartels by calling them "the guns," she accepted the reading as accurate. Best to end the conversation while she still had a shred of dignity. "Gracias, señor. What do I owe you?"

He told her and she paid him, adding a handsome tip along with the carga.

On entering Analisa y José's, Layla observed a heightened level of decor. Stunning hardwoods accentuated the understated glamour of the lobby. Intricately woven tree branches fashioned into unique works of art graced the walls, and round windows trimmed in dark mahogany were the norm, not the exception. Leave it to Mexico to take the barest, most basic materials and create eclectic and surrealistic architecture, she thought. The building's coup de grace—its ceiling—crested into a thirty-foot-high grand palapa. When she was last there, she remembered Analisa y José's as Margaritaville—Jimmy Buffet style—low-key and laid-back. Nothing fancy, but the wide beach—only footsteps from the lobby—made up for any lack of swag.

At the reservation desk, an indigenous man wearing a shirt patterned with Maya glyphs looked up from a sheaf of papers. He gave her a warm smile as she approached. The bellman followed behind with her Luis Vuitton valise.

"Hola, Layla Santiago," she said, using her real first name and the fake surname Martín used for her new passport when she made her escape from Merida.

"Por supuesto, señora. Bienvenidos á Analisa y José's. I am Arturo, allow me to assist."

"Gracias."

"A two-bedroom oceanfront suite's ready for you. Is this your first trip to Tulum?"

"No, of course not. In fact, I stayed here some years ago. My, things have changed."

A look passed over his face that she attempted to interpret but couldn't read. It seemed to spell sadness, resignation, and defeat, three of grief's five stages. In a flash, his hospitality expertise kicked in and his secret thoughts were hidden once more.

"Yes, Tulum was very different not that long ago. Heaven on earth, though those who've just discovered it believe they've found exactly that. Hurricanes in 2005 changed everything."

"The taxista told me."

"Emily was a class four and that started it. Wilma, a five, finished it off. There was nothing left. Luckily Analisa y José's had been built far back from the shoreline, and like most buildings here, made from cinder block. The owners had a foundation to work with afterwards, and insurance money came fast and was generous to anything tourist-related. The government quickly wrote and passed a law: If you were in the tourist business, insurance companies had to cut you a check within forty-eight hours after a claim was placed. Pronto."

"Amazing."

"Si. When you have a golden goose prepared to lay, you want the nest ready," he said, with a resigned smile. "We were just getting recognized by the outside world. Coco Selva, down the beach, started by a European heiress and her model boyfriend, and La Mezzanine. Yoga at the Playa. No doubt you saw them on the beach road along with many others."

Layla nodded.

"But many of the hostels and campgrounds that never held clear title, some were on ejido land—you know, homesteads gifted to the locals from the government—they just disappeared in the storm. It was a clean landscape. That's when big money came in."

"I didn't notice any name resorts."

"I mean money from bankers, politicians, others ..." He let the phrase dangle. She knew he meant cartels. "Chetumal, our capital, where the governor lives, took charge."

Again, she had to dissuade a blush. She was getting a real-life lesson in the way things worked and a general impression of how the world viewed her business dealings.

"Well," Layla began in an effort to change the conversation, "I'm glad you're still here."

He bowed his head slightly. "Gracias. Now, Emmanuel will show you to your room." He looked at her reservation form. "You'll be with us for a while?"

"Yes, I thought I'd take advantage of low season. Hot weather and summer rains don't bother me. Oh, and I'm expecting a friend in a day or so."

"If you need anything, let me know," he said, as he picked up a ringing phone.

She followed the bellman out the lobby door and down a side path made of flat concrete steps stamped with geckos, bordered by flowering red hibiscus and striped dracaena. She heard the ocean before she saw it, and was lulled by its hypnotizing rhythm. Soon they arrived at a cottage with a front deck made from zapote, and tree limbs woven into railings. Two steps up and they were at her suite.

The bellman stood at the ready. "Can I help you with anything, señora?"

"No, this is fine. Thank you." She reached into her purse and pulled out a tip. "Please leave the door open."

"Gracias," he said, handing her the key. "Don't forget the plunge pool out the side door."

After he left she stood for a moment surveying her digs, taking in the slightly salty smell of the sea, happy to be away from everything and everyone. Why she felt so comfortable on Mexico's Caribbean coast was anyone's guess. Maybe it was the breeze that caressed her. Maybe it was the lapping waves. Maybe it was the endless white sand. Maybe it was being so close to heaven on earth.

As she started to unpack she realized the clothes she'd just purchased in Mexico City would never cut it in down low Tulum. Every woman she saw sported halter tops, short shorts, spaghetti strapped frocks, or pareo sarongs. She was woefully overdressed. She placed her toiletries in the bathroom onto a counter edged with a border of white pebbles. The shower had a rainforest-style showerhead and the floor was composed of more pebbles, gray grout in between. A narrow screened window went from one end of the bath to the other, nearly touching the ceiling. The day's humidity made her feel clammy; a shower would wash away travel grunge before she explored in town.

Half an hour later, she'd showered and changed into an outfit from her last Yucatán trip. It was the only thing she owned that might not expose her as an outsider.

As she prepared to leave, the phone rang.

"Layla?"

"Yes," she said, hearing Alma's voice.

"I have news. I talked to my sister. Are you in Cancun?"

"Already in Tulum. At Analisa y José's."

"Great. Listen, Gabriella's full name is Gabriella Solano Gomez. My sister said she's working in Tulum at a hotel but couldn't remember which one. Maybe Silvia looked her up. It might be something to go on …"

"Good to know. I'll check on it. Did you find out anything else?" Layla asked.

"No, that's all. Nothing from the police."

"Let me scout around. Haven't had a chance to talk with the locals yet. Thanks for the call, Alma. I'll be in touch soon. Ciao."

Ready for exploration and another clothes shopping spree, she walked to the door and locked it behind her as she headed towards the lobby.

CHAPTER 7

"Hello again," she said to the clerk at the reception desk.

He looked up from a sheaf of papers. "Buenas tardes. How can I assist?"

"Someone recommended a hotel tour guide named Gabriella Solano. I'm not sure where she works, though."

"Hmm. Sorry, no idea, but let me ring housekeeping. Our manager might know."

"If it's no bother," Layla said. She graced him with a smile as he made the call.

"Hola, Renata? Can you come to the front lobby? She'll be right here. Have a seat."

Five minutes later a stout Maya woman wearing an embroidered huipile stood before her. "Buenas tardes, señora. How can I help you?"

"I'm looking for my niece's friend who works in one of the local hotels. Would you know Gabriella Solano?"

"Oh, lo siento. The name is not familiar. The girl who arranges the rooms for arrivals, Isabel, she's young and has many friends. You wait?" She gave a sweet smile as she watched Layla nod.

In five minutes a slender, olive-skinned woman with dark hair complete with a dramatic flash of purple along one side of her part pranced into the room. She looked at Arturo with a questioning stare. Shoulders raised. "Que paso?"

He nodded towards Layla. The young woman quickly walked over. Her long silver earrings were not to be outdone by a heart-shaped amber pendant dangling from a thin strap around her neck. On her right wrist she wore a number of silver bracelets, and her fingers were covered in rings. Her flowing pants were coordinated with a long-waisted top. She had an attractive face and piercing black eyes, her only flaw being a downturn to a wide, ample mouth. The scent of Patchouli wafted Layla's way.

"Hola. Isabel. Que paso?"

"Layla. I asked Arturo, and your manager—"

"Yeah, I know. You're looking for Gabriella?" This came out as a threat as she shifted her weight from foot to foot.

"Word travels fast. My friend's niece said she works in Tulum."

"She works at the Azul. Why do you want to talk to her?"

"Oh, I'm trying to find a tour guide who goes to cenotes and …"

The young woman looked skeptical for a moment longer. She gave Layla a thorough once over. Seemingly assured, she backed off. "Okay. Just wanted to know how you knew her."

"From my friend's niece. Do you think she's working today?"

"The day's nearly over. Maybe you can find her tomorrow," the young woman said.

"Muchas gracias. And you are?"

Again the cocky what's it to you stare. "I said Isabel."

With that she was off. Layla stood, thanked Arturo and asked him to call a taxi.

Layla felt like going to Playamar for a drink but thought it best to check out Tulum pueblo first then backtrack to hotel shops to see what she could find. Playamar could wait. The taxista dropped her on Av. Tulum, the main drag. Within an hour she'd bought a few outfits that would get her through a beach vacation. She hailed a cab, and though her final port of call would be Playamar, she asked to be dropped at the Azul. Isabel had said it was too late to locate Gabriella, but Layla thought it prudent to try.

The sandy path to the hotel lobby was lined on both sides with bushy Areca palms and ornamental banana trees. Though she'd heard that Azul was a place to be reckoned with, on reaching the lobby, she wasn't prepared for the grand display of interlocking tree branches that made up the entire space. There was a hubbub in the bar where a line was forming. Drinks were plentiful and a reggae backbeat blared from ceiling speakers. The crushing mass was a line for selfies: you in a gigantic hammock that swung over the Caribbean—a perfect backdrop, and tweetable to every being in the social media universe.

She walked back into the lobby and approached the front desk. "Hola," she said to the clerk. "I'm a friend of Gabriella Solano. Does she work tomorrow?"

Eying the attractive Latina before him, the young man placed his arms on the counter and leaned over to minimize the space in between. "Gabriella works for Maya Reál. Do you know it?"

Layla shook her head.

"It's the parent property of Azul, a real estate company. Maybe you saw the billboard in town? Maya Reál has been in business here for twenty years. It's the largest real estate developer in Tulum," he said, warming up for his sales pitch.

"She's a realtor?"

"No, the property is in the planning phase. Gabriella works for the CEO, Ernesto Torres, as liaison to Tulum's mayor. He's helping with community issues and permits."

"Sounds like a big job. How many properties will they build?"

"With eight hundred hectares?" He shrugged. "It's developmental now, but I think a thousand."

"A thousand? That's huge for Tulum!"

"Oh, no worries. They have great respect for the land. Maya Reál has always created sustainable communities, especially in the Yucatán where ecology is so important. Their motto is 'Caretakers of the Forest.'"

He could have been a voice-over for a TV commercial from an earlier era selling orange groves in sunny Florida.

"They have other projects?"

"One's finished, south of Playa," he said. "You may know it, the Maya Royale?"

She remembered passing a humongous property near Playa del Carmen in her ride from the airport. It was a blot on a pristine landscape that extended to both sides of the highway. Massive billboards announced it well in advance, one after another, displaying infinity pools, tennis courts, and bikini-clad models with Spanish Mediterranean architecture as a backdrop.

"Hmm. Well, is her office here?"

"Oh, no. She works in Tulum pueblo, close to the mayor and Maya Reál's office. You want the address?" He tapped a ballpoint pen between his fingers while he waited for an answer.

"Por favor," Layla said. "Do you think she's working tomorrow?"

"Most likely. Here's the mayor's office, too. She's back and forth."

Layla walked out of the Azul, glancing one last time at the bar where tourists were still angling for selfies before catching a cab to Playamar. Layla still remembered Tulum of old and was anxious to revive that memory and toast it, an homage to what once had been a real life Margaritaville.

At Playamar, she peeked in at the wood-fire pizza oven but bypassed the restaurant. In the far corner she noticed the owner, an expat Californian. Still here after all these years. On the beach she slipped off her sandals to feel the cool sand. Since the sun had already gone down, it was that beautiful in-between time—dusk. The crowd was sparse and that pleased her.

She'd start with a Michelada: cerveza, tomato juice, lime, ice, and a dash of hot sauce. She stretched her long legs under the square wooden table that had faded to dull red. It took effort to get comfortable in slat-style Mexican chairs but she managed. Lapping waves lulled her into a reverie and the sun's aura created a haze above the waterline.

"You'll have what?" a grating voice behind her said.

She peered around and into the piercing eyes of Isabel, the arrivals manager from Analisa y José's. "Oh! What are you doing here?"

"Duh. Taking your order?" Isabel gave her a blunt stare, defying a comeback.

"But you work at Analisa y José's," Layla said.

"You catch on quick. Guess you haven't heard about Tulum rents."

"What do you mean?"

Isabel rolled her eyes. "They're over the top! Everyone works more than one job in Tulum. Unless you're like … rich!"

"This is your second job," Layla said.

"Ja, ja, ja. What are you drinking?" She settled into a practiced slouch, hand on hip.

"Michelada, por favor."

"At this time of day? Where are you from? Chiapas or something?"

"Are you dissing me?" Layla asked.

"Only if you're from Chiapas." Isabel laughed and sauntered away.

Chastened from her reverie by a girl with a serious attitude, Layla sat up straighter in her chair and considered those who lived on the lower end of the country's social system—in other words, most Mexicans—who hustled to make a living working two or more jobs.

Moments later, Isabel was back with her drink and a word of advice. "If you're trying to pick up guys, I'd chug that and get into something respectable, a margarita or mojito. You can never go wrong with tequila or rum. You're not a gringo—thank God for that—but with that drink, you're not exactly date bait."

She sauntered off again, leaving Layla to stare at her unacceptable drink. She did what the mouthy little troll told her—chugged it and felt the liquid slide down smooth— and tried to hide the glass behind her purse. She turned, hoping to catch a glimpse of Isabel over her left shoulder, only to hear a sarcastic whisper in her right ear. "Boo! Looking for someone?"

Layla jumped. Her case of the jitters had moved to the back burner after departing Mexico City, but little Miss Purple Hair brought back her insecurities. "Hijole!"

"Oh, excuse me! Did I scare you? I forget I'm supposed to be nice to the customers."

"Yes, I didn't expect that."

"Are you always this tight-assed?" Isabel arched an eyebrow and her lips curved into a sarcastic smile.

"What?"

"Loosen up. Have a margarita. Hold this thought: tequila," Isabel said.

She wandered off towards the restaurant, and Layla noticed she'd grabbed the dead give-away Michelada glass in the process. She longed to stare out at the ocean and listen to the waves but another intrusion was coming. She sat at attention, waiting for her designated drink.

"I brought antojitos, too," Isabel said as she set a margarita on the table. Her choice— salbutes—looked divine. The crisp, palm-sized tortillas were topped with shredded turkey, pickled onions, lime, and cilantro. Layla was thankful the know-it-all was thinking for both of them. She took a bite, savoring the flavors.

"So what's your story?" Isabel asked. "Why are you asking about Gabriella?"

Layla took a healthy drag on her margarita, too healthy, as she felt the icy liquid squish her brain sideways. Hijole. Was she out of practice or was she really a dweeb? How could she be old at thirty-five?

Trying to look composed after a mind-bending iceberg collided with her head, she felt a warm rush inside, aware that the gold liquid was doing its job. Now, if she could just talk.

"Gabriella knows my niece. Well, my friend's niece," Layla said.

"So?" Isabel pulled up a chair and cocked her head, waiting for full disclosure.

"So, I said I'd be in Tulum and would look her up."

"Why?" Isabella asked.

"Why are you so nosy?" Layla asked. Finally, finally, she was getting her second wind.

"Ooh, a bit testy, are we?"

"No," Layla backpedaled. "Her aunt and I are good friends, and I said I'd look in on her."

"Doing some spying?" A sinister look crossed Isabel's face.

Good grief, she was oddly prescient. Layla had to get hold of the conversation—pronto—and take back what little dignity still existed beneath her now blushing olive-colored skin.

"No, of course not!" Layla said, hoping she sounded self-assured.

"Well, that's good, because that girl does not need any more trouble!"

"Trouble?"

"Are you like a parrot? All you do is repeat what I say!" Isabella scolded.

"Oh, no, I just hope she's not in any trouble." Real concern came into Layla's voice and Isabel picked up on it.

"You good friends with her aunt?" Her tone was softer now.

"Yes," Layla lied easily. Finally, a comfortable trait she could rely on.

"That's good. She'll probably be really happy to see you."

"Why?"

"Someone to talk to, confide in. She should have never taken that new job they offered her. It started out innocent enough, but it got crazy!" Isabella said.

"You mean the job at Maya Reál?"

"How do you know where she works?" Isabel's hackles shot straight up.

"After I met you, I stopped at Azul for sunset, to see what the buzz was about. Since I was there I checked on her schedule."

"They told you she was working with Maya Reál?"

"Yes. It sounds like a pretty big position," Layla said.

"That's not the half of it. She has to deal with that pendejo mayor, Juan Dzib."

"Is that bad?" Layla asked.

"Bad? He is the creepiest little guy I've ever seen. Beady eyes, creepy hairline, zits. Shorter than me, and with this gnarly, scary vibe. Like he only comes out at night. I wouldn't be surprised to hear he's actually a vampire."

Layla shuddered. "Oh, come on, Isabel."

"What do you know? You've never met him and you've never met Gabriella. She is one of the sweetest, most naive people I've ever met. That guy gives me the creeps."

"What's wrong with him?"

"Other than his looks? Well, everyone in Tulum knows he stole the election. He didn't have a chance against Rubén Poot. Like magic, he won with ninety percent of the vote. That's impossible in Tulum, because Rubén is related to half the town."

"Hmm. Sounds shady, but how bad can a mayor be in a pueblo the size of Tulum?"

"Oh man, you are so from out of town. Yeah, it's Tulum. Like the premier eco-resort"—she wiggled her index and middle fingers in the air—"on the planet. Do you know what that means for land prices and rentals?"

Layla looked at Isabel with new respect. "No, tell me."

"It's hot and heavy. Tulum is a gold mine, and he's got the key to the treasure box. Everything funnels through him. Contracts for streets, lighting, the school and futbol stadium, new hotels and condos, even taxes. He holds the keys to the entire kingdom, plus he's a former accountant so he knows how to juggle numbers. Everyone says he's corrupt. Not just about the elections, either."

"Sounds like you covered it all. What more could there be?" Layla asked.

"He's working close with the governor, Enrique Hernandez. The mayor's his hand puppet. That governor … talk about another piece of work. He's a rat posing as a human. Do you know what Si'an Ka'an Reserve is?"

The name resonated in Layla's brain. "An eco-reserve?"

"Oh, so you've got something upstairs, Chiapas girl. Yes, it's a million-hectare reserve. About twenty years ago, Governor Quintana who wasn't corrupt—the state was named for him—created it. He must have been psychic because he wanted to keep some of the land beautiful, preserve it. The guy had wisdom."

"Amazing he did that way back then," Layla said.

"He was married to a Maya woman. She was from Felipe Carrillo Puerto, just south, and she loved the place. Si'an Ka'an means "where the sky is born" in Mayan."

"That's beautiful. He sounds like a saint," Layla said.

"Yeah, not many of those around any more. The new governor, though, not to be trusted. They call him El Ladrón, the thief. He never saw a piece of land he didn't covet. They say he's already stolen a thousand hectares of beachfront and he's on the cartel payroll. Listen, it's been real but I have work to do. Another margarita?"

Layla nodded, contemplating Isabel's casual mention of cartel corruption.

"You're getting the hang of the Maya spirit," Isabel said, quickly back again with drink in hand, laughing. Was she laughing at her or with her? Layla couldn't tell.

"I'm going to look up Gabriella tomorrow."

"Tell her hello for me. Say, why don't you ask her to come by tomorrow night and we can all chat. Have a little chisme fest," Isabel said.

Layla took that as an act of acceptance. Did Isabel approve of her?

"Okay, thanks. After this drink I'll head back to the hotel."

"Right on, Chiapas girl."

With that she moved away from the table and began to work the steadily growing crowd.

Chapter 8

Layla rolled over in bed, awakening to an unrestrained medley of birds singing. Ocean sounds played back-up and a light breeze moved the mosquito netting around her bed. Though it would be fun to loll about, she had important things to do—first and foremost, find Gabriella Solano and see if she had any knowledge of Alma Reyes' niece.

Rather than showering, Layla chose a dip in the plunge pool, toweling off with a thick sun-dried towel. She quickly blew out her shag haircut and dressed in a gauze skirt and turquoise top.

She opted for breakfast at the beachside restaurant, ordering a pot of French Press coffee, sweet roll, and papaya. Twenty minutes later she'd hailed a taxi, and was enroute to Centro.

The cab dropped her at el municipio, an unbecoming beige cement structure near the heart of town, one street off the main avenue. Layla walked into a cool tiled hallway with office doors on either side. The first on the right was the mayor's office. She opened the door and walked in.

An L-shaped counter greeted her. Two women stood next to an out-dated printer, chatting quietly in the back of the room near aluminum-framed windows. Dented gray file cabinets long past their expiration date stood in the center of the room, offering a convenient location for workers in need of information. A phone rang, and one of the women walked over to answer it. In the far corner, a closed door looked to be a private office. Venetian blinds were pulled half-way up over a picture window with a view of the central office area. It was empty.

When the woman picked up the phone, the other turned to look at the newcomer who had entered their domain. She was twenty-something, as tall as Layla, but carrying a bit more weight. Her dark hair was pulled into a low ponytail and though not overtly attractive, her doe-shaped eyes gave her some appeal and an empathetic look made her appear vulnerable. When she saw Layla, she moved quickly towards the counter.

"Buenos dias," she said. "How can I help you?"

"Hola. I'm Layla Santiago, and I'm looking for Gabriella Solano."

"Oh, that's me."

"Gabriella, how nice to meet you. I'm here for a friend. Alma Reyes?"

"Alma, yes! From DF. How did you know to find me here?"

"You know her niece, Silvia?" Layla asked.

"Yes, we went to school together in Cuernavaca."

"I heard. Alma said she, her sister, Silvia, and you came to Tulum a couple of years ago."

"That's true. It was right after we graduated. I was hoping I could find a place for myself here, get a job."

"It looks like you did," Layla said, an easy smile on her face.

"But how did Silvia lead you to me?"

"Well, actually, I was hoping you could lead me to Silvia," Layla said.

"What do you mean?"

Layla glanced over at Gabriella's office cohort on the phone, still talking. "I thought, or Alma thought, maybe she'd been in touch with you."

A confused look crossed the younger woman's face. "With me? No, she's in DF now."

"This isn't the best place to say this, but Silvia hasn't been heard from for a few days and Alma was hoping she'd been in touch with you. She came to Tulum with a new boyfriend."

"What?" The young woman grasped the counter. "What are you saying?"

Layla looked away. When she turned back to face Gabriella, all smiles were gone. "You know that Alma was kidnapped a year ago."

Gabriella gripped the edge of the counter tighter still, her knuckles turning white. "Of course, everyone knew that."

"Well, Alma said they couldn't get to her, and she thinks they may have retaliated and taken Silvia, as a stand in."

"Oh, no, no." The girl started to shake, clearly having very little luck holding herself together.

"Listen, I found you through Isabel, from Analisa y José's. If you have time for a coffee break later, I can fill you in."

"The mayor is gone this morning. I can spend time with you now. I'll tell Gloria."

Gabriella walked briskly to the desk where her fellow worker was talking on the phone. The other woman paused her conversation, apparently sensing a problem. She held up a finger signaling she'd just be a minute, and with a few words into the phone, she abruptly hung up. The two conferred quickly, the co-worker nodding at Silvia and glancing Layla's way, no doubt wondering who could be bringing this sudden shift to what must have been a previously laid-back morning.

Gabriella dodged over to a back desk, opened the bottom drawer, and grabbed her purse. In a matter of moments she'd skirted around the counter, and was ready to go.

"Coffee?" she asked.

ꙥꙥꙥ

Five minutes later Layla and Gabriella were seated in the back garden of a juice bar on Av. Tulum, a block and a half from the mayor's office.

"Dos cafés negro," she said to the female server, looking at Layla, who nodded in assent.

Coffee in front of them, Gabriella jumped right in. "What's happened?"

"Not sure. We were wondering, me and Alma, if you heard from Silvia."

"Not lately. She texted me three weeks ago and said she was going to be in Tulum with a new boyfriend on a business trip. I waited to hear back, nada. How long has she been missing?"

"Alma last heard from her four or five days ago. She said it's not like Silvia, and she can't reach the boyfriend either. They flew into Cancun, and after his meetings they were coming to Tulum."

Gabriella stared downwards and settled back in her chair. "I should have tried harder."

"What do you mean?"

"I should have texted her again, or at least called. It was just that one text. I was busy with the new job and figured she'd just show up. That's kind of Silvia," Gabriella said.

"Were you still working at Azul?" Layla asked.

"No, I'd just made the change … to work with, um, Maya Reál, and the mayor's office."

The young woman hung her head, arms crossed, hugging herself. She slunk further down in the chair and a barely audible moan came out. Layla moved over to Gabriella's side of the table. Like an older sister, she put an arm around the young woman and gave her a tight squeeze. Then she shifted so that she could look directly at her.

"Gabriella." No response. "Gabriella!" A bit louder. "Listen, you didn't know. You had no idea what was happening. You were busy, had your hands full with a new job. None of this is your fault."

"I feel so bad …"

"Listen, we're going to try to get to the bottom of this, find her." Layla gripped the young woman tighter still, held her straight up and down. "We're going to stay on this. Believe me."

She willed the girl to look into her almond-shaped eyes, the color of charcoal. Her power of concentration would not be impeded by emotion, not at this juncture. She'd lost one young one and she was damned determined it would not happen twice. Not on her watch. Serendipity indeed. This was fucking karma.

"Are we together on this? Are we?" Layla implored.

Gabriella snapped to, apparently buoyed by Layla's strength and the mission to find her friend.

"Yes, yes," she agreed. "How do we get started?"

"We walk out that door, and we begin."

ᔕᓓᓕ

After the relative shade of the garden café, walking into bright sunshine momentarily blinded Layla. As they exited, she grabbed Gabriella's elbow and shepherded her onto a makeshift sidewalk that ran in front of the shops.

"Do you think she's been kidnapped?" Gabriella asked.

"Could be. I'm checking more info at Azul later. The desk clerk told me about your job. Do you think you could find out if they stayed there last time they were here, and if they were expected back? Her boyfriend's name is Francisco Ramirez."

"Sure. Let me have your number."

"Isabel asked if you could meet us at Playamar after work tonight?"

"Definitely," Gabriella said.

The sound of a motorbike revving up and backfiring nearby made them both stop in the middle of the sidewalk. Gabriella shouted, "What's that motorbike doing? By that car. He has a gun!"

Layla observed a black Kawasaki carrying two men wearing helmets as the noise of rapid-fire bullets shattered Tulum's morning silence. The car, veering to their side of the road, skidded. Layla pushed Gabriella towards the safety of a storefront as the noise of screeching brakes overpowered the hum drum of merchants setting up shop. Those outside their businesses, too, had scrambled from the street and inside for cover. After the noisy rat-a-tat-tat, the motorbike backfired again and skidded. The car crashed into a pole, horn blaring, narrowly missing the only other pedestrian in the vicinity.

Layla zeroed in as the bike regained momentum and zoomed off, but not before the rider turned and shot two rounds in her direction. She crouched. Bullets thunked into a concrete wall behind her.

"What happened?" Gabriella screamed. She too had huddled down, low to the street, hand over her brow.

Layla got hold of Gabriella, gripping her arm to pull her up. "It's a drive-by. Who could that motorbike be?"

"I don't know! Oh God!" Gabriella screamed again.

While most would run from disaster, Layla ran towards it. She reached the smashed car in record time, realizing the lone man inside had been hit multiple times, his torso flopped clumsily against the blaring horn. She pulled open the passenger door, reached over and gingerly pushed the dead man's limp body towards the driver's window to stop the noise. She took a closer look at the victim. He was dark-haired and middle-aged; his blood-splattered face had taken at least one bullet—his body, more. The drive-by gunmen had hit their mark. Blood was everywhere. With multiple bullet wounds it was a toss-up which had proved to be the death shot. The victim was dressed in a Guayabera shirt and jeans. A briefcase lay on the floorboards on the passenger side.

"No, no!" Gabriella's voice sounded nearly as loud as the horn had been. She had followed Layla.

Layla turned from the crime scene, backed away from the victim, car door still open. She concentrated on her new charge.

"Gabriella, get back on the sidewalk."

The girl followed Layla's instruction, head down, her motor faculties in slow motion. People were running towards the vehicle. Nearby, a woman holding a baby was crying. She clutched the child tightly in her arms in a veritable death grip.

A man approached. "What happened?" he asked.

"You were over there," Layla said, lifting her chin to the other side of the street. "You witnessed as much as I did." She quickly scanned the vicinity. Definitely not the time to be questioned on her 'why's and wherefore's' for being in Tulum. Not with her record. Not by Tulum policia.

"Listen, my friend is freaking out. Someone should call the police. I'm going to take her where she can calm down. You got this?"

"Sure," he said, his eyes on Gabriella. It was impossible to not notice the young woman's emotional state. "I got it."

A moment later Layla heard the sound of a police siren. The cop shop was five blocks away. She hurried to Gabriella's side. "Let's go back to your office, pronto."

Gabriella nodded meekly and heeded the older woman's advice. Layla walked quickly in the opposite direction, moving towards the mayor's office where she could calm Gabriella down.

"I, I know who that is," Gabriella said in a muted voice.

"What?" Layla asked. They had put a block behind them and were angling towards the street they'd just walked down thirty minutes earlier. "What did you say?"

"I know him."

"The guy in the car?" Layla demanded.

"Yes, it's Pedro Cruz. The newspaper man."

Layla stopped walking. "Who?"

"Pedro Cruz. He owns the newspaper here, *Tulum Hoy*."

"A reporter?" Layla asked.

"He owned the paper and was a reporter, too. He ran it with his wife."

"Hijole! A reporter? Killed in Tulum? Why the hell would someone kill a reporter here?"

"Let's get back to the office," Gabriella said, clearly feeling the flight not fight syndrome. "There's a lot you don't know about this little pueblo."

CHAPTER 9

Gabriella's work associate, Gloria, stood by one of the office windows that faced Av. Tulum. Though nothing could be seen from a block off the main drag, she was clearly aching to discover what the commotion was about.

"You're back! What's happening out there?"

"A drive-by, right on Tulum," Gabriella said.

"Oh my God!" Gloria shrieked.

"Yes. It's Pedro Cruz," Gabriella said, still looking shaken from the experience.

"What? Oh no, that can't be!"

"Was he a target?" Layla asked. "Had he been writing stuff?"

Gloria stared at Gabriella for guidance, saw her nod and said, "Yes."

"Like what?" Layla demanded.

"Articles about the mayor," Gloria said.

"Your boss?"

They nodded in unison.

"Hijole," Layla said, shaking her head.

"Guess taking this job wasn't such good timing." Gabriella shared a look with Gloria.

"Where is he?" Gloria asked.

"Today? At Maya Reál, meeting with Torres," Gabriella said.

"Alibi," Gloria muttered under her breath, but not without Layla overhearing it.

"Why did he have an axe to grind with the reporter?"

"Well, he wrote that the mayor stole the election … for starters," Gabriella said.

"Did he?" Layla demanded.

Gabriella shrugged before speaking. "I heard about it after I accepted the job. Isabel told me."

Isabel was like the Cassandra of Tulum. Her prophetic ramblings were beginning to become more omen than criticism. It might be wise to heed her advice. Maybe Layla could hire her as a bodyguard. She seemed to have the right stuff, or at the very least, good intel, and she was meaner than shit. Come to think of it, she had a little of Carlos's edge. She was someone people wouldn't screw with.

"Is that all?" Layla asked. Best find out the rest of the dirt before something worse happened. Though with a man lying dead in the street, things couldn't get much worse.

"She told me he's dirty."

"Dirty how?" Layla asked.

"He's making bad deals with lots of people," Gabriella said.

Gloria gave Gabriella a cool stare and shuffled her feet. As a Maya local, that was akin to screaming at the top of your lungs. The Maya never made a scene, never acted out in public. They were unreadable.

"Oh, I shouldn't be saying these things," Gabriella said. Gloria's body language had become introspective and remote.

"Gloria," Layla began in a delicate tone shifting her focus away from Gabriella. "How long have you worked for the mayor?"

"Six months. I worked for the old mayor before the election, Dzib asked me to stay on. I needed the job. My mother's sick and my father died two years ago. I have a younger brother and sister."

"Had you heard the rumors about the election?" Layla asked.

She gazed down, embarrassed. "Everyone heard about it. It's Tulum."

"Right. Anything else you want to tell me?" Layla asked.

"Is the reporter really dead?"

"Yes, I'm sorry to say that he is."

Her face fell as reality set in. "He fire-bombed his printing press," Gloria said.

"What?"

"The mayor fire-bombed his printing press a month ago. It was a warning," Gloria said.

"How do you know that?" Layla asked.

"I just know."

Layla let it slide. Why implicate a twenty-year-old Maya woman, sole supporter of four?

"Does he know you know?" Layla asked.

"I don't think so."

"Good. I won't ask you any more about that now, okay? Listen, I'm going back to the hotel to make some calls. Gabriella, what time do you get off work?"

"Five."

"I'll see you around six at Analisa y José's?"

"Si, si, Layla." The girl forced a crooked smile at her friend's friend.

"Ciao."

ㄲ回回

Back at Analisa y José's, Layla walked through the lobby and down the garden path to her suite. She grabbed a bottle of water from the mini-fridge and sat on the bed, hoping to make sense of what she'd just witnessed. She took a swig of water and decided it was time for company. She dialed Clay's number to see when he'd arrive in Tulum.

"Clay," she said. "Layla. How's it going on your travels?"

"I fly into Cancun tomorrow afternoon and I'll rent a car. Where are you staying?"

"Analisa y José's, at the end of the Tulum beach road. I have a two-room suite."

"Perfect. How's it going?"

"Today was … rough. I went to visit my friend's niece's friend. She works for the mayor and a real estate company. While we were having coffee on the main drag, when we left the restaurant, we witnessed a drive-by."

"Shooting? What the hell? Was anyone hurt?" Clay asked.

"Yes, killed actually. He was a reporter from Tulum. He'd been writing about the mayor stealing the election, and more."

"Christ, Layla. You're courting disaster these days. I hope you got outta there fast."

"I did. But I'm worried about the niece's friend. Her name is Gabriella. We're meeting tonight and I'll see what

74

she knows. Unfortunately, she's a quick study. She probably knows too much already, and it's a new job."

"Well, hang in there, amiga. Help is on the way."

"I seriously hope so. Call me when you think you'll be in. I'll be here at the hotel."

"See you tomorrow, Layla."

"Ciao," she said, and hung up.

🔲🔲🔲

Layla exited a taxi in front of Playamar around six and made her way to the sandy beach that served as an extension of the restaurant, the same place she'd been the previous night, where Isabel had, kind of, befriended her. She looked around for the purple-haired beast. Not sighting her, she pulled up a chair. It was déjà vu. Like clockwork, just as she mellowed into a pleasant haze of wave watching, the little troll came up behind her.

"Hola. You made it! Where's Gabriella?"

"She'll be here soon," Layla said.

"What are you having? A Michelada?" She gave Layla a devilish grin.

"No! Margarita, por favor."

"Oh, I see you've had your Tulum lessons. Very good. Pronto!" Isabel trotted off.

She was back with the beverage in record time. "So, how was your day?"

A horrific look passed over Layla's face, not to be missed by Isabel.

"What? What happened?" Isabel asked.

"Have you heard about the drive-by on Avenida Tulum?"

"What? No! Que paso?"

"This morning I went to the mayor's office." She watched as Isabel wrinkled her nose. "And met Gabriella to tell her the news I have for her."

"Which is—?" Isabel asked, giving her a dark stare.

Layla shifted uncomfortably in the wooden chair. "Well, you're going to find out sooner or later. I'm actually here to help find my friend's niece. She's gone missing."

"Hijole! Now you're talking a drive-by shooting and a kidnapping, in one sentence!"

Layla's eyes met Isabel's. "Yes. My friend is a journalist from Mexico City, Alma Reyes. Renowned for writing critical articles of—"

"Of those scum the cartels and corrupt officials. Everyone knows who Alma Reyes is. You think I live under a rock? She's exposed a ton of stuff on corruption. She's even written about our governor. I told you about that creep last night. Go on."

"Alma was kidnapped a year ago, maybe you heard about it."

"Of course, everyone heard about it. She's famous. She's like Wonder Woman with a side of Guadalupe thrown in. Saint Alma."

"Now she has a bodyguard."

Isabel sniffed. "She needs an armored tank. We can't lose the likes of her."

"Did you know that her paper, the *Mexico City News*, published a full-page ad directed at the cartels a few days ago, asking what they wanted the papers to write?"

"I don't read DF news. I'm strictly *Por Esto*."

"Well, a famous reporter, they called him El Viejo, was murdered as he was leaving work in front of the newspaper offices. When I talked to Alma later that night, she told me her niece had gone missing two days earlier. She was afraid it could be because now that she has a bodyguard, they couldn't get to her, so they go after easy pickings—like her niece Silvia, Gabriella's friend. Alma has reason to believe she came to Tulum."

Isabel went quiet. "Jesús y Maria. The corruption is everywhere. So how does Gabriella fit into this?"

"My uncle is a distributor for big pharma companies and hires private investigators who travel throughout the world, to source things. He's incapacitated at the moment, and I'm filling in. I had time off, and wanted to help Alma find her niece. We have a contact here in Playa. I plan to meet him tomorrow. I'm hopeful he can assist and we can discover what happened to her."

"Wait a minute. What about the drive-by? My head is spinning."

"When Gabriella and I were leaving a juice bar in Tulum this morning, two guys on a motorbike came alongside a car, right on the main Avenida, and shot into the side window. I was first at the scene—dodged a bullet myself. The victim got it in the head and the body. It was terrible."

"Hijole! So who was it?"

"You're not going to like this," Layla said.

"Tell me!"

"Pedro Cruz, the newspaper man from *Tulum Hoy.*"

Isabel's face became like stone. "Oh no, no. Terrible. Drink your margarita. I have to take a walk."

She turned quickly and strode towards the restaurant, for that one moment, speechless.

Layla looked down at her margarita. This time she sipped it slowly. She looked out at the ocean but it didn't hold the charm from a mere twenty-four hours earlier. She took another drink. As she set her glass down, she saw Gabriella walking across the sand. She appeared calmer than when they'd parted at the office.

"Hola," Layla said. She motioned to the chair next to her.

"Oh, Layla. This is so beautiful. I haven't been to Playamar for a while. Have I kept you waiting?"

"No, Gabriella. How are you doing?" she asked pointedly.

"Better. I had a little cry back at the office, and a good talk with Gloria. Friends help."

"Yes, they do," Layla said, wondering what it would be like to actually have a friend. Friends were a luxury bosses couldn't afford.

"Did the mayor come in?" Layla asked.

"No, but he called. Talked to Gloria and she told him about the drive-by."

"He doesn't know you actually witnessed it?" Layla asked.

"Right. Gloria's very protective of me, being kinda new to Tulum and everything."

"Are you working at the mayor's office tomorrow?"

"No, I'll be at Maya Reál," Gabriella said.

Isabel arrived back at the table, wearing a crooked smile on sighting Gabriella. "Hola, amiga." She put her arm around her friend's shoulder and gave it a squeeze.

"Ahh, Isabel. Que tal?"

"Well, things could be ... better. What the hell is happening?"

Gabriella hung her head as though she was responsible for the day's events. "I don't know, Isabel. It's scary."

"No lie! But listen, chica, you gotta be careful with that madman you work for. You hear me?"

Gabriella gazed into Isabel's eyes as they drilled into hers. "Yes, yes."

"I mean it. I'm not kidding. I told you that guy is a creep," Isabel said.

"You did. Well, too late now."

"Right, but you've got to act totally naive around him. He can't be trusted."

Layla interrupted. "Are you going to have a drink, Gabriella?"

"Si, margarita?"

"I'll be right back. It'll help you think straight," Isabel said and went to fetch it.

"So, Gabriella. Did anyone know the mayor was behind the printing press bombing?"

"I think people suspected it, but you know how the police are. Nothing gets investigated, anywhere. And look at Tulum. It's a pueblo."

Layla nodded. It was exactly why widespread corruption continued. Scare the shit out of the masses and the police alike—or better yet, have them on your payroll. They'd never ask questions or interview witnesses, if any were stupid enough to come forward. No small wonder why Mexico produced few heroes. Nary a one got out alive.

"Well, there's someone who might be able to help—he's in Playa, and I'm going to see him tomorrow. We need to find Silvia. After these drinks, let's go to Azul and see what they know about Francisco Ramirez. If he showed up."

"Okay. I called earlier, but my friend who's usually on the desk wasn't working until later. He might be there now."

"When Isabel comes back, we'll say goodbye and leave," Layla said.

၂၉၉

At the Azul, unlike the previous day, the bar scene was a low hum. Layla and Gabriella walked up to the front desk.

"Hola, Estefan," Gabriella said. "Como estas? This is Layla. I need your help. A friend of ours was here about three weeks ago, around the time I went to work for Maya Reál. She was with her boyfriend, Francisco Ramirez. Her name is Silvia. They were supposed to arrive again a few days ago. Have they checked in?"

Estefan smiled, reached his hand over the desk, and gave Gabriella's a quick squeeze. "Let me take a look. Good to see you, chica. I'll check the computer. Can you wait a few minutes? Ramirez, right?"

"Si, thank you," Gabriella said.

Estefan hurried into an office cubbyhole and was back pronto. "He checked in with a woman three days ago, four p.m. Housekeeping said that when she went in to clean the room the next day, their suitcases were unopened and the bed hadn't been slept in."

Layla and Gabriella exchanged a look.

"Did anyone see them after that?" Layla asked. "I have photos of them both."

"Whoa. What's going on? Is there a problem?"

"Silvia, our friend, hasn't been heard from in several days and her aunt is nervous."

"Let me check with the concierge. Can I borrow those photos?" Estefan asked.

He was off like a shot. Layla and Gabriella could only wait … and hope.

"Oye," Estefan said on his return. "Listen, the concierge remembers them. He said they did the whole selfie sunset thing. Someone sitting next to them took their photo. He only remembers because they were this stunning couple. I mean, check out the photos."

"We know," Layla said drily. "Then what?"

"Well, they took the selfie and didn't stay long at the bar. They walked into the lobby, like they were uncertain or trying to find someone, and he asked if they needed a taxi. The man said no, and five minutes later they were picked up by a black Escalade SUV."

Black Escalades! Drug dealers' vehicle of choice. Chinga! Then…poof. Up in smoke.

"But Jorge, the concierge, said right behind the Escalade a taxi zoomed in. It was a friend of his and the guy got out of his cab to say hi just as Ramirez was getting into the Escalade with the girl. He said the cabbie remembers the driver looked like one hard dude, dressed in black. Another guy rode shotgun, equally tough."

"Did he say if they seemed nervous or anything?" Layla asked.

"No mention of that. They just zoomed off."

Layla gave Estefan a perfunctory smile. "Gracias. We appreciate your help. Do you remember anything about this Ramirez when he was last here? Or does your concierge?"

"Let me ask him. Got a minute?"

This time Estefan dialed. In a few minutes a Maya man in his forties with a bum leg limped towards the counter. He wore a concerned look as though something was bothering him.

"This is Jorge," Estefan said, nodding at both women.

"Hola, Jorge, mucho gusto. Layla y Gabriella."

They shook hands. "Jorge, we need to find out more info about our friend, the young woman you saw getting into the Escalade a few nights ago."

He shook his head. "Well, I don't know anything about that."

"But Estefan said your friend, the taxista, saw the driver in the Escalade."

In Mexico, loose talk could get you a bullet through the head. If your luck wasn't holding, you'd be tortured first. The Maya concierge avoided Layla's eyes. She shifted into a higher gear. "Jorge. This girl that got into the car, she's a dear friend of mine and Gabriella's. No one has seen her since she left DF several days ago. If there is any way—any way at all—you could help us, we would be so grateful."

The concierge looked at the beautiful Mexicana and her young friend for a moment, then he started to talk. "Well, I can call my amigo who owns the taxi. Find out if he saw them in el pueblo that night. He left right after them. The man forgot his room key, went back to the desk to retrieve it. By the time he returned, Goyo, mi amigo, got a call and followed them out the drive."

"Could you call Goyo? It might help us find our friend." Layla reached into her purse and pulled out a two hundred peso note.

"Oh. Hmm. I think he may be working tonight. Do you want to take a seat?"

"They got into an Escalade and that's all anyone saw," Layla said to Gabriella while they waited.

As she spoke, Jorge, the concierge, came towards them. "My friend said he was behind them all the way into Tulum and noticed the car's license plate was hanging by one bolt. For a fancy Escalade, he thought that was weird. They made a stop outside the OXXO to talk to someone. There was a traffic jam, lots of cars, and he got stuck behind them as they drove south. They turned off at that subdivision about three kilometers from town.

"Goyo lives out that road. He was heading home to eat, and watched the SUV pull into an empty lot with a warehouse. He kept driving."

Layla nodded. This was the closest she'd come to actual information.

"You've been very helpful. Thank you so much. If you see these people again," Layla said as she paused to reach into her purse for their photos, "can you let Estefan know?"

He nodded, giving a brief smile before heading back to his work station. They watched him walk away.

"Gabriella, it's been a long day. Tomorrow you find out all you can about the mayor, but be careful. I'll meet my associate and see what he can uncover," Layla said.

The young woman nodded. "Let me tell Estefan goodbye."

"I'll call you tomorrow," Layla said, and embraced the young woman.

Gabriella walked towards the front desk and Layla went to find a taxi. At least they were one step closer to something. But exactly what that was, Layla had not a clue.

CHAPTER 10

The next morning, Layla stood in Playa del Carmen outside a three-story building on Av. Constituyentes, home to a popular realty company. It was a bright sunny day in the Riviera Maya. As she passed the downstairs office, two couples stood at the window commenting on photos of homes and condos. Another couple sat in front of a realtor at one of four desks.

Layla climbed the stairs to the second floor and spotted the name Jaime Lopez on an office door. She entered, gagging on a cloud of cigarette smoke. The A/C whirred sluggishly and, though the make-shift lobby was empty, she could hear someone on a phone in the back office. To kill time, Layla took a closer look at a collection of bullfighting photos displayed on unevenly plastered walls. Several presented a stout matador swirling a red cape; another was an aerial view of a bullring with a sizable cheering crowd. A bullfight poster held center position with smaller photos grouped around it. The matador had to be Jaime.

In Layla's world, Jaime Lopez was known as a fixer. Martín called him one of the best. Cartels had these guys stashed all over the country—they were your go-to when the shit hit the fan. Jaime's reputation preceded him.

He could easily disappear dead bodies and clean up afterwards, forge documents with an artist's flair, or arrange safe houses. He was priceless. While Layla was trying to imagine Jaime's trajectory from bullring to cartel world, a swarthy guy with a thick black mustache entered from the rear office. A cigarette dangled from one hand and he held a ballpoint pen in the other. "Hola, señorita."

His voice was a low rumble bordering on a purr. He was middle-aged, medium height with wide shoulders, and wore his thick dark hair longer at the back. A gold chain was draped around his neck and his polyester shirt was open three buttons down, exposing curly chest hair. Layla couldn't decide what look he was going for, but he displayed a congenial air.

"Hola, Jaime? Layla. Mucho gusto."

"The pleasure is mine." He stubbed out his cigarette in an ashtray and shook her hand. "How may I be of service?" he asked.

"Martín said you work with us and know the area. I'm looking for a missing woman."

"Please, come back to my office. Ándale," he said with a sweeping gesture.

As Layla took a seat, Jaime lit another cigarette. "Does smoke bother you?"

"I'm not a smoker," Layla said, giving him a cool look.

"Oye! Let me put this out! Now, where do we begin?"

Layla laid out the story. He followed her analysis closely, asked questions and took notes.

"She was last sighted at the subdivision south of Tulum? I know it. Never quite took off when things were beginning to pop. It seemed like a shoo in, but it ended up a combination of locals and low-rent expats. Lots of rebar and half-built homes," he said.

"The taxista saw her and this Ramirez guy," Layla said, as she showed him photos, "get into a black Escalade. He said the vehicle turned into a lot that was vacant except for a storage facility. That's all I know. Oh, here's their full names."

"What about Ramirez?" Jaime asked.

"He's an attorney for MBC."

Jaime raised an eyebrow.

"Yeah, could be laundering," Layla said. In their world, certain words were code.

"I'll look into him. I can start today. Do you need a lift back to Tulum? If you want to ride along to the subdivision, you're more than welcome."

"I'm expecting a friend, but the sooner you can start the better."

"Yeah, time's important."

More code. "Can I give you a retainer?" Layla asked.

"Nah. Let's see how it goes. Ready for a ride?"

ꍏꍏꍏ

At the hotel, Layla rang Alma and gave her an update.

"It's going slow," Alma said.

"At least someone spotted her. Listen, I'll be in touch after I talk to the investigator again. Keep your chin up. Oh, any leads on your friend's death?"

Layla heard a heavy sigh. "No, of course not," Alma said.

"This will surprise you—hmm, maybe not, you being in the news business. A Tulum reporter was killed in a

86

drive-by yesterday. I witnessed it with Gabriella. Broad daylight. Two guys on a motorbike."

"Those savages! Tulum!"

"Apparently the mayor's dirty and doing illicit deals. Gabriella works in his office as a liaison between him and this real estate company, Maya Reál."

"I know the name," Alma said. "They ruin paradise, but with slogans like "Protectors of the Jungle" and other catchy lies. They bulldoze mangroves, cut down palm trees, and demolish forests, then build a bunch of cheap hotels and condos. Everyone knows hotels are an easy way to launder money."

"So I've heard," Layla said. "No one can be sure if rooms were occupied, but owners declare rental receipts and deposit the cash. They don't call it laundering for nothing." As a former cartel accountant, she knew the drill.

"That's it. You said Gabriella's working for the mayor? Is she safe?"

"I warned her to say nothing about anything," Layla said.

"Should I be worried?" Alma asked.

"No, she's smart. I'll let you know when I hear more, Alma. We're making progress."

"That's what I needed to hear."

"I'll be in touch. Ciao," Layla said and signed off.

🉐🉐🉐

Since Clay wasn't scheduled to arrive for a few hours, Layla decided to take a walk along the beach, get some sun, watch the waves. She put on her swimsuit and a cover-up, located a beach towel in the bathroom, and headed outside.

Layla sniffed the breeze and absorbed the humidity of the day before she found a spot under a lone palm. She removed her cover-up and wrapped it into a makeshift pillow. Lying there, she peered through palm fronds and gazed at a cloudless sky.

Her phone rang. "Hola?"

"It's Gabriella."

Layla sat up abruptly. "Everything okay?" She could hear tension in Gabriella's tone.

"Yes, but I need to talk to you. I went to the mayor's office before going to Maya Reál this morning. It was early and he was in, alone. Gloria hadn't arrived yet and I don't think he knew I was there. I overheard him talking about Pedro, the journalist."

"What did he say?" Layla asked.

"He said, 'Another one out of the way.'"

"Well, that doesn't necessarily mean anything," Layla said.

"No, no, there's more. He laughed and said, 'That'll teach them to write bullshit about me. What about the wife?'

"When I heard that, I realized I better leave quick. His door was ajar, the blinds were closed, and he didn't have a clear view of the office, but he may have heard me," Gabriella said.

"Why do you think that?"

"As I closed the office door, I heard his chair squeak, like he was getting up. He must have entered the main office. I stood in the hallway outside with my back flat against the wall and held my breath. I could almost feel him breathing on the other side. I was terrified he'd find me there. I don't know what I'd have done if he'd come out the door and into the hallway," she said.

"Hijole, Gabriella! Cuidado! What's your schedule?"

"I'm at Maya Reál now. With Torres."

"What's his story?" Layla asked.

"After hearing things from Isabel, he's probably as dirty as the mayor. For all I know, maybe that's who he was talking to."

"Please don't implicate yourself in any way. Do you hear me?" Layla implored.

"Yes," a meek Gabriella squeaked.

"Are they doing land deals?"

"Something like that. But I can't talk right now. I'll catch you up later."

"I have a friend coming. I'll be in touch. Listen, I talked to the Playa investigator. I think he can handle things. Since it was Playa, I wasn't sure how competent he'd be, but he's listo."

"Oh, that's good news."

"He dropped me back at the hotel so I can wait for my friend. He was en route to the sub-division the cabbie told us about. He'll ask around," Layla said.

"Gotta go. Torres is waving me towards his office."

"Okay. Remember, cuidado. Ciao."

CHAPTER 11

Clay arrived at Analisa y José's around five. He called Layla from the lobby. "I'll come up and lead you back to the room," she said.

She found him gazing at the voluminous palapa ceiling, apparently in awe of its height and the lobby's ingenious interior design.

Clay's good looks would be hard to miss anywhere, but in Mexico, his height alone set him apart at a lanky yet solid six-foot-two-and-a-half inches. Shaggy, brownish hair brushed the collar of a gray silk-blend shirt, and cargo shorts and sandals completed his casual surfer look.

"Layla!" His normally low rumble of a voice boomed when he saw her, and his hazel eyes crinkled at the corners while he appraised her. "Wow, you cut your hair. Looks good."

"Clay, thank you. A change of look, for, well, you know ... How great to see you." They embraced and both appeared reluctant to untangle from the other's arms. Layla gave Clay a happy smile as she slid out of the embrace. "Isn't this place radical?"

"Looks like you found Margaritaville," he said. "Buffet's gonna be pissed."

"You should have seen it years ago, before the tourist invasion," Layla said.

"Well, it looks pretty awesome to me. And what weather."

Her eyes turned playful. "Yeah, I ordered it for ya," she said, lightly swatting his arm.

They wandered through the lobby, over the gecko steps that bordered the sandy beach to the path leading towards the cottage. "This way," she said, pointing.

"Wow, Layla, this is phenomenal," Clay said, as the ocean came into view.

"Wait till you have a margarita."

They entered the two-bedroom suite. "Over here, Clay, this room's yours."

He followed her as she gestured to a roomy bedroom with picture windows that offered killer views of the turquoise Caribbean. "Well, I'm sold. Maybe I'm in the wrong business. Should be buying and selling beachfront hotels."

"This is an eco-resort, Clay. Gotta get the language right in Tulum."

He laughed. "Oh, right. Don't want to sound un-hip."

"Cerveza?" she asked.

"Now you're talking. I'm on Mexican time."

She walked to the mini-fridge and pulled out two Dos Equis. "Beer of choice?"

"When in Rome … err, Mexico."

Layla headed to the deck. "It's nice out here. Sit. Let's catch up."

"It's only been a week, Layla."

Her tone changed. "Feels longer."

"Uh, is anything wrong?"

"I didn't want to tell you over the phone ..." There was a meaningful pause while she tried to compose herself. "José's dead."

Clay nearly dropped his Dos Equis. "Say what?"

"It's true. He died in a car chase, an ambush after he and Alfonso did a pickup at the Guadalajara plaza."

"What happened?"

Layla haltingly proceeded to tell him the details.

"Oh, Layla." He got up from his chair and kneeled next to her. "Listen, I am so, so sorry." He grabbed her hand and let it rest in his for a long moment.

"I know." She hung her head and tried to hold back tears. What an ass she was. He was barely off the plane.

"I had to tell you, right away." She discreetly removed her hand from Clay's.

"We're in a fucked-up business. This we know." He took a long swig on his beer. "More of these inside? Mine seems to be empty."

He walked out again a minute later. "So, tell me what's going on. Besides José, the poor son of a gun," he said.

"I met a woman reporter, Alma Reyes. She's famous. Not just for being a hotshot reporter, but for surviving after she was kidnapped. Her bodyguard died. She lived. Now she has more bodyguards and New Guaymas can't get to her, so Alma thinks they kidnapped her niece as payback. A twenty-one-year-old named Silvia."

"Shit. You mentioned you wanted to help her out?"

"I went up to Playa today. We have an associate who works there, Jaime. He's trying to help us track down where she went to," Layla said.

"Who's we?"

"Me, Alma, and Gabriella, a friend of the missing girl. We located a taxista who saw her niece Silvia, and boyfriend, an attorney for MBC, get into a black Escalade at their hotel."

Clay rolled his eyes.

"Yeah, I know. Bad on both counts. The Escalade *and* MBC."

"Is he connected?" Clay asked.

"Well, Alma thinks he's laundering. Has lots of money, comes to Cancun frequently. Who knows what he's doing, but there are a lot of unfortunate possibilities out there."

"Too bad he included the girl."

"Tell me about it," Layla agreed.

"What now?" Clay asked.

"Jaime drove to the sub-division today—kinda dodgy—where the taxista saw the Escalade pull in the night they first arrived. According to Azul, their hotel, they haven't spent a night there yet."

Clay looked at his beer bottle before taking another sip. "Does not sound good."

Layla's phone rang. She held up her finger and answered. "Hola? Jaime? Si. Que paso?"

She stayed quiet for some moments and nodded absent-mindedly as she listened. "Okay, okay. Ciao."

She hung up. "Jaime located what he thinks is the property. Talked to someone in the neighborhood. A black Escalade goes in and out of there regularly. Tough looking guys."

"Now what?"

"He's got a line on something. Gonna check out another lead. He'll get back to me."

"Say, if your calls are done for now, how about we take a ride to that reserve? What's it called? Si'an Ka'an? I hear it's beautiful," Clay said.

"Sure, haven't been there. The front desk guy was telling me about it. One million hectares. They're gonna keep it tourist-free except for private land and water tours, and at the end in Punta Allen, there's a little B and B. That's it."

Clay stood and grabbed Layla's hand, pulling her up. "Cool, let's go."

𒊹 𒊹 𒊹

The day was still hot when Layla and Clay jumped into his rental, a four-door Toyota. They quickly covered the distance from Analisa y José's to the Si'an Ka'an Maya arch, unofficial entrance to the biosphere. At the arrival center, attendants took notes for tourist statistics, asking questions about where they were going. On a peninsula that stretched fifty kilometers to basically nowhere, the reasoning seemed absurd.

Back on the road they were in fine spirits, recharged by the energy from the magnificence of the terrain, the jungle, and the unforgettable sea—flat as a turquoise plate.

Shortly after they crossed into the reserve, Layla wondered aloud if Clay's rental came with shock absorbers. "We can't go all the way to Punta Allen. Not today on this road," she said.

"Let's drive as far as we can until dark. I like being on this skinny peninsula with ocean all around. It's like driving in the sky."

Layla, too, gazed at the peninsula's magnificence. "There's a fishing lodge at an area called Boca Paila, and a bridge. It's about fifteen kilometers."

"Okay." Clay pointed to a wooden sign, Casa Paraiso, twenty kilometers. "Hey, I thought you said there wasn't any tourist stuff down here."

"Well, there's not supposed to be. Not even homes. I was told it was a UNESCO site and part of some foundation. 'Man and the Biosphere,' I think they called it."

"It's breath-taking, but somebody lives here other than just fish and game."

"Hmm. Maybe I'll ask Gabriella. She works for a big real estate investment firm, Maya Reál. They're working with the governor on some new project. It's gonna put a thousand condos and homes in Tulum."

Clay whistled. "In Tulum? Where are they gonna shove 'em? Under the reef?"

"No, silly. On the selva side, you know, the jungle."

"Must be huge land investments, especially with Tulum on fire like it is."

"There's a lot of turf wars. Did you notice that fenced-off eyesore near Analisa y José's? That was a land grab a year ago. They closed fourteen eco-resorts, bulldozed four. A famous Mexican movie star bought there in 2000. He knew what they were doing was illegal as hell, but he bought in again, paid twice, because he loved it so much. Some Monterrey family insists they own everything. Hundreds and hundreds of beachfront hectares. Case closed."

"Connected?" Clay asked.

"Sub-division owners, so yes, to someone. Maybe the governor. He's shady, I hear."

"Was there a communal land deal or something? With the Maya?"

"Back in the seventies, Quintana Roo's early days. I heard the president gifted the Maya twenty-five thousand hectares of farmland. Much of it was divided and shared by a number of families. The land wasn't supposed to be sold, but it was. Illegally.

"Now it's hard to know what's real or fake with the titles. The farmers moved away and the land was gobbled up by real estate moguls," she said.

"A dark legal lagoon," Clay said as he stared out at the blue abyss.

"Yep. Hey, we're coming up on the Boca Paila bridge. That was fast."

A slight curve in the road showed the bridge in the distance—actually two bridges, an old wooden wreck of one taken out by the last hurricane, and a newer bridge made of concrete.

"Should we make a pit stop? See if they got any cerveza?"

"Count me in," Layla said.

A half kilometer down the road a faded blue sign—Boca Laguna Fishing Lodge—could be seen. They pulled into a sascab lot typical of the area and parked away from the entrance. This place, a popular spot for anglers and bonefishermen, was a throwback. The pizazz factor had not yet reached Boca Laguna and Layla hoped it never would. A rusty blue truck with a faded lodge logo on the side was the only other vehicle around.

Layla climbed from the rental, instantly aware that the car's tepid A/C had provided relief from the heat wave that engulfed her once outside. She reached into the car and grabbed a wide-brimmed sun hat, placed it on her head and angled it to the side to give it some flair. Clay untangled his long legs from beneath the steering wheel, and once outside, stretched. He nodded at the building.

"Looks like something out of the forties."

As with so many things Mexican, much had been made from a handful of basic materials, primarily concrete, limestone rock, and thin slats of zapote wood. Boca Laguna Lodge was long and low-slung, a white-washed structure with thatched palapa roof. A taller round building, an add-on, sat behind the main structure. Queen palms shaded the front entrance and red and pink hibiscus bordered it along with fuchsia bougainvilleas. It was the kind of place that would be fun to get lost in for a week or two, or forever.

"Let's check it out. See if we can find a cold drink," Layla said.

They walked the short distance to four cement stairs that raised the entire property onto a dais, a makeshift seawall to preserve the foundation in case of hurricanes. Two screened French doors, encapsulated by a thin layer of zapote, needed a fresh coat of varnish. The floor was tiled in retro twelve-by-twelves, white with a wavy blue line running throughout, laid so close together that no grout existed. Inside the modest lobby stood a desk and hardwood counter, but the room was deserted. Maybe it was siesta. Maybe it always looked this way.

Layla sauntered to the desk. A service bell had a hand-written note card next to it: Toca por servicio. Ring for service.

"Well, if you're thirsty, I'd say yes," Clay said.

She rang the bell. They waited.

"Wonder if anyone's around. Should we check out the dock?"

"Okay," Clay said.

They exited the lobby through the back doors, identical to the ones they'd just entered, onto another cement dais with a patio. Plastic tables and chairs sat on either side sheltered by blue canvas umbrellas, opened wide for shade. Pot-bellied clay pots filled with more bougainvilleas splashed color against white-washed walls. They walked leisurely towards the dock, passing queen palms and a few palapas and cinder circular cottages. At the landing pier, a twenty-foot panga was roped onto one of the pier posts with two smaller ones nearby. These, along with a handful of dolphin flat skiffs with Yamaha motors, made up the Boca fishing fleet. Clay and Layla stood quietly and surveyed the landscape. There wasn't much to look at except water, sky, and the occasional mangrove islet. A great blue heron, wading in the water, was their only neighbor.

"What do they fish for?" Clay asked.

"Snook, tarpon, bonefish. At Analisa y José's, the guy told me it's catch and release."

"Magnificent."

"I agree. Want something to drink?"

"Let's go," Clay said.

Inside the lobby, two muscular men had appeared and were speaking intensely to a now materialized desk clerk.

"We need the whole place," one said in a threatening manner. He was over-dressed for Tulum, wearing a stylish black jacket and lemon-colored shirt, designer sunglasses, pricey watch, hair coiffed with an abundance of gel. The look: bespoke cartel henchman.

"But that's not possible," the scrawny Maya clerk said. His head nearly touched the ledger reviewing the reservations, hoping to manifest a different outcome. "We have guests."

That wasn't the answer the man wanted to hear. His counterpart, an equally rough sort, who apparently frequented the same tailor, stepped close to the counter, placing a heavy hand on top. He stared into the shaking clerk's widening eyes.

Layla glanced at Clay. "Move along," she whispered.

As they passed the men at the counter, Layla pulled her sun hat further over her face, angling it against a possible onslaught of stares. Clay gave a perfunctory nod as they quickened their pace through the lobby and out the French doors.

Though they could hear the continuing exchange, they chose not to eavesdrop. It seemed more prudent to move out of what could well be harm's way. In the lot, parked front and center at the entrance, they nearly stumbled into a black Escalade.

Layla looked sideways at Clay. He had the presence of mind to keep moving, taking her elbow in a gentlemanly manner, as they moved to their car parked on the other side of the lot.

"Let's get outa here," Layla whispered.

Clay nodded. No further words were needed.

The car roared into life. Without burning rubber or scattering sascab, they drove to the parking lot exit, and were on their way.

CHAPTER 12

"Head south," Layla instructed. "Drive at least as far as the bridge. If they finish their business with the clerk and go back to Tulum, we don't need them tailing us. Out of sight, out of mind."

"Agreed."

The next few kilometers were quiet except for the occasional cawing of a gull and the sound of waves hitting the shore.

Layla broke the silence. "Was he carrying?"

"Probably. Who else would wear a jacket when it's thirty-five degrees Celsius?"

Her gaze moved from the brilliant biosphere to Clay. "What's happening? Why do they want the entire lodge?"

"Beats me. Sounds like they want to make it their own personal hide-away."

"For Silvia and her boyfriend?" Layla asked. "Am I stretching it?"

"Hmm. Not sure. Maybe that's just part of it. If your pal Jaime is on it, he'll probably put two and two together."

"Look, there's Casa Paraiso. You know, the one posted on the sign right after we crossed into the biosphere. Is it a rental?"

"With a sign like that, I'd say so. Maybe we need a break after that sighting at the lodge. Shape shift or something," Clay said.

She smiled. "Yeah, I like the idea of moving my atoms."

"You always were a risk taker."

🔃🔃🔃

The sascab lane was a narrow path as white as the sand on a Tulum beach. It stretched onwards for a good way, and gave the feel of driving through a jungle, but one with a road. To Layla, even though it brought back painful memories of trekking through a similar jungle weeks earlier just hours after the plane crash, it was still breathtaking. She'd reclaimed her bad case of nerves after seeing the thugs threatening the Boca desk clerk or she might have enjoyed it more. But trouble lay close at hand—she could sense it— too close for her to feel safe or happy. Not now. Not yet.

They passed an empty two-meter palapa on stilts that served as a guard house, and kept driving. Eventually, they came upon a sizable parking lot with a lone pick-up truck. An arrow on a carved wooden sign pointed towards a sandy path through a flourish of palms.

"This is incredible," Layla said as they walked towards the villa.

Clay nodded in agreement. "Totally remote, and you got the ocean on one side and the lagoon on the other."

An unconventional beach house greeted them. Casa Paraiso, another hand-carved slab of hardwood, proclaimed. The expansive front door was positioned under an over-hanging balcony with Maya glyphs carved into a protruding border ledge. The modern stucco structure had flat slate slabs for accent plastered onto the solid white exterior. The villa was graced with areca and sego palms that bordered the entry. Clay picked up a brass door knocker at the entrance and dropped it—three times.

A young Maya woman in a knee-length cotton skirt and embroidered blouse came to their aid, opening wide the door.

"Hola," Layla said. "Would it be possible to take a tour of Casa Paraiso? My sister is getting married next year and this looks like a perfect honeymoon spot."

The young woman, trained in graciousness, nodded and showed them in.

"I didn't know you had a sister," Clay whispered.

Layla gave him a cool look. "I don't."

"You've come at a good time. Our last guests left yesterday. I'll show you around."

The tour began on the main floor. Vanishing walls were pushed in, pocket-style, to bring stunning outdoor views indoors. Though heavy foliage, palm trees, and the setback from the beach on one side and the lagoon on the other restricted full ocean views, once upstairs the vista was 360 degrees. There, the outdoor terraza sported an infinity pool for those who chose to take a swim and gaze at not one but two bodies of water.

"Lovely. May I take some photos?" Layla asked.

"Sure, but we do have a good website," the caretaker said.

While they checked out the deck, a well-dressed Mexican woman in a flowing caftan appeared on the terrace. "Hello. Sorry to disturb you."

"No bother," Layla said. "We were just looking at this amazing villa. It would be perfect for my sister's wedding."

"When is it?"

"Next spring," Layla lied.

"Plenty of time. I'm the owner, or the owner's sister, actually. Occasionally I check to make sure everything's in shape, but with Julietta in charge"—she paused and gave a smile to the young woman who'd shown them in—"I never have to worry."

"Wonderful news," Layla said, putting on one of her magnificent *give me anything I want* smiles. "I was surprised to see your villa here in the biosphere."

The woman tugged on a glamorous silver earring with a turquoise center. "Oh, my brother is governor and there was a codicil that allowed one home to be built every hundred hectares, if it used sustainable features. As you can see from the tinacos that catch and hold our water and the solar panels, we're totally energy free." She pointed to expansive holding tanks and the roof-top panels. "All we need is rain and sun."

"Your brother is the governor?" Layla asked.

She nodded. "Yes. Unfortunately he's so busy, he can never get here. He's always stuck in Chetumal, doing those things politicians do."

Layla smiled in assent. She knew exactly what politicians did. "And what's his name? I'm not from around here."

"Enrique Hernandez."

"Felicidades to both of you. Can I get your email?" Layla asked.

"Julietta can give you instructions on how to make a reservation. Will it be a large party?"

"For pre-wedding activities, twelve."

"That would work perfectly. Well, enjoy your day. Are you heading to Punta Allen?"

"No, back to Tulum. We'd like to be there by sunset," Layla said. "We better be off."

Checking her watch, the owner's sister answered, "You should just about make it."

The open road and the hope of soon sitting with margarita in hand propelled them forward.

CHAPTER 13

Enrique Hernandez, governor of the state of Quintana Roo, stood in the center of his office, for a moment unable to think. That wasn't like him. Even as a kid he always came up with a strategy, no matter if it was playing hide-and-seek on the hard-scrabble streets of Escarcega with his sister, Erwina, or running out of the frutería after snitching an orange. Just a game. That's what he'd managed to do his entire life—make a game of things and win in the process. He pondered recent events as his mind wandered.

Taller than average and strikingly thin, his clothes hung on him so loosely it looked like a stiff breeze could blow him over. His demeanor was more loan shark than politician, and his gaunt countenance did little to give others confidence.

His thoughts drifted to Francisco Ramirez, the finance attorney for MBC. Enrique had worked with MBC for nearly a decade, not always as governor, but in other ventures like the one with the cement company he and his college friend, Ernesto Torres, had co-founded. Made aware of Francisco's talents by Torres, though Enrique had a nodding relationship with the man, he had never worked with him directly. Three weeks earlier, however, he'd received a call.

Francisco had jumped in with little overture. "We need to talk about money transfers for laundering, to decide what bank accounts to use in which countries."

Enrique resisted. "That's not my job."

Francisco had persisted and continued. "A lot of cash from recent titles came from your deals—that's why I'm clearing things with you. I suggest payments be made to a bank in Grand Caymen via Liechtenstein, with fifteen percent laundered through Zurich."

"That's your territory." Enrique's objection came out like a snarl.

The banker pushed back. "Listen, Torres wanted me to firm this up."

Enrique smoothed a lock of the wavy black hair that was his singular asset and wandered over to the window. He stared at the river that lay between Chetumal, where the governor's residency was located, to the bridge into Belize, a country of thieves—thieves with no ambition. Not like hard-working Mexicans, people who worked two, three jobs to make ends meet.

As a young man he was well aware he had not a shred of Torres' looks or panache, but in spite of a less than enviable bearing, he was proud and gratified he'd won a scholarship to UNAM. After graduation, he began working with his college friend's family construction business in Monterrey.

Once NAFTA came into play, the Mexican govern-ment pushed for better infrastructure, and lucrative road contracts abounded. With a degree in chemical engineering, Enrique became a key figure in the firm. His background allowed him to massage cement compounds, saving his benefactor millions. For his efforts, he'd been well rewarded. First came the partnership in the cement company, and later on he became a presta nombre on land titles. Signing his name for Torres' gave his friend cover so it didn't look like a construction empresario owned excessive amounts of land tracts. Little by little, Torres siphoned off a parcel to Enrique here, a parcel there.

Enrique soon grasped how to play the game, and when Torres suggested he throw his hat into the ring for governor, he was all in. As governor, he'd have a heads up on new land deals. Torres promised to pay campaign expenses, and for his backing, they would later split profits on Q. Roo beachfront properties.

At first, the deals were easy pickings, but in 2014, journalists like Olivia Cache of *Por Esto* demanded more exposure on what became of public lands. Land prices rose and disastrous home and hotel relocations started; some Tulum owners refused to leave.

In an effort to regain land he'd stolen from them, several owners made side deals with the governor to reclaim their properties. Through these transactions, Enrique accumulated fist-loads of cash, and this was where Francisco came into play. The banker knew the ins and outs of money laundering, from the Grand Caymans to Panama.

The present thorn in Enrique's side was the Tulum mayor, a constant bother due to his ongoing dispute over elections with some political rag. Enrique wanted no problem buying up public lands, but the newspaper had an inside line on titles heading into escrow. Even though he'd had the mayor send a message by fire-bombing their printing press, they continued to publish.

"You're getting in too deep," Erwina warned over lunch one day.

"Don't worry," he'd told her, though he withheld Torres' news that New Guaymas cartel wanted to launder cash through the firm. The upside of a cartel connection meant protection—the cartel would take care of business, no matter how loathsome. With all they hoped to accomplish, Enrique understood that cartel muscle might well grease the wheels of commerce. And then there was the bottom line: Cartels didn't accept no for an answer.

Enrique had come a long way from that armpit Escarcega, and it was time to enjoy the fruits of his labors. With his term nearly over, he could soon relax in his villa in the biosphere. He wanted a clean slate and all banking provisions behind him.

CHAPTER 14

C lay drove to the top of the lane and approached the road leaving Casa Paraiso behind. He looked both ways. "Oh no."

Layla looked too and let out a gasp. Not far up the road, too close for comfort, was a black Escalade.

Layla lowered the sun hat over her face, slumped down in the seat and became pre-occupied with her phone. Clay assumed his normal posture and executed the turn. The road being narrow, they passed the black GM showpiece at a crawl with little room on either side. Eyes front, they could feel the pressure of glares from on high. When it was safe to have a look, Layla turned in her seat and gazed at the car they had just passed.

Layla inhaled sharply. "The license plate!"

"What about it?"

"It's hanging by one bolt. That's what the taxi guy told the concierge at Azul."

"You better call your friend and let him know what's happening," Clay said. "Something's going on."

Layla scrolled through her phone. "Jaime? Checking in. We spotted the black Escalade you're looking for. Hmm. Hmm."

"What?" Clay asked, hand up in a questioning pose.

She made a small hand gesture indicating she'd get to him. "Yes, we were taking a drive down to Boca Laguna Lodge. Who? Oh, me and Clay, a friend. He's here for a few days.

"Yes, Martín knows him," she nodded, indicating Clay was getting vetted. "Family friend."

"Well, at the lodge, we walked to the lagoon to check out the dock, and when we went back to the lobby, the clerk was being grilled by two rough guys, definitely not tourists. They told him they wanted the entire lodge for something. Not sure for what.

"That's not all. We went further south before turning around and drove into Casa Paraiso. Yeah, huge property. Did you know it was owned by the governor? I heard he was called that, too. Does that mean anything to you?" She listened intently while Clay waited for the punch line.

"Okay, I think we should meet. Any place in particular? Nada Mas? Avenida Tulum? We're south of the lodge now. An hour and a half? This road sucks. Oh, you know that?" She laughed. "Okay, ciao."

"What's happening?" Clay asked.

"He wants to meet for dinner at Nada Mas in Tulum. He has info and seemed real interested when I told him about the governor owning Casa Paraiso."

"Why?"

"Seems the governor has his fingers in a lot of pies, not all exactly legal. He's slick, though, and no one has been able to pin anything on him. He just stole another four hundred hectares of beachfront, according to Jaime. A blatant land grab, but when the media swooped and asked about it, he first refused to be questioned, then eventually broke his silence and said it was perfectly legal. He's growing his business, one Maya land grant at a time."

"Or more."

"Dinner in Tulum?" Layla asked.

"Como no?"

〰〰〰

Silvia had met Francisco at a Fashion Runway event, Mexico's society gala of the year, led by a Mexican fashion designer who had recently finished a successful show in Paris. It was invitation only and this year her family had received but a single invite. Since her father's death a few years earlier, these invitations were not as abundant as they once had been. Though her mother still held a prominent position in fashionable Cuernavaca's social ranking—hailing from a noteworthy family—her father's mega-wealth and status in the oil industry had cemented their position in fine society.

The affair itself was sponsored by a society maven, Lenora Valdez, and her mysterious husband, Silvestre Lopez Garcia. Along with a smattering of jet setters, a movie producer, and a famous New York singer, even the French ambassador to Mexico was expected to attend.

As sponsors, Lenora and her husband aimed to raise money for a local charity. Silvestre, tall and slim with a pencil-thin mustache, wore his raven hair long and slicked back. If anyone had guessed his true identity, the founder of New Guaymas Generation cartel, no one let on. His cartel had proved to be the most ruthless yet, and had infiltrated every aspect of Mexico's social order—politics, law enforcement, judiciary, high society, even gossip columns. That was Silvestre's real achievement—his ability to work his way into every nook and cranny of the social edifice.

Silvia had shopped for weeks looking for the perfect outfit and arrived at the event dressed to the nines. Her off-the-shoulder sheath was the color of a Colombian emerald, with a plunging neckline that exposed an ample bosom. Her sleek, raven-colored hair had been pulled into a fashionable up-do, making her enticing neck look longer still.

Francisco had come to hate these events, but as an eligible bachelor and prominent figure in MBC's Mexico City office, attendance was de rigueur. He hated wearing a tuxedo and privately scoffed at the city's well-heeled matrons all trying to outperform their wealthy friends. The male guests, most over forty, wore tuxedos or dark suits, Italian designer shoes, and sported expensive watches. They gathered around on the outside terraza of whatever fancy hotel hosted the event, puffing on imported cigars and sipping high-priced tequila. None seemed happy to see him and the feeling was mutual. There was one person, however, with whom he yearned to have a conversation: the founder of the event, Silvestre Lopez Garcia. On arriving, Francisco spotted Silvestre in his typical here-but-not-here position at the bar, nursing a drink. Francisco moved mechanically through the crowd, avoiding eye contact. Though the bar was crammed shoulder to shoulder with party attendees, a seat next to Silvestre materialized.

"Quite a turnout tonight," the younger man said in an effort to break the ice.

Silvestre looked the attorney straight in the eye. A moment went by and nothing was said. Francisco squirmed, feeling he was either being shunned or vetted. Finally his neighbor broke the silence with one syllable. "Si."

From that moment, Francisco started talking, as if a gusher had been unleashed. He felt a kinship with the older man, as though he'd known him forever. He first broached the topic of politics. Sensing he wasn't making headway, he ventured into the Riviera Maya's runaway growth.

"What is it that you do?" Silvestre asked half-heartedly.

"I'm an attorney for MBC. Financial acquisitions. I work in areas where there's activity. Now, it's Q. Roo."

The older fellow nodded sagely, said nothing, and returned his gaze to the glass before him.

"It isn't slowing down. Hotels are staking claims and tourist revenues continue to pour in. It's a gold rush. Assume you've been?" Francisco asked.

The question could have been rhetorical. Though hardly a talker, the older man exuded a quiet calm that brought out conversation in others. It also didn't hurt that he was urbane and well-dressed, and his charismatic wife was the belle of the ball. Silvestre turned around to face the room, searching for his better half, ignoring Francisco's question.

Lenora must have felt her husband's gaze because she did an about face. She glanced over the sea of revelers, spotted Silvestre, gave a wave and coy smile. She turned to the chic young woman at her side and steered her to where Silvestre was holding court.

"Darling," she said, placing a hand on her husband's shoulder and pecking him on the cheek. "Meet Silvia. Her father was Claudillo Castillo. He worked at Pemex with Paco Slim."

It was the first time that evening the older man took an interest in the conversation.

"Buenos noches, señorita." In a split second his personality enveloped the entire bar. "A pleasure to meet you."

She nodded and returned a dazzling smile.

"Who is your new friend?" Lenora asked, gazing appreciatively at the handsome young man next to her husband.

"Buenos noches, señora. Francisco Ramirez. A pleasure to meet you."

In that age-old precedent known as Mexican social structure, she replied, "The pleasure is mine. Do you know Silvia?" Her inner matchmaker burned inside.

Introductions made, Lenora explained it was time for the runway event. "Would you like to join us, Francisco? I've asked Silvia to sit with me. We have an extra seat."

He looked at the epitome of Botticelli's *Birth of Venus* but with dark rather than golden tresses. "That would be lovely."

It had all the trappings of a beautiful relationship.

CHAPTER 15

Silvia rolled over in a king-size bed, stretching her arms towards something or someone but found only empty space. Francisco, the debonair bachelor she'd met at the fashion event the previous night, was nowhere to be seen. She gazed around the modern, well-appointed room. High ceilings painted in light gray accented dark gray bedroom walls, and grand picture windows sported a set of closed sheer curtains subduing the morning sun, while thick patterned drapes were held back with braided cords. Francisco's designer had done an excellent job furnishing the place. She was impressed.

After last night's antics, it wasn't just the apartment's interior design that gave her pause. Francisco was a romantic and energetic lover. It had started innocently enough. After the reception, he asked if his driver could drop her somewhere. She told him her address in Cuernavaca and he said no problem. They entered his hired luxury sedan, complete with side bar and privacy window. Although she'd already had her share of spirits, when he offered her champagne, she couldn't say no—or rather, didn't want to.

After a single sip, he placed a hand on her knee, shifted her body his way and took the glass gingerly from her hand. He put an arm around her shoulders and brought her close. He began to kiss her neck with slow passionate kisses. Her body melted into the closest thing to ecstasy she'd ever felt. No one had kissed her like that before. The kisses sent shivers down her spine—and they didn't stop there. She was moved, shaken and trembling. She wanted more.

"Shall we go to my place first, before I have Felix drop you?" he asked.

She could barely get out a response.

They tumbled out of the car into the underground garage, with her leaning into his comfortable arms. The elevator doors opened quickly and he pushed the button. In moments they entered his apartment—first stop, the bedroom. The room was aglow in a soft light from corner lamps. He laid her gently on the bed and slowly removed her strapped heels, one at a time. Her body trembled as he lightly moved his hand above her knee and up her thigh. "Oooh," was all she could manage before his other arm went around her waist. She felt him move his body slowly on top of her, then his mouth was on hers. He again began to kiss her neck, the entire time keeping his hand firmly below her waist. Her body opened up to him. She was his.

🁢🁢🁢

Layla spotted Nada Mas first. She pointed to a restaurant with an overhanging palapa, a few tables tucked cozily underneath, and a neon blinking 'Abierto' sign. "That's it."

Clay pulled the car into a parking spot. They exited and walked toward the restaurant. A waiter greeted them.

Layla scanned the room and saw Jaime sitting at a back corner table. "We're joining him." She pointed at Jaime.

The waiter ushered them to the table. As they approached, Jaime stood. Layla thanked the waiter, and before sitting down said in English, "Jaime, this is my friend Clay."

Introductions made, Layla continued, "Well, I think we could use a drink. What are you having, Clay?"

"Dos Equis."

"Two," Layla said.

Acknowledging Clay, Jaime said in accented English, "So, you saw the Escalade."

"Si, it was unnerving," she told the investigator. "After knowing that was the last sighting of Silvia and her boyfriend."

He nodded in a knowing way. Driving a black Escalade was akin to displaying a family crest. "What were they doing in the reserve?"

"Trying to take over the entire Boca Laguna Lodge. Don't know why and we didn't see how it ended, but I'm sure they got what they were asking for," Layla said.

Clay agreed. "They had it all over the desk clerk."

"You saw them again after that?"

"Si. As we came out of Casa Paraiso, there they were. They must have finished finalizing their plans, and were going to Casa Paraiso. It's an odd coincidence that the villa is owned by the governor."

"There's that, and then there's the disappearance of the banker and the girl."

"Did you dig up any info on Ramirez?" Layla asked.

"I did. He's no angel, but he hasn't ruffled any feathers. Several years at MBC. Word on the street is he's in charge of laundering in the Riviera Maya."

Layla digested that piece of information. "That's what Silvia's aunt thought, too. Could that get him in trouble?"

"Maybe. If he's not playing the game right, it could get him in a whole heap of trouble. Depends how he goes about it—is he a high roller out there making a splash, or is he low-key and under the radar? Lately the DEA has been sniffing around, and with El Ladrón, you know, the governor, doing land grabs, there's been more focus on our little piece of paradise."

"Do you have any info on the lot where the Escalade went?" Layla asked.

"It supposedly belongs to some guy from Chetumal. The neighbor was reluctant to say more."

"Is it a coincidence that the governor is a guy from Chetumal?"

"Could be. Every few weeks someone shows up," Jaime said.

"Any way we can get inside the shack on the property? I mean, you?" Layla asked.

"It'd have to be at night. I'm not sure what it would accomplish, but we might find something out," Jaime said.

The waiter returned to take their order. When dinner arrived, Layla was starved. An influx of carbs gave her brain a boost. "Want to check it out tonight?"

Clay stopped in the middle of a swig of beer. "Check out what?"

"What?" A half second later, from Jaime.

"We're here, it's dark. No more cerveza. We finish dinner and head to the sub-division. You know where it is,

Jaime," she said in her best impersonation of her uncle making a demand.

He started to shake his head. Clay looked concerned and began to speak, but Layla assumed the lead and talked over them both. "No, we gotta do it. It will be six days tomorrow that Silvia's missing. Clay, you in?"

He nodded, his mouth having just clamped onto an enchilada. Jaime, looking a bit peeved, couldn't respectably say no if the other male in the group was in agreement with his boss. And besides, no one said no to the boss.

The fixer, who may have hoped to push the envelope with his new jefe, fell in line. "Let's finish dinner. I'll drive."

CHAPTER 16

They left their rental car parked in front of Nada Mas. Jaime would drive, Layla would ride shotgun, and Clay would take up the rear. The spur of the moment decision, with no one prepared for anything, was a desperate attempt at discovery.

"I assume you're packing?" Layla asked in a nonchalant manner.

"Yeah. You never know what to expect."

"Good idea, in your line of work," Clay said, tongue in cheek.

Jaime let out a low chuckle. "What, we got a joker in the back?" He smiled into the rearview mirror and winked at Clay.

Since the restaurant was near Tulum city limits, they quickly covered the few kilometers that brought them to a lonely road leading east. "This is it."

It was a black night devoid of a moon. They ambled onto the side road and passed a scattering of small houses, many lit by single light bulbs hanging from ceilings. Families were sitting in their yards or on front steps even though the sun had set long ago; it was cooler outside, in spite of the stubborn whir of ever-ready VEC fans.

"How far down is it?" Clay asked.

"Another kilometer. There's a bend in the road where the sub-division peters out."

"What else can you tell us?" Layla asked.

"Cinder block warehouse. Very basic. A large metal sliding door and a couple of barred windows—high up—in front, and a metal encased door with bars. There's one in back, too."

"You did some serious sleuthing," Layla said, throwing a bone Jaime's way.

"I waited for the neighbor to leave, then drove down the road," he pointed straight ahead. "Went another couple of kilometers, pulled over, had a smoke, and came back. Just in case he changed direction, but no one was around."

"What are we gonna do tonight?" Clay asked.

"The window in the back looked unsecured. I didn't want to hang around in the daytime to find out. It's probably locked but no bars. A good wrench and tire iron could make it come to mama."

They came to the bend. Houses had dwindled and it was darker still on this side of the sub-division.

"There, see it?" Jaime asked.

Layla, in the front seat, strained her eyes in the darkness. "I think so. Is the chainlink fence part of the property?"

"Yeah, and locked."

A sturdy-looking lock wrapped with two-inch chain links held the gates shut. "Now what?" she asked.

"Well, in my business, we don't give up so easy." He looked over at his new boss and gave her a wry smile.

She let it go.

"We'll drive farther down the road like I did and walk back. The rear fence on the property has a break in it, big enough to slip through. I've got a flashlight, a tire iron, and a wrench. Let's see what damage we can do.

"Before we get started, mind if I have a smoke?" Jaime asked, pulling to the berm.

"No, go ahead." Layla rolled down her window. The night air was sticky with humidity, not even a whisper of a breeze.

"It helps me focus. Guess it's the nicotine. Drove the wife crazy."

"You're married?" Layla asked.

"No more. She couldn't handle my hours, I couldn't handle her griping. I called her the War Department. Whatever I said, she always went to war over it. We split sheets."

"That's a new one," Clay said.

"Kinda sums it up, don't it?" Jaime asked, chuckling.

Layla shrugged and Clay nodded.

For an unplanned outing in the middle of nowhere on a moonless night, Jaime appeared nonchalant, if not relaxed. He, too, had rolled down his window and he rested his arm while taking drags on his cigarette. Neither Layla nor Clay disturbed the man's thoughts.

"You know, this is a very weird thing. An MBC banker, just disappearing like that. And with a broad. Something's going on. He's messed with someone somehow. He's compromised, or he's plain dirty," Jaime said.

Layla looked at Clay. Even in the dark she could make out his distinct profile—straight nose, firm jaw. His presence made her feel safe, even though they were in what could become a sketchy situation.

"So, did the cartel nab him because he's cooperating?" Layla asked.

Jaime took another drag off his cigarette before he answered. "If he's blabbing, he's damn stupid to think no one would find out. He was ripe for being tapped. MBC is no angel. He's the one doing their laundering, so he basically knows all. And if New Guaymas is doing business with MBC, which I heard they were, he could be in big trouble."

"Hijole. Why drag Silvia into it?" Layla asked, a tightness in her voice.

"You get to be around those guys, even our guys, and you know how it is. Ya think you're invincible. No disrespect, boss, but sometimes everyone needs to give themselves a good talking to. Get humble. Even if just for a day."

"Amen," Clay said.

"Oh, we have the Buddhist clocking in," Layla said, her voice heavy with sarcasm.

"Buddhist? What the hell?" Jaime sounded surprised.

"Yeah, Clay's my resident guru. He's gonna teach me meditation."

"Layla, be nice."

Jaime interrupted. "We can continue the conversation later. Let me grab the tire iron and wrench and see what we can find out."

He went to the trunk, rummaged around for his equipment and flashlight. "Let's go."

They followed behind the bobbing light. Clay reached for Layla's hand, placing it firmly in his.

"Now, be real careful here," Jaime said, when they arrived at the compound. "This is a little tricky. What are you wearing on your feet, Layla? Not sandals I hope."

"Sandals."

"Oh, um, be careful. We're going to walk the fence line. I'll walk next to you with the light. I don't want you getting hurt. We may have to get out of here quick, and a twisted ankle won't help anyone."

Clay followed behind Layla. The terrain was uneven and wouldn't be an easy walk, even in daylight. She kept one hand on the fence and in a few minutes got the hang of it.

"In about thirty meters, there's a jagged cut where we can slip through. Layla, maybe you should wait on this side, and me and Clay will go in."

"No, I'll go, too," she said, pushing her voice to sound fearless, not letting on she'd feel scared left on her own. Being without a bodyguard really sucked.

"I'll watch out for her, Jaime," Clay said.

"Right-o. Be careful here. Breathe in, follow me."

She watched Jaime adjust to one side and begin to squeeze in between the sets of chainlink fencing, with Clay holding it apart as much as possible. The rear of the building still looked far away, and Layla couldn't yet make out the window.

Jaime got through and held it apart for her from his side and Clay did the same from the back. She sucked it in and held her skirt around her so as not to tear it. She grabbed onto the chainlink and on stepping through, scraped the side of her foot on the metal. "Ouch."

"What?" Clay asked.

"My foot, just the top, not the bottom."

"Is it bleeding?" Jaime asked.

"Can't tell, but I don't think it's too bad."

"Well, no bandaids here. Let's keep moving."

Clay followed suit and eventually all three were on the inside of the chainlink, ready to get to the building itself and have a go at the window.

"If we can see inside," Jaime said, "we may get an idea what this place is used for, obviously for something, because according to the taxista, they were driven here by a black car."

As they approached the building, Layla looked up. It seemed a towering height. "How will we see what's inside?" she asked.

"See that inset on the window?" Jaime said, motioning upwards.

Clay strained his eyes. "Some of the cinder blocks are offset. You want me to give you a boost. I'll cup my hands, and you try for the ledge?"

"Si, let's give it a try."

Layla stood back. "Should I hold the light for you?"

"Better turn it off," Jaime said.

"I agree," Clay added.

Clay took the position as booster, cupped his hands, and waited for Jaime's weight. He was much taller than Jaime, with a solid build, and not an ounce of fat.

"What if you can't reach the ledge?" Layla asked.

"Let's not over think this, boss," Jaime said, preparing for the boost.

He, too, was solid, and though shorter than Clay, had a readiness that defied understanding. Layla flashed on the bullfighting photos. Of course he had an edge. He'd outrun bulls.

Clay's boost still put the shorter man under the ledge, even though Jaime was standing on tip toe. Clay stood patiently as Jaime looked upwards, teetering, while he considered the next move. Layla watched nervously from below as Jaime's right foot searched for any small crack or uneven block that could be used as leverage to reach the window. His first attempt nearly dropped him on top of Clay.

"Crap!" he said in a loud whisper as he hit the earth lightly.

"Easy, Jaime, easy," Clay coached.

The cartel fixer took a moment to reconsider. "I see an edge that might work."

"Go for it," Clay said. "Let's try again. Should I give you a bigger lift?"

"Okay. Got my eye on it. Let's go."

Layla held her breath. Clay boosted the lighter man, watching him scramble for position on the nearly vertical surface.

"Ohh," Jaime said, falling back into Clay's already cupped hands as the Canadian readied himself for the added weight. "Not again."

"Listen. Next time you'll get it. You need a second?" Clay asked.

"No, ready when you are," Jaime said.

"Let's do it."

Clay boosted Jaime a third time and Layla could hear his scuffling feet as he searched for any crack in which to rest his toe. "Got it—think I got it!"

"Bueno," Layla whispered from below.

"Made it!" Jaime said in a loud whisper. "Can you throw me the flashlight?"

Clay's toss was too high and it ricocheted off the building, falling back to earth. Layla scrambled after it on the dark ground.

"Do you see it?" Clay asked.

"Looking," she said as she scuffed her feet around in the loose dirt. "Here it is."

She picked it up and moved towards Clay, handing him the light. "Ready?" he asked.

"Go!" Jaime repeated.

This time the fixer deftly snatched the moving flashlight from the air while managing to tightly hold onto the ledge with his right hand. "Got it!"

Layla breathed a sigh of relief and Clay again stood at ease.

Jaime expertly turned the light on with one hand and shone it into the warehouse window.

"What do you see?" Layla asked.

"Give me a minute, slight glare." From below they saw a systematic spot of white move back and forth. "It's a big room—nearly empty. Several chairs. Looks like a concrete floor. There's a counter at the far end, close to where you drive in. Two steel cupboards, double doors. A battered wood table, a few empty bottles. Not much more. I'm coming down. Gonna jump. Watch out."

He leapt to the ground, limbs folded inward, falling expertly into a roll so as not to injure himself. Did he learn that in the ring? Layla wondered.

Jaime rolled over and pushed himself up, rubbing dirt from his hands onto his pants. He flipped off the flashlight. His face was no longer visible in the dark. "Whew." He was breathing heavily.

"What do you think?"

As she asked the question, they heard a noise that sounded like a car approaching. Next came gates creaking open.

"What was that?" Layla asked.

"Someone's here!" Clay replied.

"What should we do?"

"Get out, fast!" Jaime said.

The three invaders started towards the break in the back chainlink fence. "Layla, be careful," Clay instructed, as he watched Jaime move through the slip.

"Hurry," Jaime urged. "Get positioned to move once we figure out what they're doing."

"Right," Clay said. "Layla, you okay?"

She pulled her skirt around her body, gingerly moving through the chainlink fence. "Si."

Clay deftly navigated his oversized frame through the fence as though he were a gazelle. For a big guy, he had great moves. Probably the Aikido training, Layla thought.

"Now what?" Layla asked.

"We wait. Quietly," Jaime instructed, placing an index finger over pursed lips.

They heard the gate scrape back into position, a door open and slam. Someone said, "Keep to the left, over there. Over there."

"Okay, but what about him?"

Layla's head jerked wildly to look at Jaime. She heard a car door slam.

"What about him?" the other voice demanded.

"Who?"

"The banker. Who else? Inside, cabrón."

"Right, man."

Layla, Clay, and Jaime stayed still against the fence, trying to overhear any snippet of conversation they could, not daring to move. Another car door opened and more conversation spilled out.

"Step down, step down, pendejo!"

"Grab his arm. Hijole! I can't do everything. I'm driving here."

Disorganization appeared to be the status quo. Layla listened, trying to decide how many men were involved in the late night visit. The car, previously at an idle, moved. She heard the brakes again and a car door open and slam shut. Two men and a hostage?

She heard shuffling of feet and voices again. "C'mon. Move it. I've got you, pendejo. Are you going to open the door?"

"I had to park, cabrón. What's your hurry?"

"Well, what do we do with him?"

"Get him inside and shut up."

"He can't see, asshole. He's blindfolded, remember? Give me a minute."

After a bit more maneuvering, the slow-moving trio went inside the warehouse, firmly closing the door. The cavernous building took on an eerie glow when the lights turned on.

"Is it safe to move?" Layla asked, letting out a shaky breath.

"Yeah," Jaime answered. "Clay, you good?"

"Yep. Let's get outa here."

They returned to their original formation and slowly moved along the chainlink fence until they were at the corner, adjacent to the building and the parking lot. Layla spied the Escalade inside the lot. From their vantage point, the dim lights of the warehouse glimmered.

"They said banker," Layla said aloud. "What will they do to him?"

"Maybe nothing. Maybe something," Jaime said. "But we want nothing done to us so we'll chat later."

If one of the rough guys had forgotten something in the vehicle and came back out to retrieve it, things could get dicey. For thirty meters, the fence gave them not an ounce of cover.

"Move, move," Clay said.

Layla could do that, and the three of them, regardless of the dark night and dodgy ground, kept close to the fence and propelled themselves towards the road.

"No light until we're well away from the warehouse," Jaime said. "Careful until we reach the car."

Along with the close call, the humidity was making Layla sweat. No one spoke. Inside the car they'd have cover. As they settled into Jaime's Toyota, quietly pulling shut the doors a few minutes later, Jaime said, "Well, now we know where Ramirez is. But where the hell is the girl?"

CHAPTER 17

Layla rode shotgun in Jaime's Toyota, stunned into silence. No one uttered a word. That was the million dollar question: Where was Silvia?

Layla began. "I've got to call Silvia's aunt. What do I tell her?"

Jaime glanced over at his jefe sitting next to him. "You tell her the truth."

"She'll be upset," Layla said.

"Yeah, of course she will, but we're putting this puzzle together. If everything was cool, we wouldn't be in Tulum on this wild goose chase at all."

Clay agreed. "You gotta let her know the boyfriend has been sighted. I mean heard, I guess. Was it him?"

"Has to be," Layla said. "They said banker."

"They've split them up for a reason. Is there anyone else involved in this little love-in that I don't know about?" Jaime asked.

"I've talked to Silvia's friend, Gabriella. I told you that. She works at the Tulum mayor's office and Maya Reál. She's the liaison between the mayor and the developer. A guy named Torres."

"*The* Torres from Monterrey? Construction?" Jaime asked.

"I guess so," Layla said. "Why, do you know him?"

"Everyone knows who he is, boss. He's big, real big. A player."

"And there's the mayor's other assistant, a Maya woman, Gloria. She seems to know what's happening in Tulum."

"So that's it?"

"Oh, and there's Isabel."

"Who's she?" Clay asked from the back seat. "You have a gaggle of girl assistants, Layla."

"She works at both Analisa y José's and at Playamar on the beach. She's really up on what's happening with the hotel scene and land deals. Hey, we can stop by Playamar, grab a drink and see if she's working. Are you up for it?"

"That's a no-brainer for me," Clay said.

"Sure," Jaime agreed. "We'll pick up your car from the restaurant and head over to the beach. The night is young, and maybe we'll find out something new from one of Layla's chicas."

ꓵ ꓶ ꓶ

Playamar's business always picked up after dark. On weekends music started around nine and went late. Clay pulled into a parking spot a few cars down from Jaime.

"Nice spot," Clay said as they moved towards the restaurant. Music wafted from indoors, Caribbean rhythms with steel drums. Layla decided to sit outside, so they could better converse.

"Playamar goes way back," Jaime said. "Haven't been here lately."

"Oh, there's Isabel!" Layla spied her sashaying towards the bar, drink tray in hand. "Go ahead and look for a table outside."

Layla moved across the room and came up behind Isabel. "Hola," she said loudly.

Isabel turned so quickly Layla nearly bumped into her. "Oops, sorry!" Layla grabbed the girl by the shoulders and gave her a quick hug.

"Hey, Chiapas girl. What are you doing here? Did you come out from under your rock to see how the tourists live?"

"No, no." She grabbed Isabel's elbow and moved her to what could be considered a quiet spot in the rowdy restaurant. "We discovered something. Something important."

Isabel's mouth dropped open. "Well, what?"

"We know where Silvia's boyfriend is, but it's not good."

"What about Silvia?" Isabel demanded.

With a forlorn shrug, Layla proceeded to tell Isabel where she, Jaime, and Clay had spent the past hour.

"This is creepy! So, the boyfriend's kidnapped and they have him blindfolded in a warehouse?"

Layla nodded. "Yes, but no sight of Silvia. At all. Jaime, you know, my Playa contact, thinks they're moving them around, to not bring attention to the situation. Clay thinks so, too."

"Who's Clay?"

"Oh," Layla said with another shrug. "A friend from Canada."

"As in male companion, Chiapas girl? Hmm. When were you going to tell me about this new development?"

"Stop. It's nothing, we're just friends. Old friends," Layla lied. "Come over and I'll introduce you. We're searching for clues. Anything that may give us a push in the right direction."

"Well, I heard from Gabriella earlier today," Isabel said.

Layla perked up. "Did she have any info?"

"She said that Torres was talking about doing some sort of expedition in the biosphere for a special investor group this weekend. Impromptu."

"Si'an Ka'an? Where in Si'an Ka'an?"

"There's not much there. At the Boca Laguna Lodge."

"No!" Layla nearly screamed. A fellow tourist who'd been idling nearby gave her a strange look and moved farther away.

"What?" Isabel demanded.

"We were there this afternoon. We saw a black Escalade."

"The Escalade from when they arrived?"

"Apparently so. The taxi guy who saw them told the concierge the Escalade license plate was hanging by a single bolt, with two big guys in dark suits riding inside. Bingo! When Clay got here, we thought we'd take a little drive and stopped in at Boca Laguna. The road was too bad to go to Punta Allen that late in the day."

"I know. I live here. Go on."

"We were going to grab a drink, but no one was at the desk so we walked to the dock. When we returned, the clerk was talking to two rough tipos, overdressed for the beach. They were demanding the entire lodge this weekend. We kept walking, and outside the front doors, there it was."

"Oh, no. It was them. At the Boca Laguna Lodge, and Torres is gonna be there, with Gabriella. What is going on?" Isabel asked.

"There's more. We got out of there fast and drove further south. Didn't want them tailing us all the way up to Tulum. Went into that Casa Paraiso, do you know it?"

"Of course. Beautiful villa, secluded."

"We were just killing time. Ended up meeting the owner's sister. You'll never guess who the owner is."

"Tell me!" Isabel barked, stamping her foot.

"The governor," Layla said.

"No! Something's happening."

"Si, si, si," Layla said. "But what?"

"These are not coincidences, Chiapas girl."

"Listen, I'll go find the guys. Can you bring over three margaritas?"

"Sure. See you in a few," Isabel said, darting off to get their drinks.

Layla moved away from the bar and went in search of the guys.

Clay and Jaime had nabbed a table and she hurried over, grabbing a chair and excitedly taking Jaime's arm. "You're not going to believe this."

"They're outta alcohol?" Clay deadpanned.

"No, silly. Isabel's here and she has news from Gabriella."

"Now tell me again who Gabriella is," Clay said. "The friend?"

"Yes, and guess what happened today. At her job with the developer, Torres, he told her they were going to have a little impromptu getaway for angel investors at—"

"Don't tell me," Clay, the quick study, said. "Boca Laguna Lodge?"

"Yes! What are the odds?"

"So, the mayor's in with Maya Reál, Torres' development, and did you say the governor knows the Tulum mayor?" Jaime asked.

"We're not really sure, but Isabel, who works here and at Analisa y José's …" Layla began.

"Go on. Go on!" Jaime said, apparently as short-fused as Isabel.

"Isabel said the governor's dirty."

"Well, we have quite a pot brewing," Clay said.

At that moment, Isabel sidled up to the table with refreshments. "Hola, I'm Isabel, and I come bearing drinks." With a devilish grin, she set a margarita in front of each of them.

"Hmm. Let me see if I can figure this out," she said. She nodded at the former matador, hand on hip, drink tray stowed under one arm. "You're Jaime from Playa."

He grinned. "Guilty."

"You must be the Canadian," she said in English, giving a long look at Clay who seemed to enjoy her eyes feasting on his handsome face. "Clay?"

"Present and accounted for," he said.

"Okay, I want to know everything." She pulled up a chair and plunked herself down.

"Not so fast, chica," Jaime said. "You have some info, too. What's this about the Boca Laguna Lodge? I want to hear it first-hand."

Not afraid to take center stage, Isabel warmed to her role as informant. "So, Gabriella told me that Torres—you know Torres?"

Three heads nodded. "He's set up some last minute event with his primo clients at the Boca this weekend."

"Any known reason?" Jaime asked.

"Investors. She's expected to be there to meet and greet the guests."

"How many are attending?" Clay asked.

She turned her attention to the Canadian. "Gabriella thought around a dozen."

"Is this usual? Last minute events?" asked Jaime.

"She hasn't worked for Maya Reál or the mayor long—it's all new to her."

"Speaking of the mayor's office, have you heard more about the drive-by?" Layla asked.

"No, but Gabriella may know more."

"I'll call her in the morning," Layla said, looking at Clay. "We'll get a briefing."

"Did you actually lay eyes on Silvia's boyfriend?" Isabel asked.

"No," Layla said, "but apparently he was blindfolded because they had to lead him from the SUV to the door. They called him the banker."

"Where's Silvia?"

"That's the big question. Why did they divide them?" Jaime reached into his pants pocket and pulled out a pack of cigarettes.

"Oh God, a smoker?" Isabel demanded.

"Si, do cigarettes bother you?"

"Uh, yeah. Like me and everyone on the planet. Couldn't you take up a more suitable vice, like laying land mines or something?"

"Hijole. You got an attitude, chica," Jaime said.

"That's the second time you called me chica. My name is Isabel, and you, caballero, may refer to me as such. Now I have work to do." She stood abruptly and marched off.

Layla cocked an eyebrow at Jaime. "Maybe it's time to finish our drinks and leave. There's probably no way in hell she'd bring us more after that exchange. Plus I still have to call Alma." She picked up a paper napkin and began to play with it.

"Good idea," Clay said, pulling out his wallet and placing a stack of pesos under his margarita glass. "That should cover it. Ready when you are, Layla."

"Jaime, I'll call you tomorrow and we'll form a plan on how to proceed. Thanks for driving."

"Sure, boss. No problem." He fiddled with his pack of cigarettes. "Are these really as offensive as everyone says?"

Layla looked at him. "I told you yesterday I don't like them. Guess Isabel feels the same. Doesn't anyone else say anything?"

"Don't have a lot of close amigos. I never much thought about it."

"Well, your wife wasn't a fan either, right?"

"Yeah. Okay, got it. We'll talk tomorrow." He pushed away from the table. "Thanks for the drink, amigo," he said to Clay, patting him on the arm.

"My pleasure."

"Vamos?" Layla asked Clay.

He nodded and the three headed out.

CHAPTER 18

"Alma!" Layla spoke loudly into the phone from her hotel room at Analisa y José's. Clay had retired to the front deck with beer in hand. "Como estas?"

"Okay. Have you heard anything?" the reporter asked. The pain in her voice radiated through the phone line. It was going on day seven.

"We've uncovered some info. I'll start with the most significant. We know where Francisco is … but not Silvia."

"What? How can that be?" Alma asked.

Layla proceeded to detail their evening from start to finish. She ended with the promise that she would find out as much as possible from Gabriella in the morning.

"Why would they split them?" Alma asked.

Layla didn't want to share all her feelings regarding the separation issue and hoped her tone carried confidence rather than despair. "It might be easier for them to move one person around rather than two."

Alma sighed. "It could be as simple as that. Let's hope so. I've been to the biosphere—it's a lonely place. Is it unusual to have a meeting so far away from everything?"

"Maybe. That's why I'll see Gabriella tomorrow. It's also odd that the governor owns Casa Paraiso, where we saw the SUV turn in. His sister was there, and she didn't hesitate to tell us he owned it," Layla said.

"He's famously dirty, even by Mexico standards. In bed with the launderers and the cartels ..." Her voice drifted off. "Hiding money in a number of accommodating countries."

Alma sighed. "Why did Francisco take Silvia with him when he knew it might be dangerous?"

"Unaware. Not thinking," Layla said.

"Stupid ... it makes me so mad. Poor Silvia. Well, let me hear from you when you know more. Gracias, Layla. Ciao."

Layla moved to the mini-fridge and grabbed a cerveza. She wandered onto the front deck and sat down next to Clay. The breeze was heavenly, and even though it was dark, she could see the palm trees swaying.

"Hola, amigo."

"Hi, Layla. How'd she take it?"

"As well as could be expected. She's anxious. Can't figure out why they were split up. What's your take?"

Clay sat in silence before answering. "Easier to manipulate if they're separated. He won't be watching every move that's made."

"Do you think her life's in danger?"

"Could be. Kidnapping's never good. You gotta look at it from their perspective. What are they trying to attain?"

"First off, I'd guess control over Francisco. Somehow he screwed up. How?"

"Jaime said he worked for MBC for a long time. If he's their attorney, that means he holds secrets, and if he's also their chief laundryman ..." He paused mid-sentence.

"He knows a lot. If the DEA did a swoop, lots of maybes," Clay suggested.

"Oh, God," Layla whispered.

Could Francisco have put himself in a very unpredictable situation, hoping for leniency on the other end? He would know the cartel, any cartel, not just New Guaymas, would retaliate. Is that where Silvia came into the picture? Were they using her as a shield—or a carrot?

"But it wouldn't be the feds," Layla said aloud to Clay. "They're as complicit as the cartel, sometimes worse." So well she knew the players.

"This is their retaliation, and with the girl, she can be used to make him do their bidding," Clay said.

"Hijole," Layla said. "This sucks."

"You're not going to know what's happening until you talk to Gabriella. Even then, you're still going to have to connect the dots."

"Why are Torres' investors going to Boca Laguna? It's so remote."

"Hey, that's probably why. Like when someone wants a meeting in a sauna—it's off the grid. No one would ever be able to tap the lodge. Not at such a late date."

"True." She sat and thought about that for a minute. "Who are his investors?"

"You can ask Gabriella for a list. Have Jaime do a profile and see how it adds up."

"When will we find Silvia?"

"Let me think about it over another beer." He stood and stretched his long arms high overhead, empty beer bottle in hand.

"Sure. Can you bring me one, too?" Layla asked.

"I'm your willing servant." He gave her hand a light squeeze as he walked towards the front door. She couldn't help but notice his tanned calves with their toned muscles and leg hair such a soft blond it was barely noticeable. She'd never seen him in shorts before. Easy on the eyes.

CHAPTER 19

Layla rose early, anxious to get on with the day. She walked into the living room, noticing that Clay's door was still closed. Since he'd only arrived in Mexico the day before, he was surely in time-zone hell. Her first instinct was to make coffee to clear the cobwebs. After locating ground beans and a coffee maker, she started the brew. In minutes the aroma filled the room. She grabbed a cup and her phone and walked out the front door. Standing on the deck, she looked at the soft waves, a psychedelic turquoise. They drew her to the shoreline. She wanted to hear them crashing, to obliterate all thoughts. She yearned to curl into them—let herself be taken by the current.

The ankle-deep water felt warm on her feet. By August the Caribbean would be the temperature of a bath tub. She let the calm set in, knowing this might be her only moment of meditation for the day. After a short reprieve, she turned around, looking for a spot to make a call. She located the same palm she'd sat under the day before, wrapped her pareo around her waist, and plunked onto the sand.

Gabriella answered on the first ring. "Hola?"

"Gabriella, como estas?" Layla asked. "I have news."

She quickly caught the girl up on the prior day's events. "Tell me about the impromptu meeting at Boca."

"It's a two-day affair. Torres has requisitioned the entire place. He's even invited the governor and the mayor," Gabriella said.

Layla felt her blood pressure rise. "The Tulum mayor? And the governor? Can we talk today? I need to be there during the meetings. I have a real strong feeling that Silvia's disappearance is connected somehow."

The younger woman let out a sigh. "Really? Could she be there, too?"

Layla paused before speaking. "She could be. Actually, she could be anywhere in the entire state. That's the problem. Has anyone mentioned MBC?"

"Um, actually, yes. I heard the mayor say something about someone from the bank."

"Which office will you be at today?" Layla asked.

"The land management company," she said. "It's a block off Av. Tulum. A dark green building with rows of palms out front. Not far from the mayor's office. Here's the address."

Layla jotted it down. "Is your friend okay?"

"You mean Gloria? Oh, yes. She's my rock. Never wavers," Gabriella said.

"I'll bring Clay, too. We'll see you at ten. Ciao."

Layla clicked off the phone and took one last look at the ocean. Time to leave the waves behind. There was business to be done and a girl to be found. Weird how she'd changed hats and was playing detective. It was a good thing neither El Patrón or Martín could see her now. They would be floored—or disgusted.

Clay and Layla parked and walked into the development office of Maya Reál in Tulum. Gabriella stood behind the counter.

"Hola! How are you, Gabriella? This is Clay."

"Mucho gusto, Señor Clay," she said.

"Just Clay. A pleasure to meet you, too."

"Can we go out for coffee?" Layla asked, as she peered into a back office where a well-dressed middle-aged man lounged behind a desk, talking on the phone.

"Yes, I'll tell Señor Torres."

She stepped away and walked to the office, knocked lightly on the open door, and indicated she was going out. The dark-haired man, who had put a hand over the receiver, took a curious look at the visitors and waved his hand at Gabriella, indicating all was fine.

"So, Gabriella, what's happening?" Layla asked ten minutes later as they again sat at the nearby juice bar. "Any word on the dead reporter?"

"The mayor told someone on the phone that the police are investigating, then he chuckled, like it was some big joke." She gave Layla a disgusted look. "My friend heard it, too, and she was really angry."

"I hope Gloria remains calm," Layla said in a stern manner. "You may have to explain how important it is she doesn't let her feelings out. The mayor can't know she suspects him."

"Of course," Gabriella said, looking down. "But she's lived here her entire life and has seen so many changes for the worse. She gets angry."

"Well, that's understandable, but if our hunch is right, the mayor is not only determined, he's dangerous. Do you want me to talk to her?"

"No, no, I can handle it."

Layla wondered if she could. "Okay, when will the Boca Laguna meeting happen and who's attending?"

"Friday. He finished nailing down the group. This is for you." Gabriella handed her a list.

She quickly perused it. "Why so last minute? Any idea?"

"No. He was keeping to himself about it until the last possible moment, and all of a sudden he needed me to send out directions. That's how I got the names."

"I'll scan it and send it to Jaime," Layla said. "Where can I find a scanner?"

"I can send it from the office."

"Would that be dangerous if Torres catches you?" Layla asked.

"I'll tell him it's for preparations. I can manage," Gabriella said, straightening her back as she accepted her role in their parallel cover-up. "What's his email?"

"I'll text it to you. What time will it begin?" Layla asked.

"Opening remarks are in the evening, but Torres will be there around one to check things out. The mayor is riding down with us," Gabriella said.

Layla groaned. "That's awful."

"I know. I hate being anywhere near him since the motorbike death squad!"

"You've heard nothing else about it? Just the phone conversation?" Layla asked.

The young woman shrank back in her chair. "Only that the dead man's wife is very upset and is calling him out. Saying first he fire-bombed them, now this—her husband's death. She's telling everyone he did it."

"What's her name and can you get me her number?"

"Of course, it's Flora. I'll give Gloria a call." She punched in her friend's number.

"Hola, Gloria. Can you text me Señora Flora's full name and number. Yes, at the newspaper office. If she's not there I'll find her home line."

A moment later, Layla heard a familiar ding. "Here it is. Flora's name and number." Gabriella showed it to Layla.

"I think I should call her."

"Go ahead, Layla. Anything else for you?" Clay asked.

"No, thanks," she said as she stepped away from the table.

Ten minutes later, Layla was back; her face was scrunched up and she was nibbling on her thumbnail. She brushed her dark hair back from her forehead before she sat down. "Guys, looks like we have a lead."

Clay and Gabriella, who had been speaking quietly, both stopped. "How so?" he asked.

"Flora has incriminating information. Not good. I don't think the mayor was only into monetary corruption. I think he was also a sexual predator."

"What?" Gabriella's head snapped up from her juice glass.

"Flora told me about the rite of spring dance, where a school girl in ninth grade is chosen to be the queen of the colonia."

"Yes. Gloria said it was a rigged system to find the prettiest girl. The town fathers promote her as queen for the festival. They pay for her dresses, the float, and flowers."

"That's not all, Gabriella. Did Gloria tell you that, too?"

She looked down. "I know what you're saying. It happens a lot."

"They take advantage of the girl, don't they?" Layla prodded.

Gabriella hung her head. "No one's supposed to know, but the men who promote her have a chance to … you know. Gloria said it happens very late, after the festivities. They get her drunk, pass her around to whoever paid for her to be queen."

"Did Gloria tell you this?" Layla asked.

She nodded.

"Flora said her maid, Fabiola, has a gorgeous daughter. Fabiola's a widow with three kids. Hard to provide for them all on her salary. Her oldest daughter, Marisol, is fourteen going on twenty. She's beautiful but fragile. Often sick, misses school.

"The publisher's wife said when she heard Marisol was chosen as queen, she was excited and said as much to Fabiola. Fabiola acted strange, though. Flora forced it out of her. She said it was all a ruse—the girl ends up deflowered, and the family, usually from the poor side of town, is disgraced," Layla said.

Clay had been listening. "Good God! That's terrible! What happened to the maid's daughter?"

"Well, Fabiola is no dummy. When she came to work after the festival, Flora asked about it. Fabiola said Marisol got sick and couldn't go."

"She sidestepped the system?" Clay asked.

"Yes, a poor Maya widow outfoxed the foxes. They were beyond angry, especially Dzib, who'd made the arrangements. Fabiola refused to budge and kept the girl inside the house for days. Couldn't prove if she was sick or not."

"These are serious offenses," Clay said.

"Can any of that—predatory stuff—apply to our missing Silvia?" Layla asked. "Is that why they split her and Francisco?"

Gabriella, who had been looking extremely glum, burst into tears. "Oh no! Not to Silvia!" she gasped. "Please not to Silvia."

Layla put an arm around the girl's shoulder. "Listen, Gabriella, we're going to find out where she is. With your help, and Gloria's and Flora's. With Jaime's and Clay's help, and mine. Now listen. This is the plan—this is what we're going to do if they've kidnapped Silvia for a weird sex game. Are you willing to help?"

The girl nodded.

"Okay, here goes."

CHAPTER 20

"Jaime, it's Layla. You got the list?"

"Si. Tycoons, boss. How'd Torres manage to get all these guys in one room?"

"It hasn't happened yet, it's tomorrow, but things are looking pretty dodgy. I've been hearing more about the mayor. Over the top slimy," Layla said.

"We had that figured out after he fire-bombed the newspaper. Got more?"

"I talked to Flora, the dead publisher's wife. Seems her husband was working with Olivia Cache. You know who she is, right?"

"The journalist who exposed the sex ring in Cancun?"

"Si. According to Flora, her husband was on the verge of dropping another dime on Dzib. Everyone thought it would be about land grabs, but it was about his connections to the sex industry and trafficking. In Tulum, Isabel said everyone more or less expects phony real estate deals. But sex—with underage girls—that's off-limits. Way off-limits."

"The river runs deep."

"It does. Listen to this." Layla caught Jaime up with her conversation with Flora. "Maybe that's how the mayor got started."

"And he just built on it from there, but how does this relate to us trying to find the girl?"

"Francisco may have cooperated with the DEA. Flora also told us he was in pretty deep through MBC. Everyone thinks reporters on these small newspapers are simply reporting tourist stats or restaurant openings. Some of them are damn good. Because Cancun is such a wild west show, the corruption runs both north and south. According to Flora, Francisco could well have been a connection inside the DEA. They did a drop about four months ago. They found out the Cancun Airport manager was … cooperating with cartels. No comments, Jaime."

She paused and took a breath. "According to Flora, the DEA didn't stop there. Because of Olivia Cache's work outing Cancun's sex industry in *Por Esto*, they went undercover and started sniffing around, checking out how the money flowed from trafficking, and stumbled onto laundering operations. I'm guessing that's how they found Francisco. The DEA demanded he do one last job, one more name and they'd put him into witness protection. He was compromised and on the way out. Then he met Silvia."

"Love hurts," dead-panned Jaime. "So …"

"So. What did you come up with on the list?" Layla asked.

"Business and banking guys. No pols. I guess the friendly governor is the only politico we're looking at. What are you thinking?" Jaime asked.

"Don't forget the mayor. They've blocked off the lodge at Boca all day tomorrow and Saturday until six p.m. Sunday. It'll be a helluva private party, complete with a raffle."

"A raffle?" Jaime asked.

"I think they plan to use Silvia as the prize."

Jaime snorted. "You're kidding!"

"No. I think Torres is using her as bait. It'll be a two-fer. He'll prove to Francisco and the governor you don't mess with him. You don't double-cross your jefe. Let that be a lesson to you, Jaime," Layla joked.

"Boss, that's not even funny."

"Sorry, I couldn't help myself," Layla said. "But ... Torres is tight with New Guaymas cartel. They're running the show, according to Flora. They work with him, laundering money through his construction business and leaning on his connections with MBC. That's where Francisco came in."

"When did the DEA compromise Francisco?" Jaime asked.

"My guess? Four months ago, when they did the Cancun Airport catch."

"What are we going to do about it, and how do we find the girl?"

"Funny you should ask. I was going to talk that over with Clay, and Gabriella. I have a plan. Can you swim?" Layla asked.

"Say what? Of course I can swim. What does that mean?"

"Well, put on your water wings, or at the very least a lifejacket, Jaime. We're going to take a little cruise on the high seas."

ㄹ 回 回

Muyil, south of Tulum, is known for Chunyaxché, one of the Maya's oldest pyramid sites, unique for its access to the Si'an Ka'an Biosphere through lagoons. Because it's located twelve kilometers inland, the Maya dredged a canal system to reach the ocean. This took on utmost importance to Layla and crew, as that pathway would soon carry them north to Boca Laguna Lodge.

Bordered by mangrove swamps, the canals are difficult to navigate even for experienced seamen. Layla's next task was to find someone who already had their sea legs.

ﭏﯕﯕﯕ

Though Layla was furiously trying to connect the dots on the Boca party and Silvia's whereabouts, many unknowns were left hanging. Gabriella was the best resource for logistics. They headed over to the mayor's office, where she was working that afternoon, to discuss event timing.

"We're alone," Gabriella said, when she saw Layla and Clay. "The meeting room."

Though Tulum could well be considered one of the world's most famous eco-resorts, the municipio didn't spend an extra peso on the pueblo's governing faction. The spartan meeting room desperately needed a coat of paint and the mismatched furniture looked worse for wear. Gabriella shut the cheap paneled door behind them.

After taking a seat in a folding chair, Layla began. "There's no way we can exit the lodge from the road and stay safe. We'd be sitting ducks."

She flipped her burner open and shut, a newly acquired quirk, as she thought things through. "It's vital that Clay and I check out the lodge. Flora's husband heard a day before he was murdered there was going to be a grand gala held by Maya Reál, and the remote meeting could well include under-age girls, compliments of Dzib. Do you have a mock-up of the property and who's staying where?"

"I do," Gabriella said. "I was working on it before you arrived. Twelve plus Dzib, Torres, and the governor. Fifteen rooms. The lodge has eighteen. Can I reserve one for you?"

"Good idea. We'll be coming in from the ocean—I think that's safest. But we can't go merely on Flora's gut about Silvia's whereabouts," Layla said. "That's why we have to get down there before they get the party going."

"Will Jaime be involved?" Gabriella asked.

"Yes. Also, he packs heat, something we don't have. Hopefully they don't either. Clay?"

"These are businessmen looking for a good time. They're not outlaws per se." He gave Layla a meaningful look. "It's Mexico. I don't think they'll be carrying."

Gabriella pushed back her chair and stood. "If you go to Boca today, let me know. I'll be down tomorrow morning. There's one cottage at the property's south end that's more remote. Number eighteen. I'll leave it open."

"Flora's probably right, but we don't want to set up a boat from Muyil, get there and no Silvia. Speaking of a boat, does Gloria have connections with anyone in Muyil?" Layla asked.

"I'll tell her to call you. But remember, Muyil is twenty kilometers from Tulum. Plan for travel to and from there, plus the boat ride, which will be slower at night. You're going to need not just a seasoned guide, you're going to need a Maya blessing."

"Ojalá, Gabriella, ojalá!"

CHAPTER 21

"Gloria, you know everything about Tulum," Layla said as she looked at the young Maya woman. "How long have you been working in the municipio?"

Gloria stood beside Layla on the street in front of the white-washed Palacio Municipal under a spreading almendrón. The day was hot and the humidity was edging higher by the minute. "Not long, but I've lived here my whole life. I've seen Tulum go from a pueblo to forty thousand people. Can you believe it?"

Layla wiped her hand across her brow. Though she was gradually adjusting to the heat, it felt like she was standing inside a pressure cooker. "Is it working out?"

Gloria snorted. "Developers like Maya Reál push for development. New construction destroys the mangroves, not to mention the reef. My cousin dives and sees so much bleached white coral. That means it's dead forever. With no reef, we have nothing."

"Tourists will no longer come," Layla said.

"Hmmph. I'm not worried about tourists," the Maya local replied in a huffy tone. "What about our ocean? Will it be destroyed for us and future generations? Even now the amount of refuse ..." she looked at Layla. "You know what

I mean, right? The nitrogen in the water … over the top. The Yucatán sits on a layer of limestone, a fragile shell of freshwater underground cenotes, many used for drinking water.

"Eighty percent of the eco-properties don't even try to filter their waste and flush toilets directly into the mangroves or right into the ocean. That's what development has done for Tulum. More like eco disaster. Meanwhile, people pay five hundred dollars a night for a palapa hut with cold running water and no electricity, while just below the ground—we're standing on top of it—runs the world's largest underground river. It flows to the sea, and the sea is connected to the reef …" She let out a disgusted sigh and pushed her long black hair over a shoulder before adjusting wire-rim glasses. "But they keep building."

"Is your cousin still diving?" Layla asked.

"Si, si. He knows the hidden spots like Puntas Sanas not far from Carrillo Puerto. Ojalá, there are still jobs for Maya on the water—diving, fishing."

"What do you mean?" Layla asked.

"Guatemalans are undercutting the locals for construction work. They charge less and the hotel builders have replaced them with cheaper labor. We Maya are like a subspecies."

Layla thought about that for a minute. First take their land, then the jobs?

"Well, I have a job. I need someone to take us by panga from Muyil to the Boca bridge."

"My cousin knows lots of guys with boats."

"Can you call him for me? It'd be late Saturday afternoon. Could be a day, could be two. They must be able to navigate through the lagoon at night."

"I'll call him now."

🔲🔲🔲

The text dinged in Layla's purse. She reached for her phone to retrieve the message.

"Clay, I've got to call Alma," Layla said as they drove back to Analisa y José's.

"It's the best way," Clay said. "She's gotta know."

Layla bit her lip. She hated the thought of telling Alma that her gorgeous niece could soon be the prize for a group of hedonistic assholes in what sounded like a members-only sex club.

As Layla prepared to text Alma, her phone rang. "Bueno."

"It's Gloria. My cousin has a friend with a panga. Pedro. He'll do the job for you."

"Great! When should we talk to him?"

"Do you want to meet him in Muyil?" Gloria asked.

"Let me check. Clay, Gloria found a boatman. Want to drive there?"

"Sure. Where's he at?"

Layla placed a hand on Clay's arm, indicating a momentary delay. "Gloria, is he far from Tulum?"

"Twenty minutes at most. Here's his number. Not many street signs," Gloria said.

"Got it, Gloria, ciao! Clay, I'm calling Pedro."

Moments later Layla connected. "We can meet you in twenty minutes. Past the pyramid site, at the dock? Sure.

"Clay, we'll go straight to the dock. His boat is *Damael*. I'll text Alma now."

Clay glanced her way. "Just do it."

"Finished. Here's our turn-off. Dirt road, parking lot," Layla instructed.

A white-haired Maya man emerged from a palapa to collect the parking fee. "Not sure how long we'll be," Layla said.

He shrugged and waved as they walked towards a worn white panga with *Damael* painted on the side. In the boat, a local was tidying up. When they approached, he turned to greet them.

"Pedro?" Layla asked. A young man in his early twenties faced them. He had a rangy build with raven hair pulled into a ponytail. His faded T-shirt was thoroughly soaked. Even though waves hit the panga tipping it from left to right, his stance remained firm.

"Si. You are Layla?"

"Yes, and this is Clay." She looked questioningly at the Maya's damp appearance and took a longer look at the panga and its faded paint job.

"You're good? And the boat?" Layla's tone conveyed her apprehension.

His laugh defused her uneasiness. "I just washed everything off from a fishing trip. Smelly." He waved his hand under his nose. "I didn't fall overboard, if you're wondering why I'm all wet."

Layla's attitude took an about-face. *Calm yourself. You're not even halfway through this madness.*

She gave a wan smile. "I'm thinking we'll need your services tomorrow or the next day, late afternoon. Around six. How long is the trip up to the Boca bridge?"

"At night? Could be two hours. It's an hour to navigate through the canals to open water."

"What's the moon cycle?" Clay asked.

"New moon, it will be dark."

"I'm still waiting to hear when we should be at the lodge," Layla said. "We'll be picking up a friend and bringing her back to Muyil. Not sure how long it will take."

"If Gloria sent you, I'm good with it."

"I'd like to pay you half now," Layla said as she reached into her purse, "and the other half when we finish."

The Maya local's eyes widened as Layla passed him a hefty clump of pesos. In witnessing his surprise, Layla smiled. "If Gloria said you're good, *I'm* good with it."

"Muchas gracias."

"De nada. So tomorrow, but that could change," Layla said.

"Señora, I am ready when you need me. Do not worry."

"I want to tell you, this job"—she glanced Clay's way as she said it—"is a bit unusual. It could be dangerous. Does that bother you?"

"Life is dangerous, señora."

She and Clay shared a look. "Please, call me Layla."

Pedro looked at her feet. "Your sandals, Layla. Do you have other shoes?"

"I do, and long pants."

"Long sleeves, too. Even in the Caribbean there can be a breeze at night."

"No problem. Okay, hasta pronto."

CHAPTER 22

Layla and Clay drove back towards Analisa y José's amidst a cluster of merging traffic on the two-lane road south of Tulum. As they edged closer to the tourist mecca, the crowd of cars and delivery trucks grew more concentrated.

"Looks like everyone's going to Tulum or Playa," Clay said.

"So are we. Want to hit Playamar for dinner, or try Tulum?" Layla asked.

"Doesn't Playamar have a wood stove pizza oven?"

"Si, one of my favorites."

"Layla, you say that about every meal we have in Mexico."

She laughed and lightly swiped his arm. "You calling me out on my foodie pleasures?"

"I know you. Playamar it is."

Twenty minutes later, they were settling into a table at the restaurant. Layla looked around as she sat down, searching for Isabel. "Isabel has to be here. It's her second home."

Clay corrected her. "You mean second job?"

"Um, yeah. She said everyone in Tulum needs at least two to stay alive."

"Right. I heard the locals barely get by, and I don't even live here."

"There she is," Layla said, happy to change the subject. "Isabel!"

Isabel spotted them and made a beeline for the table. "Que tal, amigos?"

She actually looked happy to see them. As soon as she opened her mouth, Layla realized why. "Ojalá! You didn't bring that cretin with you."

"Jaime? Did he bother you that much?" Layla asked.

"Um, si. I don't call him tipo and he insisted on calling me chica. I won't have it."

"Do you get that a lot from customers?" Layla asked. "We know guys can be stupidos."

"That's a nice way to say it. I'd say pendejos would be more accurate."

"Isabel!"

"What? Now you don't swear in front of our Canadian amigo?" She gave a devilish wink in Clay's direction as she watched Layla blush. "Por favor, señorita Layla."

Isabel made a bowing gesture, then her body shot upwards. With hand on hip, drink tray under her arm, she said, "Get a grip or I'll tell Clay you're from Chiapas."

"I thought my secret was safe with you."

Both women laughed while Clay tried to figure out the joke. "Glad you're having a good time. Meanwhile I'm dying of thirst."

"At your service, Clay," Isabel said. "Two margaritas." She fake saluted him and sauntered off to get their cocktails.

Clay said, "She's a trip. So, how are you feeling about everything?"

Layla shifted in the wooden chair and stretched out her legs under the table. She took a quick glance at the Caribbean. The motion of the ocean gave her a sense of balance. Maybe she should move closer to it; better yet, buy a boat, live on it—absorb the sea's abundant energy. "I'm nervous about tomorrow. We've got to drive down. I have to text Jaime and ask him to pick us up early. Gotta do our legwork before Pedro takes us to the Boca bridge."

"Well, you could text him now, before our margaritas. I'd like to do a little serious drinking tonight." He gave her a meaningful look.

Layla fidgeted, rubbing her palms along her skirt. "I need to relax, too."

Isabel waltzed up with cocktails. "Anything to eat? Antojitos. Dinner?"

"We're thinking of pizza," Layla said.

"Try the Margherita." She first looked at Layla, then Clay for confirmation.

After they finished eating, Isabel came over and pulled up a chair. Several tables had cleared and it was quiet except for the low buzz of conversation from other diners.

"What's happening?" she asked.

Layla looked at Clay. "It's been busy. Talked to Gloria and Gabriella and the publisher's wife. We're heading to Boca with your favorite new friend tomorrow."

"Any particular reason?" Isabel asked.

"I'll catch you up more after we get back," Layla promised. "There's a lot going on and I don't want to muck it up by talking about it. Just say I'm superstitious."

"That's cool. I cross myself every time I spill the salt," Isabel said.

"Pizza was great. How about another round of margaritas?" Clay asked.

"Claro. That's what Tulum's all about. If there's no fiesta happening, make your own."

They watched her walk towards the bar. Under the table, Clay placed his hand on top of Layla's. "That was good. We don't need to share everything with everyone."

His hand felt warm; could be from the heat of the day, or was it just ... the heat? She let hers settle into Clay's larger one, feeling comforted by the simple gesture. She'd had no human contact since the morning she and Carlos ran from Don Guillermo, when he'd held her in his arms after she learned that Lupita had been killed. The same day the plane crashed in the Yucatán jungle, and the day Carlos died.

Not to be ignored, even if she was just delivering cocktails, Isabel re-emerged, drinks in hand. "Your margaritas." Somehow she dominated every conversation.

"Muchas gracias," Clay said, slowly removing his hand from Layla's but not before giving it a light squeeze.

"I'm taking off. Have an early day at Analisa y José's tomorrow. Are you okay?"

The couple's glance caught Isabel's attention. "I guess I answered my own question." She backed away with a slight wave. "Hasta luego."

"Let's toast," Clay said after Isabel had departed.

"To what?" Layla asked.

"Catching a break. To the Maya gods."

Layla rested her hands on the table in front of her margarita and pondered what Clay had just proposed.

With eyes closed and the position of her hands, she could have been praying. "I hope they're listening," she whispered. "I really do."

🔳🔳🔳

The couple got to Analisa y José's a half hour later after finishing their drinks. Evening seemed to be the only time of day the Tulum beach road wasn't overrun by vehicles of every kind. They were quiet until they reached the property. In the lobby, Arturo manned the front desk, gazing into a computer screen. He looked up.

"Buenos noches. Someone sent you a gift. It's in your room."

"A gift? What could it be?"

"Well, it's in a bottle and has a little burn."

"Tequila?" Layla asked, feeling an immediate surge of pleasure.

"Oh, I gave it away!" Arturo dead-panned.

"Maybe we should run back to the suite. Wanna race, Clay?"

"No need. It will be waiting for you when you get there," the attendant assured her.

They wandered out of the lobby onto the gecko steps that led down the dark path towards the beach and their private bungalow. As Pedro had predicted, it was nearly a dark moon. A handful of constellations shone above as they picked their way along the walk to their cottage. "Say Layla, how's your foot doing from the other night?" Clay asked.

"You mean the cut from the fence?" She stooped down to touch the jagged edge.

"Yeah. Is it okay?"

164

"It stings a bit. Maybe I should pour a little of my gift on it," she said.

"Let me look at it when we get to the room. We don't want it to get infected."

"Oh. Don't bother, Clay."

"No, no, no. You know I'm compulsive about health stuff."

"Not just meditation and martial arts?" she teased.

"No. The body in general," he said as they walked up the stairs to the dark deck of their cottage. Layla rummaged around in her purse and located the key.

"In we go, and then it's Dr. Clay to the rescue," she said.

Two corner lamps had been turned on and the light enveloped the room in a romantic, iridescent glow. Layla had already set down her purse before spotting a handsome bottle of Don Julio on the counter.

"Oh, just what el doctór ordered." She glanced at the card. "From Alma. How nice. Can I pour us both a shot while you're examining the patient?"

"Sure. I work better when I'm drinking."

She walked to the counter, took an appreciative look at the tequila, and twisted off the cap. Shot glasses sat on a bamboo tray alongside a wooden vase filled with bougainvilleas. She poured the tequila into them and walked back to where Clay had plunked himself on a pillowed chaise lounge positioned near the front door. An evening breeze blew in, billowing the suite's gauze curtains from side to side.

"Here, Layla." He moved over and patted a spot to his right. "Now, which foot is it?"

"This one," she said as she started to undo the strap at the back of her left sandal.

"Have a drink first," he ordered. "To your health. Salud."

They looked into each other's eyes as they downed the amber liquid. "Another?" he asked. "Before the doctor performs his duties?"

"By all means."

He got up and was back in a moment, bottle in hand. "Your glass?"

She handed it to him, accidentally brushing his fingers in the process. She felt her face flush, and brushed it off as the tequila talking. He poured two more shots. The heat first burned her throat, then it hit her chest. Finally her head recognized the familiar buzz.

"So good."

"I think the doctor needs one more before he begins," Clay said. He grabbed the bottle from the floor where he'd placed it. "Hand her over."

She obediently gave him the glass, still feeling the burn of the liquid and the reliable mood shift that chaperoned good tequila. He poured another round.

"Time to look at the patient."

He gently pulled the unstrapped sandal from her foot and held it lightly, heel side down, in both hands. He moved it slowly back and forth, checking out the small ugly gash where the fence had torn her flesh. "A little ragged. Does it hurt?"

"Not as long as you're holding it." She looked at him a moment too long. Damn, the tequila was doing its job.

He moved his hand towards her ankle. "It didn't do anything here?" he asked.

"No."

"How about here?" He looked at her as he lightly massaged her calf.

"No, it's fine." She breathed deeply, feeling her heart begin to race.

"I'll pour a drop of tequila on it," he suggested. "Like in the movies."

Clay moved her foot to his knee and found the bottle. He opened it, poured a tiny bit into his shot glass, and dribbled a drop on the wound. She cringed.

"Did that hurt?"

"No," she lied. "Let me see." She craned her neck to get a look.

Again, he held her foot, and gently moved his hand in a slight caressing motion from foot to ankle to calf. She leaned back on the chaise lounge, totally relaxed. "Feels good."

He moved a hand to her thigh, pushed aside the gauze skirt exposing her long legs, and touched her flat stomach with the other hand, nearly covering it. Her body trembled as he did so.

"Layla," he spoke her name softly, passionately. "Layla," he repeated, as he moved his powerful frame steadily closer. He held her in his arms for a long moment before running his hand along her side, up her rib cage, his lips following behind in easy, expressive kisses.

His face was soon level with hers. He shifted her head slightly to the side as he kissed her neck. She closed her eyes and melted into his caress. A sigh came out that sounded like a purr.

"You're beautiful." He breathed the words into her ear while he caressed her hair, gently pushing a strand away from her face. They shared a passionate kiss.

"Clay ..." she managed to murmur as she wound her arms tighter around his waist.

His voice was a whisper when he said, "Should we move this to the bedroom?"

Her kiss was a clear answer, so he scooped her into his arms and carried her out of the room.

CHAPTER 23

T he phone rang just inches from her ear. What time was it? Ooh, her head. Stop the ringing! Grab it, grab it, she said to herself as she looked around the room and spotted Clay on the far side of the bed, sheets wound round his muscular torso as though he'd just attended a toga party. Hijole! What had she done?

"Si," she managed to whisper.

"Boss, did I wake you? It's Jaime."

"Um, no. I mean, yes. I mean, can you give me a minute?"

"Sure. It's early. Tried to call last night but no answer," Jaime said.

She located her skirt lying on the floor and wrapped it around herself like a dress. She dragged herself into the living room, shutting the door so as not to wake Clay.

"We're going to Boca today, right?"

Her mind shifted into focus. "Yes, of course. You'll drive?"

"Yeah. Heading out now. I'll be at Analisa y José's in fifty minutes. You said you wanted to get a jump on it and I didn't hear from you last night, so I decided to drive and dial."

"Good, good. Gotta grab some coffee and a shower, but we'll be ready when you arrive. Give me a call from the lobby."

"Sure thing, boss. Ciao."

Now for damage control. Hijole! She'd slept with Clay. What a disaster! Well, not really a disaster, she thought as she remembered the delicious sensations she'd experienced the night before. How was she going to deal with this? A man in her life who was not a bodyguard? That was a new one.

She tiptoed over to the kitchen and got coffee brewing. She splashed water on her face, combed through her hair with her fingers, then drummed them on the countertop as she mentally organized the day while waiting for the coffee to finish. After a cup she'd call Alma and catch her up on their activities and prepare her for the unpredictability of the weekend to come.

A familiar beep sounded from the coffee maker, and she grabbed two cups from a bamboo cupboard and set them side by side on the counter. She filled one with hot black liquid and blew on it to take the heat off. She walked to the front door with her phone and stepped outside into sunlight so bright it made her eyes squint. Damn. Hangover. She moved down the stairs towards the ocean. Once on the beach and close to the lapping waves, she plopped next to the same palm she'd befriended the day before. Her fingers did the walking and in moments, Alma picked up on the other end.

"Layla, I got your text. I was going crazy not knowing what was happening."

"Alma, we were in Muyil yesterday with a boatman. You know it?"

"Um, south of Tulum? Pyramid site?"

"Yes, but we were there because it has a port and dock. We hired a boatman who can take us up to the bridge at Boca Paila, where the lodge is. We have reason to believe Silvia is there."

She heard a gasp on the other end. "What? Gracias á Dios!"

"Not a hundred percent sure but we think we're very close. This morning me and Clay and Jaime, the investigator I told you about, are driving down and looking around, to see what we can find out. I only have a minute but we're making progress. I won't go into it on the phone. You may not hear from me until Sunday, but please try not to worry. I'm on this and so are a number of other people. We're doing our best to find Silvia, okay?"

"All right, Layla."

"Good, and thank you for the bottle of Don Julio. I had a chance to taste it last night," she said, as her thoughts strayed to the sensual evening she'd spent under its influence with Clay.

"Was it good?"

"I can't even begin to tell you," she replied, tongue firmly planted in cheek. Her mind flew to the memory of Clay's splendid torso—how he moved over her with a gentle but steady rhythm; how the memory of his touch made her quiver, even now in Tulum's bright sunlight. "Listen, you will hear from me. We gotta let this work its way out."

"Okay, Layla, okay," Alma said, signing off with her requisite, "Ciao."

Layla leaned back against the familiar palm and drank a gulp of coffee. Get going, she said, more to the coffee than to herself. I need a lift, pronto. The drink had reached the perfect temperature. She took another sip and realized it was time to move. There was a lot happening in her world, and none of it would be accomplished by hanging out on the beach with a cup of java.

🁢🁢🁢

Back at the suite, Layla was surprised to see Clay standing at the counter, wearing shorts that sat low on his hips, no shirt, drinking his own cup of coffee. "You're awake, and you found the coffee." She tried to smile normally and wondered how that was playing out.

"Yes, I did. Thank you." He gave her a sexy grin. "When I reached over, I discovered I was alone in bed—empty except for a sheet and a pillow. Seemed like a good time to get up."

"Oh … um, I didn't want to wake you, so I left the room to take Jaime's call."

"What's up?" Clay asked, shifting into a more business-like tone, all the while sipping coffee.

Layla walked to the sink and rinsed out her cup before setting it on the counter. "He's on his way. Should be here in a half hour. Looks like we're taking another road trip."

"So, who showers first?" Clay asked, a playful expression on his face.

Layla blushed. What was wrong with her? She'd just had sex with this hunk less than eight hours ago; he'd seen her in the buff, made her feel unbelievable things—things she'd never felt before. Get a grip, she told herself.

She gave him a look. "Why not shower together? Save water." Finally, she was getting her groove back.

"I'm all for conservation. Ready?" He grabbed her hand and led her into the ensuite bathroom. "But you'd better take off your—dress? Need help?"

He pulled her closer and undid the ties from the skirt that served as a makeshift bodice. It fell to her feet and she nimbly stepped out of it and moved towards the shower. "First one in rides up front."

She could feel his eyes on her butt as she leaned in to turn on the water. "Your best asset," Carlos had always told her. "And you know how to move it."

She turned halfway around, well aware of the power her body wielded, and reached for his hand. "What are you waiting for?" She stepped into the glass enclosure.

Layla's eyes were closed as she stood under the stream of lukewarm water, so she didn't see Clay's arms before he folded them around her and pulled her to his chest. By that time water was flowing over them, like a waterfall in a rainforest. He tilted her face, eyes closed, towards his own for a lingering kiss. She reached up, wrapped her arms around his neck and leaned in. She was beginning to like Tulum more every day. She could easily get used to life on the Caribbean coast.

CHAPTER 24

"So Alma knows what's happening?" Jaime asked Layla, who was riding shotgun in his four-door navy Toyota Corolla. They bumped along south of the Si'an Ka'an arch, moving steadily towards Boca Laguna Lodge.

"Yep. I told her about Muyil and our trip to Boca today but didn't go into detail. Let her know we had reason to believe that Silvia was being held at the lodge."

"How are we going to check that out, boss? They're not gonna let us just waltz in. Shouldn't we be dressed like timeshare salesmen or insurance adjusters? Someone whose got a legit reason to be there?"

"Insurance adjusters …" Layla rolled it over in her mind "You're a genius. That's it!"

"We're not exactly dressed right," Clay said. "I'm wearing surfer shorts."

"We tell them we're at a conference in Playa, and since we were nearby, management asked if we'd check in at the lodge before our weekend of fun after a week of seminars. Being ass kissers, we jumped at the chance to do their bidding."

"And since we're in the Riviera Maya, today's not only casual Friday," Clay said as he adjusted the collar on his short-sleeve shirt, "it's casual dress week."

"Perfect cover," Jaime said. "We say their corporate package can be given a hurricane upgrade, but we gotta see if they're up to code. Meanwhile, we have access to the entire property."

"Brilliant!" Layla turned around and gave Clay a grand slam smile. "We got this, guys. We can check the dock and let Pedro know the best place to pull in."

"But wait. They'll want to know the name of our company," Clay said.

"We're a sub-contractor for their insurance company. Hopefully they'll say, 'Oh, ING,' or whoever. We say yes."

"Oh man," Clay said with a groan. "Undercover insurance agents. Isn't there a telenovela like that, Layla?"

She laughed loudly as though the remark was hilarious. She still hadn't gotten over her shower experience. "Not yet, but I'll be in touch with my producer."

"Are you guys on something?" Jaime said, giving Layla a sideways glance. "You're acting loco. I didn't think you did drugs, boss."

"I don't. Just hungover. Alma sent a bottle of Don Julio to the room. You know, too much of a good thing." She pulled down the car's compact mirror and pretended to fix her hair, looking for Clay in the backseat. He winked.

"Alma sounds like a cool lady," Jaime said.

"She is."

Twenty minutes later, the trio came to the lodge turnoff. The parking lot was empty except for the navy service truck. "Looks like we've got the place to ourselves."

"Today's the day Torres and the mayor are coming?" Jaime asked.

"Si. Ahead of the crowd." She opened the door and stepped into blinding sunlight reflecting off the sascab lot. Clay and Jaime followed suit.

"Whew. Hot one already." Layla waved her hand back and forth in front of her face. "Gabriella told me they'd get here early to set up. There's a ballroom with a palapa ceiling."

"Showtime," Clay said. He nodded ahead to double French doors where an attendant stood watching their arrival.

"I'll do the talking," Layla said. She marched up the stairs and waited for Jaime to pull open the door; the attendant was too slow to do the deed. She gave him a cool look, assuming her authoritative position. She moved towards the front desk, with Clay and Jaime in tow.

A counter clerk—different from the previous day—stood behind the desk, watching their progress.

"Good morning. Is the manager in?" Layla asked.

"He's unavailable. Can I assist?"

"We're insurance agents representing the Office for Hurricane Preparedness. We're here to inspect your property; we're in the area for one day only."

"Oh, sorry but we're closed to the public today. We have a conference coming in." He checked his watch. "Very soon in fact. It's taking over the entire lodge through Sunday. I'm afraid we can't accommodate you."

"Unfortunately, it must be today or never," Layla stressed. She, too, looked at her watch. "As you know, hurricane season begins June 1, and we have the entire state of Quintana Roo to cover as well as Chiapas and el Yucatán."

The counter clerk shook his head slowly back and forth.

"No big one since Wilma," Jaime said, butting in. "When was that? Oh, yeah, 2005. It'd be a shame if you didn't have the extra coverage because we couldn't inspect your facility."

Clay got into the role, putting on a sour look. He decided on a different tack. "Is there anyone else on the property that could give us clearance?"

The clerk, looking glum and pulling on his shirt sleeves, brightened for a moment. "Um. Well, there's our accountant. He should be here any time now …"

Layla's haughty look had replaced her Tulum-at-the-beach face. "I didn't get your name."

"Bernardo. Bernardo Octavio Perez."

Layla pulled a notepad from her purse. "I'll tell our manager you denied us access."

"No, I didn't say that." The clerk was now backpedaling. "I have to ask the accountant."

"Well, I suggest you give him a call," Clay said as he moved closer to the desk. He loomed above the Maya clerk, whose height barely reached the Canadian's shoulders.

The clerk nodded dumbly, turned, and went to a phone on a rear credenza.

The crafty trio gave tiny fist bumps as they waited for the action to begin.

Bernardo was back. "Roberto said he'll be here soon. Would you like to take a seat?"

"We'll get a head start. May I wander into the back offices?" Layla said.

The clerk gave her a strange look. "Is that necessary?"

"You won't believe what they ask for. Building materials, composition, ceiling height."

"Go ahead." He waved towards the back office. "Or maybe I'll just show you the way."

"The men can start outside," Layla said. "How many cottages on the property?"

"Eighteen."

"Any rooms in the main building?"

"Only one. A studio for the general manager, if he shows up and needs to stay over."

She watched Jaime and Clay walk through French doors that led onto a wide deck leading down to the cottages. "May I see it?" Layla asked, pulling out her thousand watt smile.

"Certainly," Bernardo said, falling into line. "It's through the sala." He walked to the end of the counter and pulled up a partition. "This way, please."

A wide doorway led to the sala, which Layla assumed would be used for meetings or meals. Since they were smack dab in the middle of nowhere, a restaurant would be a necessity.

"Where is your kitchen?"

"North of the lodge. In a separate building."

"Is anyone there now?" Layla asked.

"The cook and her helper. It's not a large party, and she's been doing this for years."

"Is she always on the property?"

"If there's a big party, she and her assistant sleep over. There's a room with a couple of beds built onto the kitchen. These fishing parties," he said with a shake of the head.

"Up early? Angling for the prize dorado?"

He looked at her appreciatively, realizing even though she had the looks of a city girl she knew her way around a fishing pole. "Si, si. They're early risers and many are very demanding."

"Is it a fishing party this weekend?"

A shadow crossed his young face. "Um, ahh, no. I think it's business. A closed party. Even I won't be working, once the guests arrive."

"Hmm. Maybe a secret birthday for someone special? Or famous?" Layla pushed.

"Oh, they don't share information with me. This time I didn't even get a guest list."

"Is that unusual?"

He shook his head. "Well, yes, actually. I haven't worked here that long, but they usually want a name, email, and cell for everyone attending. In case of problems. Medical or whatever."

"And if they're famous or politicians, sometimes it's best to keep things undercover." She let her arm accidentally brush Bernardo's hand.

"Oh, excuse me. My, what a lovely sala," she said, acting intentionally flustered by the unplanned touch.

"They use it for dinners, too. We have a lot of parties of ten or twelve."

"Is this the unit that your general manager stays in, if he sleeps over?"

They'd entered an area off the sala. Though the room was small, it had all necessary creature comforts. In the back, a door led to a bathroom and shower.

"Perfect for someone who needs to rest after a long day. Especially with that road."

"Right. Let me show you the ballroom," the clerk said.

"Sure. This must be a good job." They walked out a back door and into the compound.

"Hmm, I guess," he answered.

"You don't sound very enthused."

The clerk nearly stumbled when he heard Layla's comment. "Oh, no. It's a good job."

"What's not to like?" Layla pressed.

No answer.

"Let me guess." Layla pulled out her notepad and began sketching cottage placement while they walked. Gabriella said one sat farther away from the others. "Management?"

"Oh, no, I never said that."

"Nothing wrong about not liking your boss. I have the same problem, actually," Layla said.

Sensing a kindred spirit, the clerk perked up. "Really?"

"Yeah, he's a real pendejo. Ayyy!" She feigned a blush. "I don't usually get carried away with that type of language, but I think we share common ground."

"Yeah, I guess so."

"What don't you like about your boss?" Layla asked.

"Oh, in my opinion he hangs out with the wrong people."

"Meaning?"

"Well, if there's an opening, he'll invite Cancunese down. For long weekends."

"Family, friends?"

The clerk shook his head. "No, bigwigs, the mayor. Business owners. Sometimes …others."

Layla took the cue. Her origin story followed her wherever she went. "But they're paying customers, right?"

"I guess."

"Are they rude?" Layla kept sniffing around, trying to get a fix. Were these captains of industry or narcos like herself?

"Not rude. Crude is a better word. Some are politicians."

Layla sensed she was making progress. "The lodge must be booked months in advance. I'd assume you rarely have openings."

"During hurricane season there's usually a lull. Coming up."

"Aah, yes. First of June. Do they stay the entire weekend?" Layla asked.

"Usually, but they're much more demanding than the fishermen. These guys want everything round the clock. They get stupidly drunk, and then there's the girls."

Layla's interior barometer jumped sky-high. "Girls? Working girls?"

The clerk scowled. "I shouldn't be saying this, but it bothers me. Some are professional, but others are very young. I don't think they come willingly."

Layla snorted. "Sex slaves?"

"Hijole," the clerk moaned. "I said too much."

Layla stopped in the middle of the path. "Listen, I won't tell anyone what you told me, Bernardo. Don't worry."

In the distance Layla spotted a dark-haired man in his thirties walking towards them.

"Here comes the accountant; please don't say anything."

"Is that what's happening this weekend?" Layla asked.

Bernardo shrugged, looking down. "I think so."

Layla put on her queen bee act. The man approaching could give her pushback.

"Buenos dias." The accountant had the bearing of a company man. He was attractive with a medium build, dressed in khakis and a Guayabera shirt. The look could be a uniform or a lack of fashion sense.

"Hello. I'm Layla and I'm here with two others that represent your insurance company."

"Roberto Guevarra. You mean ING?"

"Why, yes. Since it's almost hurricane season, we're at a seminar in Playa, and our manager asked us to do a quick check on the lodge. With last year's activity, we want to assure ING that Boca Laguna is up to code to qualify for the special addendum, and make sure you've taken proper measures."

"Yes, we've done a lot of upgrades this year. No doubt Bernardo has told you." He smiled benevolently at both of them. Layla wasn't the only one with charisma.

"He's been most helpful," Layla said.

"Have you seen the dock yet?"

"My associates are on the grounds now and plan to check on it."

"How long will you be?" Roberto asked, looking at his watch. "I'm expecting people soon. We have a private party all weekend."

"Bernardo mentioned that. Sorry for being last minute. With so many properties to check, I think my director was a little overwhelmed because of the Playa conference."

Roberto smiled again, showing straight white teeth. "I'll be in my office if you need me."

🔹🔹🔹

Clay and Jaime had moved swiftly after departing from the main lobby. Clay had already surmised that Jaime's organizational skills were well beyond his pay grade; he possessed an uncanny ability to view the whole enchilada. Clay watched as the former matador's eyes darted from spot to spot, no doubt inputting mental notes as he whizzed along. "This set-up's not too bad," he told Clay.

Jaime had what Clay would call situational awareness—something that had kept many a dealer, bodyguard, or jefe alive. "What's your take?"

"Well, the cottages all line up in a row, in front of the lagoon. The dock juts out from the center of the spread. There's a lot of privacy, and that'll help us remain undercover."

"Gabriella reserved the southern most cottage for us. It'll be empty, if we need it," Clay said.

The fixer spotted the cottage. "Good work. I want to see it." Once there, he checked the door. It wasn't locked and he pushed it open. "Coming?" Jaime asked.

Clay followed. The curtains were drawn, making the room quite dark.

"Hit the light." In a mumbled voice, Jaime said, "Where to hide it."

"Hide what?" Clay asked.

"Close the door."

In spite of the oppressive heat, Clay again did as Jaime directed. He watched him pull a nine-millimeter from under his loose polyester shirt. "Whoa. Game changer."

"I have another in the car. But we're gonna need to carry during this little circus. The stakes are too high. Entiende?" Understand?

"I do. There's the SUV guys. Can I see it?" Clay asked.

Jaime handed over the piece. "Now we find a safe place to stash it."

They looked around the sparsely furnished cottage. "Bathroom?" Clay asked.

It was roomy with an old-fashioned commode, the tank on top and a ledge above. "Hey, Jaime," Clay said. "How about up there?" He pointed to the ledge.

"Can you feel around, check if it's damp?"

Clay was the perfect height for the job. "Sure." He reached a long arm around behind the tank. Even he had to stand on tiptoes. "A cinch no maid would look up here."

"I'll wrap it," Jaime said, grabbing a hand towel. "So no sticking when we need it."

"Good idea, but why leave one in the room?"

"As back-up, or if we're frisked. Or if the other one gets wet. We're on the water."

"Are you driving down?" Clay asked.

"Yeah. We need two escape routes. They won't recognize me. You had a brush with the SUV," Jaime said.

Clay nodded. "Let's run that by Layla. We'll come in by panga, then meet up with you—maybe here in the cottage. It's positioned far enough away from where the activities will no doubt take place."

"We can have Gabriella hide the key under the mat or somewhere."

"Hand me the gun," Clay said after he watched Jaime wrap it in the towel. "Up we go." The gun disappeared onto the ledge above the toilet tank. "Ciao for now."

"We'll see it this weekend. Now let's find Layla and figure out what's happening."

CHAPTER 25

The car hit a pothole on the Si'an Ka'an Road and Gabriella's body shifted in the seat of the Tsuru. Even with seatbelt fastened, she came very close to the mayor. His skin had an unhealthy glisten, and the gel he used to smooth back his grungy hair looked an inch thick. Beady, rodent-like eyes completed the picture. He reached over to touch her arm, taking any option to close the gap between them, even a mere bump in the road. She shrunk from his slimy touch, a scowl forming on her usually impassive face.

"Eww." She brushed off the spot where his hand had touched her.

"What?" Juan Dzib asked.

The mayor was so preoccupied he missed Gabriella's exaggerated movement of wiping his paw prints from her arm.

"Oh, nothing." She was sitting next to a murderer, riding alone with him on a deserted beach road in the middle of a million-hectare biosphere. "These bumps upset my stomach. Had something to eat last night that didn't sit right," she lied.

"Nice of Torres to ask you to come. Too bad he couldn't ride with us."

Silence was the easiest way to endure the long, endless road. It had become her mental armor.

"Will you stay the entire weekend?" the mayor asked, ruining her reverie. His voice sounded like a cross between a screech and a whine.

She ignored the question. He cleared his throat and gave another try. "Are you in Si'an Ka'an the whole weekend?"

"What?" Playing dumb was a worthwhile ploy. She'd at least come away with something after years of mockery and jibes from older brothers who loved to harass her. She could stonewall.

"The whole weekend?" he repeated.

"What about it?" she said, to needle him.

"Are you staying?" the mayor asked.

"Hmm? At Boca Laguna? Not sure. It depends on whether Torres wants to drive back on his own. I have to set things up."

The mayor continued driving, avoiding what bumps he could. After their brief exchange, Gabriella decided she could eliminate the need to genuflect at one of the stations of the cross, assuming she was in a church-going mood on Sunday. After the joyless ride she was on with Dzib, her penance was done.

🈁🈁🈁

Layla left Bernardo at the front desk and walked briskly out the French doors to look for Clay and Jaime. With no immediate sign of them, she stood for a moment to get a better idea of cottage placement. She spied cottage eighteen, appreciative of its lone position away from the others. She walked in that direction and paused before the door. She gave a light knock.

"Who's there?"

"Layla."

Jaime opened the door. She entered and stood in a semi-darkened room steeped in heat and humidity. The clammy smell of the tropics invaded her nostrils. "What's up?"

"I brought an extra piece. We're leaving it here," Jaime said.

"Oh. Where is it?"

"The bathroom, hidden on top of the commode," Jaime said.

"Could come in handy, huh?" Layla asked.

"Not sure how this is gonna come down, boss."

"Now what? We have a piece stored, we got the lay of the land. Should we split?"

"How do we know if Silvia will be here?" Clay asked.

"We'll have to chance it. I talked at length to Bernardo. These events happen periodically. It's tweaked him. He's young but not so naive any more," Layla said.

"What did he say?"

"He said it's common practice for the manager to bring down Cancunese. Bigwigs, hotel owners, and there are always girls. I asked if they were working girls, and he got angry. He said many don't want to be here—whatever that means—and they're young. Under-age."

"Whoa. So, what's our plan?" Clay asked.

Layla looked down at her hands for a second before speaking. "We leave. I'll call Gabriella and tell her the cottage is perfect. Ask her to leave the key—somewhere. Ideas?"

Clay walked to the door and looked around. There was a pot with a sego palm to the right on the stoop. "Under the potted palm?"

"Not exactly original, but it'll do. I'll tell the accountant that we've reviewed the property and we're gone."

"You got it, boss."

Clay opened the door and ushered Jaime and Layla out. They departed from the stoop quickly, to avoid being seen near the site of their upcoming rendezvous.

"It's eleven. Gabriella should be here soon. I'll call her." Layla scrolled for the number.

"Gabriella?"

"Si," she said. "Hello. Yes, we're very close to the lodge, Señor Torres."

"Okay. You can't talk. We're heading out. The cottage is perfect. Leave the key under the potted palm. We'll be back, not sure when. We may have evidence. Not a hundred percent, but enough for us to return. Everything okay?"

"Si. Todo bien. Adios," Gabriella said.

Layla put away her phone. "They're almost here. We'll figure out timing as we drive."

They passed quickly through the lobby, where Bernardo manned the front desk. "Leaving?"

Layla motioned to Clay and Jaime to keep moving. "Yes, thank you. We'll be in touch."

She scooted out the French doors. Jaime had already started the car and Clay was in back, window down, waiting for the A/C to kick in. Layla took the front seat and turned around to check on Clay as Jaime backed up and turned towards the road. He looked left, preparing to head out, but a cloud of dust from the north deterred him: a fast-moving black Escalade emerged from its nucleus. He inched back into the lot, allowing the oncoming vehicle wide berth; the whirling dust resembled a Saharan sandstorm. The SUV bypassed the lodge, making no attempt to slow down. Layla kept her back to the road and faced Clay, who had lowered his head. The car whizzed by, leaving Jaime's Toyota in a haze. Two suited men rode in front. The passenger had completely turned and was fiddling with something in back.

"Boss, I think they're in that car."

"Who?"

"Silvia. The guy riding shotgun's either got a sick dog in back or a baby on board. I have a feeling about this."

"Where are they going?" Clay asked.

"Not to Punta Allen. Wait. Casa Paraiso? The governor's house?"

"Perfect hideaway," Jaime said.

"The best. No one around, probably not even the sister," Layla said.

"Do we follow them?" Clay asked.

"Not too closely, but yes," Jaime said.

As the cloud receded, Jaime pulled onto the road. "Did they check you out?" Layla asked.

"The driver looked this way, but I never get a second glance."

Clay eyeballed Jaime. Except for a meaningful mustache, he could easily fade into a crowd, perfect cover for the work he did. Unlike Clay, he'd attract little attention.

"Here we go. The chase scene," Jaime announced.

"You're being dramatic," Layla cautioned.

"Hey, this is the first step, boss. We're on to something, and it involves two people who are being held against their will."

"You could be right," Clay said.

"Follow that car."

CHAPTER 26

Near Casa Paraiso, a cloud of dust hovered over the lane leading to the isolated villa.

"Now what?" Clay asked.

"We have to follow, but the car will be a giveaway. Walk in?"

"You know how far that is, Layla?"

"Yes, but we need to check. Jaime, drive south. Can you pull over? Stash the car, or park it. The two of us," she glanced at Clay, "will see what's happening and verify if Silvia's there."

"What about Francisco?"

"Him, too," Layla spit out, trying to not look riled. "The problem."

"Every crime has a problem, boss. Maybe he couldn't help it."

She pursed her lips and blew her hair away from her forehead, ignoring Jaime's soft sell. She let it go. "Hopefully we'll get full details later."

Francisco was a selfish idiot, she thought. To introduce an innocent bystander into a laundering scheme was unconscionable. Money laundering had no small players. It was big time.

"Jaime, can Clay borrow your piece?" Layla asked.

"Sure."

They'd followed the road a kilometer past Casa Paraiso. "Listen, I'll drive you back to the top of the lane and find a place to wait it out. Call when you need me," Jaime said.

"Gabriella thought it was tomorrow. If things change, we could be doing an about-face."

"True. Okay, here's the gun, Clay. You guys check the house."

"Let's do it," Clay responded.

꒰꒰꒰

Jaime dropped them and continued north. The dust had settled after the SUV's dash down the lane, but, to avoid discovery, Layla and Clay would have to dart into unwelcome jungle that secluded the house from the road. Their safety precaution, Jaime's nine-millimeter, was stashed in the back waistband of Clay's shorts. They trudged towards the house and after walking a good way, spotted the SUV in the drive, encouraging them to edge deeper into the trees, not far from the entryway.

"The front door's in the center. Did you notice any others when we were inside?" Layla asked.

"I think the kitchen's off to the left. Let's dart across the road and check it out."

Layla nodded before looking both ways, ready to make a dash. Good a plan as any, she told herself. A light breeze rustled the palm fronds above them, and she was thankful for it.

They closed in on the villa's entrance near the parking area and saw a path had been cleared. Still hidden by trees,

Clay pointed to the house's left side where they could take shelter before inching closer. Once safely out of sight at the corner of the house, Clay zeroed in on the Escalade.

"By the scuffed dust, I'd say more than one person got out of the back door."

Sand surrounding fancy villas was raked with the precision of a Zen garden if the caretaker expected to keep his job. Something had definitely occurred; it looked like two—maybe three—sets of feet had shuffled out of the car. Were they dragged? Drugged? Oh God, she thought. Silvia is close.

"I can feel her," she whispered to Clay.

He put an index finger to his lips. They stood in silence, settling into a stealth rhythm. Luckily, they were shielded from the sun by the shadow of the two-story dwelling and shade from another palm grove growing on the north side of the property. A narrow path for beach-goers had been cut through to the ocean.

"Watch and wait," Clay observed. "Been on a stake-out before?"

Layla wrinkled her nose. "Former life—cartel accountant. The brain behind the computer."

"Right, but I figured you knew the drill." He gave a quick squeeze to her sweaty palm.

"I'm nervous," she admitted.

He nodded at the looming house. "Not a good position. We wait. At least I like the company."

He was trying to keep it light. Her own thoughts—not so good. She felt close to a meltdown. Even though she came across as composed, she wanted to scream. Practice, however, had become practicality in the world she inhabited.

She'd gleaned techniques from watching her uncle in one tight spot after another. He maintained.

She had no idea how long they'd been there when she heard an unidentifiable noise inside the house. Like a chair being dragged across a tile floor—for a long ways.

She shrugged her shoulders in Clay's direction. He raised an eyebrow and again placed a finger to his lips. Though it could be anything, they both knew it was far from that. They stood like stick figures, barely daring to breathe. Then it came. What began as a howl became an unholy ear-shattering scream. The front door flew open. They hugged the side of the building tighter still, Clay close to the corner. Together they saw her as she dashed into their line of vision—the girl from the previous day. She tore out of the house, running as if death itself were chasing her, but instead, it was one of the henchmen trying to keep up. With his Glock trained on her backside, he yelled, "Fucking stop! Stop! Or I'll shoot."

The girl either thought she had the stamina to run the distance, dodge the bullets, and live another day, or she didn't—but something made her run for it rather than await her future inside.

A shot rang out. The gunman, tailing her and on the move, had taken aim, as though tracking an animal. His pricey jacket exposed not a crease and his movements disclosed experience. He was a gunman out for sport, a practiced eye trained on his prey. Another shot rang out. The girl continued to run, now into the thick jungle of palms. She was well into the grove, and though he followed, she seemed to be pulling out of range, dodging his pursuit. He fired again. Down. He'd struck her as though she'd been a target at a shooting range, but from the backside. Time stood still for a split second before a flow of blood began forming a shallow pool around her body. It would soon attract an army of insects and animals, nature's clean-up crew. They would dispose of her earthly shell unless the gunman decided to do the decent thing—dig a grave and bury her.

Clay pushed Layla farther against the wall. Layla stared down in shock, yearning to get a glimpse of the fallen woman—a girl really—that they'd met a day earlier. Both Clay and Layla knew what came next would be calculated and meaningful. The gunman broke precedent and jogged towards the girl's body.

His sharp reaction echoed through the previous silence. "Hijole!"

A yell came from inside the house. "What the hell, cabrón?" his partner yelled as he barreled through the door.

Layla couldn't see henchman two, but Clay's vantage point would allow him to watch the man's movements as he raced towards the fallen girl. Sharp voices rang out while they overheard the exchange.

"Muerto?" the second asked.

"Of course. Chinga, now we gotta bury her."

"We?" the second gunman asked. "I said to take it easy. Why you losing it, pendejo?"

"She was crying and asking questions, too whiny, once she saw the girl."

"Hijole! That doesn't mean you let her slip out the door and kill her!"

"She made a run for it. I couldn't stop her."

"What, you getting old, cabrón? Should I tell Torres?"

"Shut the fuck up. She made a move while I was getting the tape on the other side of the kitchen. I never thought she'd go for the door."

"After what you did to the banker? Are you kidding? I told you not to let her see him."

"Oh, fuck him. Now we only have two to take care of, not three."

"After you worked over the banker, it's more like one-and-a-half. It's a good thing the beauty didn't see what you did to her boyfriend or she'd never be up for the party tonight."

Layla tugged at Clay's shirt. He turned and she mouthed the word, "Tonight?"

The shooter snorted. "Chinga, with what we're going to give her, she won't know her own name, much less who she's screwing."

"What about the body?"

The duo had turned away from the building while deciding their next move, making it impossible to hear them, but from body language, they both knew what was up. It was an ancient question, one that had plagued humanity going back to Cain: where to bury the body?

As the henchmen's voices rose, Clay and Layla heard, "Get a shovel."

"Where?"

"Find one, pendejo! I didn't fucking shoot her."

The gunman turned abruptly, and Clay slunk back into the shadows of the house. With no garage or caretaker's cottage on their side, the gunman would look for tools elsewhere.

"They'll put her in the jungle, not far from where she fell," Layla said, in a whisper.

They watched from the sidelines while the two struggled with the girl's body, carrying her deeper into the grove. Moments later, one walked from the grove towards the garage and emerged with two shovels. As he passed the spot where the girl had fallen, he paused and laid down a shovel. With the other, he scraped dirt over the blood then scuffed it around, careful to follow the trail until it dwindled, in order to cover all evidence that a killing had occurred.

In spite of the death they'd just witnessed, Layla tempered her mindset. Though she'd not retained the mantel of cartel head for long, she was confident her DNA would pull her through. She could handle whatever was thrown her way. Not to mention that other thing: she had a strong desire to continue breathing.

CHAPTER 27

Still sidelined while waiting to see what Torres' henchmen planned to do, Clay and Layla kept silent. They could only watch and wait as they squatted against the villa wall, close enough to the ocean to hear waves lapping on the shore; the road was far away. Clay occasionally sneaked a peek to gauge how the job was going. The men had hung their pressed coats on a fallen palm near the driveway. They heard digging, and twenty minutes later Clay and Layla saw both henchmen at the perimeter of the grove, gathering rocks.

"What're they doing?" Layla asked.

"They'll cover the grave with rocks," Clay said, "to discourage animals from disturbing the body."

More disrespect, as though death wasn't bad enough, Layla thought.

She knew this was merely a knee-jerk reaction. Every move they made breathed self-preservation and that alone. No doubt they planned to be well out of range should a blunder occur. After a couple rock-collecting trips, they heard grunts as the two hurled raunchy zingers at one another. With Yucatán temps soaring, they'd be in need of a shower before attending to the real business at hand:

delivering Silvia in one piece to the triumvirate of Torres, the governor, and the mayor, along with a host of immoral businessmen.

"Take the fucking shovels back to the garage," they heard one henchman bark.

It sounded like the tit-for-tat exchange overheard a couple of nights earlier at the warehouse.

"Me? I did most of the digging."

"For Chrissake! Just do it!"

The bickering continued as one of the guys picked up a shovel and his coat, and the other did the same. Every man for himself. They walked to the garage, threw the shovels inside, and hiked back to the front entrance, breathing heavily. The door closed behind them.

Layla tugged at Clay's shirt. "There's no need to guess what's going on. She's inside."

Clay nodded. "Let's get out of here. We'll wait a minute then run over to the trees."

"Bypass the fresh dug grave," Layla said, stating what Clay had avoided, "and walk fast to the top of the road."

"It sounds like they beat the hell out of Francisco, but Silvia's in reasonable shape."

Layla wiped sweat from her brow with the back of her hand. "Until they drug her for the event. What time is it?"

"About three. We gotta get a move on. It's happening tonight. Call Gabriella and the boatman, but first, Jaime."

"I don't think we can stop her from being drugged," Layla said, almost a question.

"We can't go in there, Layla. Not the two of us with one gun. We're going to need Jaime's help. We'll show up at the lodge tonight and deal with it."

Her confidence from twenty minutes earlier had fallen to a moody low. "I feel awful. Hot, depressed." Not to mention she was spinning from yet another déjà vu moment. Why were young girls dying around her? Who the fuck was she? The angel of death? "God, I think I'm hungry. How can that be? I just witnessed an execution. I should be throwing up."

The impact of the killing scene had crept up from behind and tapped her on the shoulder. Please stop thinking about Lupita, she prayed.

"Let's get up to the road and figure out what we can do to at least change the eating and humidity part, okay? Find a place to take a shower, maybe in Muyil," Clay said. He read her immediately, her thoughts laid out clear to him, like a page from the I Ching. "Don't fail me now, Layla. You're made of stronger stuff than that."

CHAPTER 28

Their call to Jaime brought the matador in record time. The thick tangle of palms alongside the road served as a convenient hiding spot while they waited. Jaime barely stopped the car, but like pros in a sports car endurance race, they were prepared. He was the driver, they were roadies at the pit stop, awaiting the next challenge. Their determination level had spiked, too, since they'd viewed the kidnappers as killers, and the cover-up—burying the body. Would Torres or Dzib care? Had they known the girl would be there? She was an innocent bystander whose life had ended by merely showing up for work. Layla wondered who the decider was in all this. She began to fear for Gabriella, having witnessed one young innocent being shot and killed, with no concern from the man who employed her.

"What's up?" Jaime asked. He looked at the two of them suspiciously. "You seem off."

Though slightly winded, Layla began. "We witnessed a killing. The caretaker, a young woman, was shot dead by the henchmen from the warehouse."

"Chinga de Madre! What happened?"

"We sneaked through the palms close to the villa where we saw the Escalade," Clay said. "The sand around

201

the car looked messed up, like there'd been a scuffle. Fifteen minutes in to us holding up the wall, we heard a noise. The door burst open and the girl shot out of the house."

"She was hauling ass, as though she was running from the devil himself," Layla said.

"Sounds about right," Jaime said, pulling down on his mustache as he frowned.

"One of the guys was on her, with a Glock. He shot twice …" Layla paused, recalling what she and Clay had just witnessed. Her eyes glazed over, her voice became listless.

"And for a split second I thought she could pull away, dodging in and out of the trees, but somehow the sucker nailed her." She gripped the cushion of the car seat and stared dumbly at the floorboards. "Damn, another one down." On my watch.

"Boss." Jaime's voice was stern with a tone of finality. "You know the business we're in. There are no saviors here, no heroes. If it's anyone's fault, it's the damn banker's. To bring a girl into this shit-hole? He took a chance with her life, and she's not out of the woods yet."

"He's bearing the pain now," Layla said.

Jaime glanced over. "What do you mean?"

Clay continued, "One of the guys said he was pretty messed up. Don't know how bad."

Jaime mulled that over and let it go. "So, what's the timeline?"

"Oh, it's tonight, not tomorrow. I've got to call Gabriella and Pedro, let them know it's on, and"—she said before letting out a sigh—"they're gonna drug her before the party."

"Makes sense. No worries of a scene if she's all drugged up," Jaime said.

Layla put a hand above her brow and rubbed her fingers across her forehead. She shifted in the seat and stared out the window. The caretaker's murder had brought up feelings she didn't care to examine. She was raw inside. "I feel bad," she whispered under her breath.

She never exposed feelings to underlings. That showed weakness. But Jaime had an avuncular quality, a stand-in for Patrón—measured, old school. Regardless, that was no excuse. Time to get a grip. In her game, you rode the wave or you ate it. There was no in between.

His voice broke into her thoughts. "She'll get through the drugging. It's the rest that we're worried about. Like what happens afterwards if we don't intervene."

She looked over at him. "Okay, got it!" she said with an edge, suspending the feel-good relationship between master and minion.

Her voice had shifted an octave, taking on an assertive air, dismissing his comment in an offhand manner. "I'll call Gabriella and see when it starts. She's there now. The mayor was her chauffeur earlier. What time is it?" she demanded.

"Nearly four."

Layla scrolled through her phone. "Hola, Gabriella. It's on for tonight. Can't talk, but we'll be taking the boat up with Pedro, right after dark. We'll go to the cottage—when you can get away from the crowd, we'll see you there."

"Is everything okay?" Gabriella asked.

"No, but we're moving forward. Silvia will be there, not sure about the banker. You'll be coming back with us, most likely riding with Jaime. You will not be staying at the lodge, got it?"

"Okay. Thank you. Tonight at nine in the ballroom," she said, signing off.

"It's at nine in the ballroom," Layla repeated. "Pedro next."

She dialed and connected with the boatman. "We're on for tonight, not tomorrow. Should be in Muyil in an hour. I'll need to find a place to grab a bite to eat and shower. We've been running through the jungle. Your cousin's in Muyil? Great. See you soon."

"You got that set up in record time," Clay said. "Punch it, Jaime. We're heading south."

CHAPTER 29

Torres hadn't planned on the governor's inability to navigate the politically charged landscape that the state of Quintana Roo had become. They'd gone to university together; the governor came in as a scholarship student, whereas Torres hailed from one of Monterrey's most prosperous families. In spite of different backgrounds, they had somehow connected and complemented each other, both in school and later on when Torres brought the earnest graduate into his father's construction business.

In time, Torres introduced Enrique to fraudulent land deals, enlisting his help. Things cruised along until the Tulum mayor stepped in and befriended the newbie governor, tempting him with land grabs, assuring he'd lend a hand creating titles. The governor's alliances began to shift as Dzib made promises to assist in cashing out on deals if Enrique played the mayor's game. Torres became miffed. He had no desire to share the governor with Dzib, and to add salt to the wound, the mayor's sexual predilections were beginning to draw public attention.

It wasn't that Torres was opposed to sex parties. If one was wealthy, a well-connected wife with family pedigree along with a sexy mistress was standard fare. If that wasn't enough, there were various sex clubs where men like himself let it all hang out. Over the centuries, probably since time immemorial, men had flaunted wealth and power to gain access to the most beautiful women on the planet. But back to Dzib. That damn mayor had muddied the waters.

"Señor Torres?"

The contractor's reverie had been disturbed. "Yes, Gabriella?"

"I have your orders for seating assignments. What time can we expect everyone?"

He looked at the young woman he'd recently hired. She wasn't particularly attractive but her body mirrored a style depicted by the European masters—a bit fleshier and rounder than what modern women strove for, but then, he'd always enjoyed a full-figured woman.

"Around nine. We'll have drinks and start the light supper directly after and …"

"Can I drive your car back to Tulum?" she said, interrupting his thoughts a second time.

"What?"

"I'm not feeling well. I told the mayor. I'll leave it at the office and catch a taxi home."

He pondered her suggestion. Actually, he hadn't really thought about where she would be once things got rolling. He'd assumed the mayor would have made arrangements.

"Yes, that will work. Take my car."

"Thank you. I'll need the keys. If I start to fade, I won't have to bother you later."

He began considering logistics—where to put the girls before they were showcased to his colleagues in the ballroom. Dzib had ordered drapes, one job he managed to finish, and the night's grand prize would be the banker's squeeze. After the weekend activities he'd throw her back into the water, not so different from the bonefish anglers at the lodge. If they drugged her she wouldn't know what happened. As for Francisco, his crass disloyalty would be dealt with later. The kidnapping, so far, was working in his favor. Since Francisco had no idea what was coming, there had been no struggle when the cartel slugs picked him up at his hotel. The girl was unexpected, but there was no way to not include her, or Francisco would have guessed the ploy. Tough luck for the girl. He guessed her at twenty-one, a little older than the others, but her accidental presence had worked out very well indeed.

🎵🎵🎵

"I'm heading to the dining room, to check on things," Gabriella told Torres.

"Okay. I'll be in the lobby. Later you can find me at my cottage. Number one."

"Of course," she said, and left the room.

Once she was gone, Torres began to think about retribution. Francisco's stance on handling things had raised eyebrows from politicos high up the food chain, those involved in crafting international banking statutes. He'd been asking for more meetings with key players; Torres loathed the interference. He didn't need the pressure of being put under a microscope with associates questioning his financier's actions.

Money laundering was something Torres had never considered. With the graft he collected by short-changing state and federal governments from bridge and road contracts, he was riding high. His ploy was two-fold: first, overbid the project, promising a kickback to those reviewing the bids if he scored, and second, cut the composition make-up in the two staples of the trade—concrete and rebar. He'd relied on the governor to handle these issues before politics became his calling.

Torres' accomplishments had made him a star, not only to the public, but the cartels had eyes on him, too. His wife, a society maven, had begun hosting charity events with the wife of Mexico City's Silvestre Lopez Garcia. He was a mysterious one, or had been until Torres accidentally discovered he was the power behind the throne of New Guaymas Generation cartel. By the looks of Silvestre, it was obvious cartels were no longer run by shit-kickers driving pick-ups and listening to ranchera music. Silvestre wrote the book on cool—a real Cary Grant, tight with everyone from law enforcement and the judiciary to high society types. Along with his glamorous wife, Lenora, they ranked high in the city's social register and regularly attended posh events. Soon after Torres' wife ingratiated her way into Lenora's company, the cartels came calling.

"Señor Torres," his secretary had said one day. "A Señor Morelos is on the line."

"Can you take a message?"

"He said he must speak with you directly. He mentioned Señor Silvestre Lopez Garcia."

Torres picked up and spoke to the associate of his wife's friend's husband. Since he was well known in the construction world, he assumed more business would flow his way. An appointment was scheduled.

When Morelos came into the office, he was accompanied by another fellow. As the men settled into the conference room, both declining coffee or water, they got right down to business.

Skilled at reading body language and anticipating the unspoken wishes of his clients, Torres got the ball rolling. "What type of construction do you need?"

"Me and Vasquez are in a different business than what you're used to," Morelos said.

"Oh, don't be so sure," Torres said, subduing a smile. "You'd be surprised at the extent of our company's scope. I've been in business twenty-five years, and that's not including how long my father ran the company."

Morelos gave a sideways glance to his partner. "We're dealing in the financial sector."

"Oh, building for a banking project?"

"You could say that."

"Banamex, Scotia, MBC?"

"We mainly deal with MBC."

"Will the project be in Monterrey?"

"Quintana Roo."

"Hmm, a long way from here. But I know el Yucatán is growing by leaps and bounds."

"Si, but by banking project, we mean we need your assistance in putting money through one or more of your construction accounts. You know, to clean the money. Look legitimate."

Torres shifted in his chair. "Excuse me, I'm not sure what you mean." Though not yet alarmed, their strange request had gotten his attention.

The other fellow, Vasquez, leaned in, placing his elbows on the sleek conference table, its glossy finish reflecting his image like a mirror. "You'd be laundering money for us."

"Oh, gentlemen ..." Torres began, performing the exact opposite move that Vasquez had done, but in backwards motion, to distance himself from not only the words he'd heard but from the man who uttered them. "You must have me confused with someone else. I run a legitimate business." He placed both palms flat on the table and let out a small chuckle, to defuse the unappealing subject at hand. "I do construction."

"What about concrete composition?"

"Excuse me?"

"Composition of your concrete. The mixtures," Vasquez said. His look had gone dark. He was the fixer, the one who would take out kneecaps for starters, or if things didn't go his way, worse. His gaze never left Torres; he was a cat eyeing the canary.

"Why yes," Torres said. "Concrete is a composition of various materials."

"But your composition is off."

"What are you talking about?" Torres asked.

"Let's not play games," the other man said. "You demand discounts from your suppliers, then you lower the standards on materials for your clients. Double dipping."

"That's ridiculous. I've worked with federal and state governments for decades and they never ..."

"Of course they never," interrupted Morelos, his voice growing louder as he settled into a rhythm. "They either didn't know you were screwing them or you cut them in on the profits."

"I beg your pardon, that is incorrect."

Morelos smirked. "No need to practice your manners on me. I didn't want to go this route, but you give me no choice."

Silvestre's impeccably groomed goon brought out a meaningful leather folder. When they displayed photos of his family, Torres knew his world had crashed. Particularly disturbing was the mention of his son's athletic prowess. They clucked over his daughter, but lingered long over a picture of his wife in a low-cut evening gown.

Morelos stroked the photo, holding it up for him to see. When he leaned closer and said in a low voice, "Your wife is very pretty," the point was made.

In a strange twist, a man who always gave directions would now be the one taking orders. They wanted him to invest in Mexico's new gold mine, Quintana Roo, and here he was. A luminary among businessmen in Mexico's financial capital, Monterrey, now stuck in outback Quintana Roo, sifting through land deals and expected to launder profits through his company to a string of international banks.

That's where Francisco came in. He'd ingratiated himself with Mr. Big from DF, and Torres had to play the laundering game or be exposed for cheating the very corporations he did business with. Adding another layer of shit, Francisco could be working with the feds. In Mexico, gossip was quick to circulate. Was the governor in on it? Torres thought not. He'd known Enrique since university, and though not the sharpest knife in the drawer, he wasn't a turncoat. Between the cartel's money laundering demands and rumors of Francisco being compromised, this was the opposite of a win-win. In fact, Torres couldn't decide which outcome would be worse.

But Francisco's dubious status had brought things to a head. The loose talk flying around construction circles had to end, and Torres was the only one capable of putting a lid on it. Why Francisco had dragged a beauty into the hellhole of the Q. Roo reckoning was anyone's guess. Of course, Francisco had no clue that this weekend would be *his* reckoning, but Torres didn't take lightly to veiled threats. One didn't grow up working construction in Mexico without learning how to squeeze the opposition. Destroy and conquer—that was his father's motto.

Torres hadn't made it this far in life without seeing a few storm clouds on the horizon. Even though it might not look like there was a way out, his instincts told him there was always a way through.

CHAPTER 30

When Francisco Ramirez accepted a position at MBC, he was groomed from the bottom up, keenly observed for his performance under pressure. He possessed the callow veneer of an outright con man with an ability to pull the wool over anyone's eyes. When the bank directed him to convince smaller banks to illicitly open additional accounts in their clients' names, he didn't flinch.

The process had a name—structuring—with an odd nickname: smurfing. His boss explained how to do it. "You make small money deposits into numerous accounts, but stretch it out over time, Francisco."

While big time launderers worked with Asian banking entities, because Mexico was close to the Caribbean—with amoral countries like Grand Cayman, Nevis, and Panama as neighbors—these locales would be used instead.

"You'll execute a complicated sequence of transfers. So many that banking oversight won't recognize what's happening," his boss instructed. "Here's how it works. First, cash is placed into a new venue. Second, we do what we call layering. It involves more complex transactions that camouflage the illegal source. Lastly, we've got integration."

"What's that?" Francisco asked.

"Getting your hands on the cash. These transactions get deposited or integrated—risk free—into accounts that are now sanitized."

Even a former Mexican president fell under the launderer's spell—the corruption in Francisco's country went that high. At one time currency exchanges had proved an excellent way to clean money, and the former politico was the sovereign of Cancun due to the number of exchanges he owned.

Service industries worked well, too, and hotels had become popular laundering vehicles. As explained to him, no one truly knew how many guests stayed at a hotel on any given night. Hotels could claim full occupancy—even without guests—and create sizable receipts. Bank deposits would reflect erroneous guest arrivals for unseen business. Clean money. Foolproof.

လြလြလြ

Francisco's slicked back hair gave him a rakish look, and his ripped muscles came from lifting weights. A confirmed obsessive compulsive, he organized his desk before leaving for a meeting with a CEO of a Panamanian bank.

He waited in the lobby for the elevator. Riding up, he checked his tie in the mirror and patted down his hair, a final approval on his dapper appearance. The bell rang and he exited. He hadn't seen much of this particular banker lately even though he was one of their main guys. Once a schedule had been established, meetings were the exception not the rule.

He entered a subdued lobby where a woman with high, sharp cheekbones that proclaimed indigenous roots greeted him. "Señor Francisco Ramirez?"

"Yes, here to see—"

"Señor Montejo. Please have a seat."

Her phone rang. She looked at Francisco, nodded, and beckoned him to follow.

The hallway was a collage of oil paintings and certificates in gilded frames commemorating services rendered. At the end of the hall she opened the door to a spacious, well-appointed board room. Three men sat at one end of a twenty-foot conference table, eight foot across at the center, tapering down to an oval on both ends. They spoke in hushed tones. The conversation halted when Francisco appeared.

The man at the head of the table, Alberto Montejo, stood as Francisco came to greet him. He was fifty-six with a graying mustache, and due to his years and a sedentary lifestyle, carried some girth around the middle that extended upwards to the jowls of his cheeks. With a pleasant manner and perpetual smile, he resembled a jolly south-of-the-border Santa Claus. The other two men stood and they shook hands while introductions were made.

"Have a seat, Francisco," Montejo said. "Thanks for coming. Señors Eduardo Gomez and James McArthur are with the Financial Action Task Force or FATF, an intergovernmental body that promotes anti-money laundering policies. Because Panama has been on the list since last June, alongside countries like Afghanistan, Sudan, and Syria, here at Pana-Bank we needed a refresher course in how to strengthen government supervision in the financial sector. We want to fully cooperate with regulations, so we can continue to do business with MBC."

Francisco wasn't prepared for a meeting with financial regulators alongside the very man involved in one of their largest money laundering schemes. He shifted in his chair and looked longingly at a water pitcher sitting center table, aware that reaching for a drink could make him appear anxious. Posturing rule number one: Accept nothing.

"FATF," Montejo said, nodding at the two gentlemen, "has had some concerns about Panama. I've had a crash course in how to keep Pana-Bank healthy and rule-bearing to the core.

"Panama's had limited regulation of bearer shares exclusively owned by whoever physically possesses them. They told me bearer shares are vulnerable to money laundering—few records are kept of buyers—and selling them is easy. With new international changes this year, under Panamanian law, transparency is more difficult to achieve. The original share owner isn't required to turn it over to an authorized custodian such as a bank or an attorney."

As Francisco realized the meeting bordered on an indictment, he got hold of himself. He cleared his throat, complemented by a shake of his well-coiffed head.

"Excuse me, Señor Montejo, with all due respect, it's very interesting to know how the FATF works, but I'm not sure where MBC fits into the conversation."

Eduardo Gomez, man in charge, placed his elbows on the mahogany table and peered around their host in order to make eye contact with the banker.

"Let me explain. We're regulators for the regulators, Señor Ramirez. In other words, we're well-schooled in what goes on in some countries' banking institutions. This past half year we're focused on Panama and the number of transactions certain banks—Mexico's in particular—have been making there. Our superiors suggested it was time to pay a visit. Not only to Señor Montejo"—he nodded to the man at the head of the table—"but also to the Mexican bankers he does the most business with."

"Oh," Francisco demurred, "I'd love to be considered in that league, but I think you have us confused with another financial institution."

"Well, maybe I'm overstepping boundaries by giving you information on Panama and why the country is in a gray area with FATF, but in going over paperwork, Pana-Bank has made it very easy for companies to be formed, due to the country's banking stipulations. We've been following their transactions for a while now. There are serious legal loopholes that have been leap-frogged over, and this often leads to"—he paused, considering how to communicate in the most delicate manner—"improprieties later on."

Much to Francisco's chagrin, the conversation continued in this vein. He slowly retreated into his own private world as the voices in the room faded to a hollow hum. He couldn't help but notice Montejo's usually placid face become more dejected, as though he realized he was falling down a very steep mountain, one meter at a time. After his soliloquy, Gomez did a wrap.

"We have an associate coming to see both of you within the week. Here you go," the number one enforcer said as he rummaged in his wallet and pulled out a stark white card with plain block lettering. "Señor Montejo already has one."

Francisco could have not been more surprised if the card had been imprinted with the name of Satan himself on it. Instead it bore the name of a gringo, and behind the name in capitals, DEA. Underneath the hideous black letters it read Financial Securities Division.

"Wait, wait." Francisco struggled to keep his voice calm. "Neither MBC nor Pana-Bank has business with the DEA."

"Well," Eduardo Gomez paused, too politically correct to smirk before saying, "you do now."

With that, the two financial enforcers stood, gave a curt nod to a humbled Montejo, and did a last round of handshakes. Francisco knew those handshakes were the beginning of a devil's agreement—a trail of tears. Though the enforcers strode out of the room and out of Francisco's life, the residue they left behind was just the beginning of a nightmare that would soon rule his soul, making a 180-degree turn from what he'd previously experienced in his up-to-now sublime existence.

Chapter 31

"Jaime," Layla said. "Can't you go faster?"

"Boss, we're on a sascab road and I'm doing the best I can."

"Twenty kilometers an hour?"

"What should I do, kick in with more horsepower? You got a mystery plan?"

"Floor it."

"No way. Pedro's waiting for you. All due respect, boss, you got pre-game jitters. Don't go squiggly on me."

Clay reached over the seat and put a hand on Layla's shoulder. "He's doing it, Layla. We'll get there, but we better talk about our plan. Like how this is gonna play out."

"Clay's right. Maybe it's good we got some time, because I have no idea what the hell we're doing," Jaime said.

"Let's discuss it now." Her tone immediately mimicked the timbre she'd learned from watching El Patrón. Direction with inflection, Patrón had instructed. Fake it until you make it.

"Clay?" she said, looking back at him.

"Okay," Clay began. "We start with Pedro. He'll help us get some grub and wash up before we head into the lagoon. He said it could take a couple of hours at the very least."

"That means it'll be dark when we arrive. Do we go right to the cottage?" Layla asked.

"I say yes," Jaime said. "Got any idea where I should park while we're figuring out how to get our hands on the girl?"

Clay joined in. "Wasn't there a side road behind the lodge, near the kitchen? Where they drop off supplies? I think I saw it when we checked out the dock."

"Yeah, I think so. After I drop you, I wait two hours at the biosphere arch, then head down to that spot by the kitchen and wait to hear from you," Jaime said.

"Si, si," Layla said. She nodded as it all coalesced in her mind. "That's it."

"Then what?" Clay asked.

"We wait. To see where they'll be hiding Silvia, or stashing her I should say," Layla said.

"Do we make a run on it? Take down whoever's holding her to release her?"

"Too risky. He's going to have the goons," she said, thinking about the henchmen with powerful builds and killing temperaments.

"It's going to have to be a reveal," Clay said in a monitored tone. "None of this is going to be what we expect. It couldn't be planned if we placed a million on it."

"He's right. Once you reach the cottage, call me when you need me. We have to see where they're taking the girl before we can make a break for it with her," Jaime said.

"There'll be cars in the parking lot, for cover. I don't suppose they'll have parking lot attendants," Clay said.

Layla shook her head. "This is a sex party, Clay. The fewer people around, the better. The desk clerk said they even send him home. Every man for himself. They carry their own luggage, no room service. The kitchen staff leaves immediately after dinner."

元元元

The last thing Silvia remembered was being picked up at Azul with Francisco. The two strange men in the car were intimidating—big and rough around the edges—but Francisco had held her hand. She loved his protectiveness and figured all would be well. He didn't explain where they were going, business of some sort, and she hadn't asked, even when they left the subdued lights of Tulum behind. She'd heard wealthier businessmen had deserted their ocean properties and moved inland, to escape the hassles that came with beach-front ownership in the world's top tourist resort. Once in the jungle, they converted ranches into veritable fairylands with splendid villas, nature trails, exotic gardens with koi ponds, and swimming pools with waterfalls.

She didn't start to panic until she heard the worry in Francisco's voice, when he asked where they were going. She had tugged on his shirt sleeve, leaned in and whispered, "Something wrong?"

"No, mi amor," he'd said softly, and nibbled her ear in a teasing manner.

A little later they turned onto an outback road, passing a derelict subdivision filled with makeshift homes, many half-built, a combination of rusted rebar and broken dreams.

The entire area emitted the scent of danger. That's when Francisco again asked, "Where are you taking us?"

There had been no immediate answer, and in spite of the pot-holed road, the driver had sped up, jolting them in the backseat from side to side. Neither she nor Francisco were wearing seat belts, causing them to jostle against each other. She fell into his lap. He pushed her up abruptly and stuck his face into the front seat, staring at the driver and demanding, "Where are you taking us?"

The next sequence of events would forever remain in her memory. The man riding in the passenger seat pulled out a gun with a long barrel, nearly the length of a forearm, and with a snarl said, "Shut the fuck up or the girl gets it!"

Their early evening cocktails had worn off long before but the fact that he was singling her out as a possible victim in a situation she had nothing to do with made her head spin. She shrieked, loudly. The dude in the passenger seat swung around. With his free hand, he slapped her face. She had never been slapped before. When Francisco got in his face and yelled, "Hey, man! What the hell?" the gangster leveled the gun at him.

"You want a taste of that, too? Or you want my friend here, with the double barrels?"

He grinned and in a taunting voice said, "Cálmate."

Francisco pulled Silvia close, turned her face to where she'd been hit, and in the darkness, tried to inspect the damage. "Oh, mi amor," he murmured. "I'm so sorry. Does it hurt?"

She ignored Francisco's concern for the smack to her face. "Where are we going?" she asked, scared and embarrassed to have been hit. Her tone was more whiny than she intended when she repeated, "Where are they taking us?"

"I have no idea," her once debonair lover admitted as he slunk lower into the soft leather of the Escalade's rear seat. He looked away. He was on a rutted road in a sea of black, where shadowy silhouettes of half-built homes stood dejectedly in a derelict subdivision.

CHAPTER 32

The governor's sister had agreed to go to Chetumal for the weekend at her brother's request. He had a problem and needed her advice. Enrique always consulted her, but that's how she'd arranged things. A self-acknowledged control freak, she'd put that in place early on. As kids, when he thought he was stealing an orange for himself, it had been at her urging. His little legs running fast into the tienda to find the perfect ripe Valencia, and dashing out at record speed, so he could offer a prize to his sister.

Even now, Erwina reviewed the books before they were sent off to the state treasury, in order to keep an eye on the number of titles they owned not only in the Si'an Ka'an Reserve, but in the entire state of Quintana Roo. Beachfront land, worth millions and millions of dollars.

Torres, their childhood friend, had first urged Enrique to take part in unsavory Riviera Maya ownership deals, where land was the new gold. But stealing titles, if you were caught, could bring troublesome consequences.

Recently, the Tulum mayor had wormed his way into her brother's graces by floating promises of additional beachfront titles. Dzib had misappropriated these from the Maya, who'd been gifted the land by the government in exchange for working it. For Quintana Roo to attain Mexico statehood, the constitution had required a population of eighty thousand. The land grants assured the head count was good.

Erwina wanted to be rid of both the mayor and the construction magnate. Worse, she feared he had talked Enrique into money laundering—a likely imprint of a cartel demand. One last round of deals, he had promised. She pressed him on it, and he listened.

Once in Chetumal, her brother explained he'd received a last-minute request from Torres to meet him and the mayor in the biosphere. He had insisted on going, saying they were also calling in the MBC guy, a smooth-talking banker with a law degree. So, she would stay in Chetumal while her brother departed to meet Torres at Boca Laguna Lodge.

She told Enrique, though, if she got too bored, she might take the Mercedes and drive to Casa Paraiso. He'd begged her not to. Now she needed to talk with Julietta at the casa, but no one answered at the villa. Erwina was puzzled. Julietta was relentlessly on point. Never without her cell phone and willing to do anything to keep her happy, Julietta was an obedient lap dog. Erwina decided to try once more before bothering her brother.

One, two, three rings … "Hola!" she nearly shouted, but the voice wasn't Julietta's.

"Si, Señora Erwina?"

"Hector? Hector! Why are you answering Julietta's phone? Where's Julietta?"

"Oh. Señora Erwina. Yo no se. She is not here. The house is locked. I found her phone outside when I arrived to do yard work. Maybe she dropped it. A car was here, and there was activity in the driveway."

"Activity?" she scoffed. "What do you mean? Like futbol?"

"Oh, no, nothing like that. The driveway is a mess. I have to clean up and prepare for the next guests."

"There are no guests for two weeks, Hector!" she all but screamed. "Can't you remember the schedule? What do you mean a mess?"

"Like something was dragged across the sascab and ..."

"Wait, wait. Can you get into the house?" she interrupted.

"No, señora. Remember? You don't trust me with the key," Hector said.

"I never said that. I just said I wasn't going to give you a key."

"Oh, yes, señora, yo comprendo."

She detected a note of sarcasm. "Where could she have gone, and why lock up the house? There's nothing for kilometers."

"Si, verdad. The palm trees in front—they look different. Maybe someone was here."

"What do you mean?" Erwina asked.

"They're usually *suave,* smooth. The fronds are torn and there's scattered dirt."

"Why would that be?"

"I don't know. I just got here. The garage, it's messy. Someone used my shovels."

"They're not your shovels!" Erwina barked.

He paused before speaking. "I'll look around more. Maybe Julietta went to the beach."

"Get a grip! She was working! She would never take beach time!"

"Señora," he said, in the calm tone he used on superiors, "I am telling you, she is not here. She is not in the house or she would answer the door."

"Something is wrong, Hector!"

"That is possible. Should I clean the garage before I leave?" he asked.

"No! No! I'm coming up. Can you wait for me?"

"Señora, you are hours away. Is there an extra key? One you hide if you need to get in."

She stifled a scream. Keys were from a bygone era. Now there were lockboxes, security codes, Alexa.

"Of course not. I have a code for the house."

"What is a code?" he asked.

She exhaled loudly, then remembered a friend's story after they'd bought a villa in Akumal. The Maya couple hired as caretakers had to be taught how to turn off lights and shut doors on leaving. The story came rushing back to Erwina. She brushed it off in her characteristically cavalier manner.

"Hector," she continued in a deliberate tone. "I will be there as soon as I can. Clean the garage, rake the driveway, and look around to see if you can find anything, *anything* that would let us know where Julietta might have gone."

"Si, señora."

🀫🀫🀫

Jaime's car pulled onto the road that led to the Muyil dock. "Where to?"

"Pedro said go left at the 'y' and the house is second on the left."

In a few minutes they were in front of the boatman's cousin's abode.

"Okay, boss. And Clay?" Jamie looked at the Canadian. "You know where the piece is."

Clay nodded. "Yep. The bathroom, and in my backpack I got a box of ammo. Thanks."

"No problem. Our plan is I wait for your call," he said, looking at Layla, "and we take it from there. With the girl."

Layla gave a solemn nod. "Yes, Jaime. We'll call, and hopefully we'll know where to find Silvia."

She lifted her chin as she'd seen her uncle do countless times, grabbed her bag, and got out with Clay. Jaime executed a perfect three-point turn in the sascab lane and pulled away.

Pedro's cousin's property, surrounded by a ring of coco palms and bananas trees, was cordoned off in front by a rickety chacá fence. Pedro had seen the car arrive and was out the door before they got to the threshold.

"Hola. We're here," Layla said.

"Bueno. Ándale," he said, his arm sweeping towards the house.

Twilight was upon them. It was still warm but not uncomfortably so as it had been at Casa Paraiso. A light breeze filtered through the cocos as Layla stepped beyond the gate. She caught the scent of night blooming jasmine, just beginning its evening rhapsody.

"Adelante," a female voice from inside said. "In the cocina."

She followed the voice into the house, where she met a mid-twenties Maya woman with dish towel in hand, wearing glasses that sat low on her nose. She pushed them up with a wet finger. "You are friends of our cousin. Bienvenidos. Soy Martína."

"I'm Layla, the pleasure is mine. This is Clay."

"You will have dinner with us, yes?"

"That would be lovely," Layla said. "Would it be possible for me to wash up first?"

"Of course. The baño is in back." She pointed to a curtained area. Layla, bag in hand, was more than ready to wash off the heat and humidity of the day. En route to the bathroom, the aroma of pibil chicken hit her nose. She knew to savor the moment as life had taught her that pleasure might not last much longer than that. Best to grab this momentary calm before an evening that could well reach epic proportions, with an unknown outcome that would either be the best or the worst case scenario.

CHAPTER 33

Night had fallen by the time they finished dinner with Martina and her husband. Pedro looked at Layla.

"Is it time?" she asked.

"Si, señora. The night is dark, the panga is ready."

That was all Layla and Clay needed to hear to push back their chairs and ready themselves for the next leg of their journey, this time by sea. After a polite barrage of compliments, they followed Pedro to the door.

They walked the short distance to the Muyil dock where the twenty-foot fiberglass boat was indeed prepared for the journey. Since it was a dark moon, Pedro had a powerful flashlight he'd use if needed, but Layla guessed that as a competent captain and local, he knew the routes and the canal so well it would go unused.

"Will others be on the water tonight?"Clay asked.

As he readied the Yamaha motor, Pedro said, "Sometimes there are pangas with contraband, but they don't bother locals."

Layla well knew who those pangas belonged to: cartels carrying marijuana or cocaine. It didn't really matter how product got to market, just so it got there, and using mules was the oldest method on record, one package or kilo at a time.

"If we do see another panga, though, it will be best for you to lie down, Layla. I'll cover you with a blanket. No need to bring unnecessary attention."

"How fast does this baby go?" Clay asked.

Pedro's pride of ownership came through even in the darkness. "My Yamaha Sportsman has forty horses. Not many pangas can catch me. Why? Will we be chased?"

"I doubt it, but it's good to know what ya got under the hood."

Pedro pushed off, and they settled in for the journey. After starting the engine and making sure that all was well, he stood in the stern—straight as a sentinel—his hands in the pockets of gray cotton pants. He watched the water while the boat skimmed along at a steady clip. Layla sat in the middle and Clay in the bow while Pedro guided the panga through an intricate series of canals that would be hard enough to commandeer in sunlight.

After they'd been at sea for a half hour, Layla decided it was time to check in to see how he felt about waiting it out.

"It could be a long night, Pedro. We hadn't told you, but someone kidnapped my friend's niece. We're going to try and get her back."

There was silence as he digested the info. "You said it was dangerous," Pedro said. "That is very dangerous."

"We might have to wait a long time, but it's best that you stay with the boat. You know the Boca dock, but it wouldn't be a safe place to tie up. Is there an alternative?"

"Let me think about it." After several moments, Pedro spoke, "I have an anchor, and there's a cove south of the lodge near the bridge. I could wait there until you need me."

"How far away is it?" She asked.

"Ten minutes, fifteen at most."

"Well, if that's the best we got, that's what it will have to be," Clay said. "Right, Layla?"

"The timing ... I hope we're not being chased and our friend has all her faculties," Layla said to Pedro. "Before you drop us, you'll need to show us that cove, in case we need to get there. Also, we'll show you the cottage we'll be in, if there's last minute changes and we can't make it to the boat."

"The cottage is the last one at the lodge," Clay said.

That agreed upon, everyone settled into their thoughts and meditations: Pedro steering through watery terrain he knew well, day or night; Layla settling in for a journey seeking to locate a missing girl; and Clay, observing the biosphere's night sky. Even the stars appeared muted, as if they, too, were in alignment with the mission. Only if one looked long and hard enough did the moon cast a shadow. The lapping sound of water on the panga against the Yamaha's steady hum was the calmest it would be for them over the next several hours. Time to sit back and enjoy the ride.

᠊᠊᠊᠊᠊᠊

As Jaime sped north on highway 307 towards Tulum, and Clay and Layla sat in Pedro's panga listening to the hum of the outboard while they traveled north, Erwina, too, was on the move. After talking with Hector, she became more rattled, realizing something was amiss with Julietta. Before putting on sensible strap sandals, a pair of cargo pants, and a long sleeve tee, she went to her room and extracted the Glock 43, nine-millimeter, from its hiding place. Enrique had bought it for her, explaining it was all about safety.

"I'm now the governor," he had said, "of Mexico's thirty-first state. We're in Chetumal, a frontier town. Not much better than Escarcega."

She lowered her head. Though Chetumal was the wild west, she prayed it had some leverage over that shit-hole Escarcega. The capital of Q. Roo, Chetumal was where even the Belizians came to buy appliances straight off container ships docked in its port. Chetumal had a recklessness to it, an outback mentality; if it had a slogan it would be "Anything goes." A place where even people might be sold.

Though Erwina rarely went out alone, it was good to know she had back-up that could be stashed in purse or pocket. She'd practiced shooting the lightweight nine-millimeter when she took her handsome German Shepherd, Elegante, out for walks. A last minute decision included bringing the dog along. He'd not only provide company on the lonely drive, but security. She decided to take the shortcut, a road south of Felipe Carrillo Puerto, that was bumpy as hell but cut off an hour's time.

She located a heavy-duty flashlight and a blanket to throw in the back seat along with bottled water. Planning for everything and anything, she popped into the kitchen and grabbed a stack of corn tortillas and tossed them in a bag with some bananas. After putting a leash on her dog, she went to the front entryway where she asked the houseman to have the chauffeur bring her car around.

"May I ask where you are going, señora?"

"To Casa Paraiso. Since it's late, I'm taking Elegante with me," she said.

The man stepped back and eyed the massive animal. Mexicans in general weren't big on dogs. No one in the governor's mansion liked Elegante; Erwina knew they were afraid of him. In turn, the possessive dog sniffed warily at the houseman.

Erwina was ready. She had Elegante, the Glock, and a four-door gray Mercedes that looked like a tank but drove like a dream. She was off.

🔲🔲🔲

Things were picking up at Boca Laguna Lodge. Torres appeared stressed and the mayor—the mayor was missing in action. Gabriella was en route to the dining room and planned to take a quick peek at the kitchen to check with the cook, Clarita, and her helper. She would make sure all was ready for the attendees, and, as had been suggested by Torres, the kitchen staff could leave. That was her exit strategy, too. With no idea how the night might unfold, she planned to soon be many kilometers away from Juan Dzib. She was freaked out that she'd ridden alone in a car with him, down the Punta Allen road. Her overbearing older brothers had lectured her to never get in a car alone with a man she did not know. She'd been fifteen at the time.

"Why?" she had asked.

The boys were in their late teens, attending college at UNAM in DF, and though Cuernavaca was hardly the outback, DF was one of the world's largest cities. "How would you get away if he decided to take you somewhere?"

"Take me where?"

"Some place where he could hurt you. Men can't be trusted," Rico said, straining to make her understand something her teen brain could not yet wrap itself around.

"Shouldn't I trust you? You're a man. Well, kind of." She smirked and he pinched her on the arm, hard.

"Ouch! Why did you do that?"

"Listen," Marco had chimed in. "Not all men are like us. Rico's right, Gabriella. They're stronger than you, too, and you're an attractive girl. They might want to take advantage of you. No riding alone with strange men in cars, okay?"

Marco thought she was pretty? That news warmed her heart. She had always liked him better than Rico. So, she had listened, especially since she now knew she was attractive. Proof positive: her brother had told her so. But Gabriella had gone against their advice and ridden with Dzib yesterday. Even though it was work, she had felt weird sitting next to him. When the car had zigged and she had zagged, accidentally brushing against him, she had the feeling he wanted to put his hands all over her.

In the kitchen, she looked for the cook. She touched the key to Torres' car lodged safely in her pocket. Her ticket to ride. Once she checked that kitchen preparations were in progress and after she helped check in the club members—that's what Torres had called them—she'd beat feet outta there. The group would be arriving shortly; it was almost eight.

🜁🜁🜁

The last thing Silvia had said to Francisco, before the worst thing happened, was, "Why? Why, Francisco?"

She had had to whisper loudly. The disgustingly well-dressed brutes in the front seat had turned on the radio. The music helped and allowed her to think things through; the radio gave her cover.

Francisco had hemmed and hawed, whispering to her that he didn't know. She turned to look at him even though it was dark inside the car.

She elbowed him hard in the ribs. "Liar."

"Ouch."

"Tell me now!" She had to whisper again. Her face hurt where the asshole had slapped her and she had no idea where they were going. "What the hell is going on? Tell me!"

Even though the darkness hid his facial expression, he gave off an uneasy vibe. He leaned towards her and whispered, "It's me."

"Yes, it's about you," she said in a huff. "I have no business with these people. You know who my family is?"

Everyone knew who her family was, the stuff of legends. Her father had been one of the Pemex 'flacos,' a handful of young entrepreneurs that Paco Slim had hand-picked to work in his one man conglomerate, the only corporation in Mexico authorized to sell gas and oil. The chosen ten had been given the keys to the city, and through Slim's auspices, were assured fortune and fame. Her father, now deceased, had been Slim's favorite. Taken in the prime of life, everyone had said at his requiem that bordered on a state funeral. In a packed cathedral, Slim, one of the world's richest men, had given the eulogy. Flash forward and here she was sitting in the back of a black Escalade. When it had pulled up to the Azul forty minutes earlier, her first impulse had been caution, but she had thrown it aside. Due to her family's reputation, she'd been warned about kidnapping. Now she was kidnapped. They would pressure for ransom.

"Did you make a deal with them to kidnap me?" Silvia asked.

Francisco nearly choked. "Of course not, mi amor. I love you."

"Cut the sexy time crap. You know who I am," she said.

"That's not it, I swear. They don't know who you are," he said.

"What? Well, why are we being driven down this lousy road by thugs?"

"It's me, I'm …" He couldn't immediately get it out. Finally, he said, "I'm wearing a wire."

"A wire!"

"Shut up! I mean, keep it down," he said.

"Why are you wearing a wire? For who?"

"The CEO of MBC, but he must have gotten a heads up."

She whispered loudly, "The bank CEO? You were going to tape him? Why?"

"Because of money laundering," Francisco said.

"Money laundering? Who?"

"My bank. They were going to indict me unless I cooperated."

"Who was going to?"

"The DEA," he admitted.

"The DEA? Who the hell are you?"

"I didn't start out doing it, really," he said.

"Well, it looks like you ended up doing it! You're not only a liar, you're a rat, and now I'm stuck with you in the back seat of this goddamn car."

She shook out of fear as a short gasp escaped. She pulled away and turned to look out the window—only darkness. She sat in the back of a cartel car and it wasn't even for her pedigree. She had been warned about these very things: Escalades, cartels, dirty money and dirty politicians. Silvia had listened to no one and followed her heart and her loins into a stupido's bed. She could be tortured. Raped. Killed. Five minutes earlier, she may have pleaded innocence, but lover boy told her he was wearing a wire.

MBC had been in trouble even while her father was alive, charged with multiple counts of money laundering. Alma had written about it. If they found out Alma Reyes was her aunt, she would definitely be tortured. She let out a sigh; slowly tears came. A few at first, then they flowed like water from the tap. She collapsed against the seat, as far away from Francisco as possible.

Fuck!" she whispered loudly, "Fuck!" Because truly, she was fucked.

卍卐卍

The Escalade pulled in front of a dodgy warehouse a few kilometers past the subdivision. That was her line of demarcation—where and when her life had changed. Right after they passed it, reality shifted from a promising future to no future at all. The goon who'd slapped her got out to unlock the gate. He swept open the chainlink fence and the Escalade rolled in. The driver pulled to a stop near a two-story warehouse with corrugated tin roofing. The first goon locked the gate behind them.

The driver turned and barked, "Get out of the car!"

The other goon swung open Francisco's door and dragged him out before reaching in for her. She opened her mouth to scream but he dove into the back, clamped a hand over her mouth and yelled, "Shut the fuck up, bitch!"

The evening was proving to be a number of firsts. She'd never been called a bitch before. She struggled to wrestle free of his arm, but he overpowered her. She kept quiet and followed the other goon, who was leading Francisco towards the locked warehouse.

"Got the key?" he asked, turning to look at the man holding her arm.

"No, I thought you had it."

"Puta de Madre! I told you to grab it!"

"From where?"

"In the glove box, douche bag."

Goon number two eyed her with a sinister stare. "You going to stand here, quiet like?"

She gave a short nod and gazed down at her feet.

He moved away and jogged back to the SUV. She stood staring at Francisco's back. The goon returned with the key and handed it to his accomplice, who was strong-arming Francisco. He let go and unlocked a hefty metal padlock that was bolted on a chain into the building itself. He swung open the door; his hand searched for a switch. As the room flooded with light, Silvia saw what would be her quarters for how long into the future, she had not a clue. This, now, was her new reality.

CHAPTER 34

Hector didn't worry too much about Julietta not being at the villa. She was a good employee, conscientious to a fault, always striving to comply with the demands of their fussy employer. He assumed she'd accidentally dropped her phone. Maybe a boyfriend picked her up and in her excitement, it fell from her purse.

He had no further time for reflection because he had work to do. Though la señora wouldn't arrive for hours, by then it would be nightfall. He liked to get things done sooner rather than later. After chores he'd go down to the sea, wade into the warm water, find a palm for shade, and take a siesta.

Hector started by getting the rake from the garden shed and carefully scraping the sascab into a neatly lined pattern. It looked beautiful after he finished, as though he had created order in the grains of sand. When he'd first started working for Señora Erwina and was told to rake sand, it seemed a crazy task. But now, three years later, he found it soothing to make the sand look untouched. He took his time as he did with all his jobs. Erwina usually paid by the day, not by the hour, and because he had to wait until she arrived, no hurry.

After he finished, he put the rake back in the shed, closed the wooden doors, and latched the black iron lock in place. His next job would be to straighten the garage, doors flung wide open. The shovels had been thrown inside—helter skelter—caked in mud. Dirt was strewn across one side, as though whoever put them back simply didn't give a damn.

He found the push broom in a rear corner and began sweeping the dirt into a single mound. Later he'd get the dustpan, throw it back into the grove, and trim the fronds with his machete. Even though la señora would arrive at night, tomorrow was another day, and the raggedy leaves would draw attention. His task in the garage finished, he grabbed the machete from a hook on the wall, picked up the brimming dustpan, and walked to the grove. With so much damp mud, two trips would be needed. Though he didn't scrutinize the trees much on his first clean-up round, on the second, he observed a trail snaking deeper into the grove. He mused that possibly there had been a burglar, Julietta spotted him, and rather than face the music, the culprit had run into the palms to hide. Natural curiosity led him to the narrow trail, well aware the grove grew thick and close at the center.

The path had been beaten down so it was easy to follow. He walked a bit before it widened. That's when he saw something unusual, something that didn't belong in the coconut grove: a number of rocks stacked side by side over a raised section of soil. The dirt around the sides looked fresh, similar to the soil he'd thrown back into the jungle. He studied it for a moment before it came to him. He couldn't bring himself to say it. He hated to even think it. It looked like a grave.

241

🎋🎋🎋

The panga was now on the open sea. Layla was glad she had packed a long-sleeved shirt. Though Pedro had placed a blanket nearby for her use, she told him no worries.

"We're ten minutes from the bridge," Pedro said. "I'm going to slow down near the cove; you'll be able to see it from the water. Got a flashlight?"

Clay said, "Yes, plus we'll be carrying on the way back."

"A gun? It's going to get serious?"

"We're stealing a kidnapped girl from some very bad men, Pedro. Men who plan to use her as a sex slave," Layla said.

"Sex slave? At Boca Laguna?"

"Si, bigwigs from Cancun. We think the governor might be there, too."

He shook his head. "Ayy! This country. Ever since those pinche tourists started coming, nothing but problems. With land and titles, with firearms. They ruin the reef by standing on it when they snorkel, and hotels dump their waste right into the ocean. Guns used to be against the law in Mexico. A farmer could own a .22 rifle; that was it. My father had to fill out papers to register his. Now every pinche gang or cartel guy, they're packing an automatic. Los malos."

Layla felt a blush rush up her neck to her cheeks, glad the night's darkness concealed her face. She knew what Clay was thinking, thankful he was who he was, stating nothing to no one, ever. "Si, si, those pinche tourists, they brought all the problems," she murmured, denying her existence and ignoring his use of the common nickname for cartels.

"And the gringos," Pedro said.

"Yeah," Clay threw in, taking the load off Layla, "those damn gringos. I'm glad to be Canadian."

ᘒᘒᘒ

Erwina's car skidded at the top of Casa Paraiso's lane. Driving for well over two hours had given her time to think. She feared something had happened to Julietta. There could be no other way the girl's phone would be lying on the ground, and neither would she abandon her post. They were kindred spirits. A sense of respect crossed both sides of the aisle, no matter who was employer, and who was on the payroll.

The rumbling of the Mercedes' heavy frame woke Hector, who had dozed off in a hammock alongside the garage. Elegante sat in the car and though everyone knew about the big Shepherd, Hector had never before laid eyes on the giant. Erwina slammed on the brakes and stopped the car, but left the brights on. Though motion sensors would trigger automatic lights once she got closer to the front door, for the moment the driveway was dark.

"Hector!" she yelled.

He sprung from the hammock and was at her side in a moment. "Señora Erwina! You are here."

"Have you been outside this whole time?"

"Yes, of course. I told you I have no key."

She snorted. "Oh, that. Well, come with me into the house. Let's see if there's any message from Julietta."

"Your dog, he will stay in the car?"

"Oh, no. Get him for me. The leash is in the back."

Hector caught his breath before answering. "But Señora, your dog doesn't know me. It would be best for you to let him out."

"Hector, he must learn to know you. Get Elegante!"

Cowed by her demand, the Maya man inched his way towards the Mercedes. A growl emanated from the car's interior. Dogs smelled fear; Hector shook with fear. He had no use for dogs. Dogs carried rabies.

"Are you coming?" Erwina shouted, nearly at the front entrance, lights now illuminating the doorway.

"Okay," he whispered.

He reached for the car door. "Perro, perro," he said in as calm a tone as he could muster. "It is only me, Hector, your mama's obedient servant."

The growl got lower. "Come, boy, come Elegante. We'll go to the house. I have water."

With an insane burst of confidence, he swung open the back door and the giant German Shepherd leapt out. Hector shrieked, but the dog ignored the Maya local and trailed after his mistress, better than any bodyguard.

Elegante ran to Erwina's heels as she put the code into the security panel on the side of the building. The dog sat his huge haunches down beside her, watching as her finger tapped in the digits. "Come, Hector. I want you with me. Don't lag behind."

Hector bounded behind the dog and he and Erwina entered the house together.

What lay before them was bedlam. Chairs had been overturned, furniture upended, drapes pulled from their rods. The kitchen spelled disaster—a state of total disarray—with the table pushed to one side. On it sat a roll of duct tape next to a knife. Liquor bottles were scattered everywhere, broken glass lay strewn across the floor. A wide scrape scratched into the terra cotta floor went from the refrigerator at the back of the lengthy room to the entryway where a chair lay on its side. Dirty dishes and food packaging covered every conceivable inch of counter space.

"What's happened here?" Erwina shrieked. "Did someone break in and kidnap Julietta?"

"I don't know," Hector said, a fearful shadow crossing his face. "I've seen no one this entire day. No one." He made the sign of the cross as he spoke.

Ghosts were around, or at the very least, souls in flight. In a flash, it came as a revelation. "Señora," he said in a whisper.

Erwina darted through the downstairs in a surge of energy, flipping on light switches, gauging the damage, gasping at every turn. She ran upstairs. A blood curdling shriek bounced off the walls and tile floors, echoing throughout the concrete house.

"Hector!"

The Maya man, stepping lightly through the disorder on the first floor, jumped at hearing her scream and stormed up the stairs. He saw Erwina standing at the threshold of the master bedroom, shaking. The dog passed him on the way up and sniffed the air at the doorway.

Tears streamed down her cheeks. "What's happened here. Hector, what has happened at Casa Paraiso?

"Look, look at it." She pointed to the tile floor. "Blood."

He pushed past her into the bedroom, sidestepping the blood. The room resembled a cluttered depository of household articles, thrown into a pile. The bedspread had been torn from the bed, cast onto the floor along with scattered towels, as if someone had tried to clean the blood flow but tired of the effort. Ropes were tied onto a wooden chair that had been dragged in from elsewhere, more duct tape, another knife, liquor bottles scattered about. Unidentifiable odd wires and small electronic parts with receivers were torn to shreds, strewn across the floor as though an electrician's box had been upended, contents tossed in every direction. Bedding had been removed, exposing a bare mattress.

"Oh God, did they torture my Julietta?"

He touched the arm of his employer in a gentle manner. "Señora Erwina."

Just then he felt a nudge from behind. He jumped, let out a yelp, and turned quickly, arms in fighter stance.

It was that damn giant of a dog, sniffing his backside. He let out a relieved sigh, in preparation for what came next. "Señora," he repeated. "I think I know where Julietta is."

"Where?" she demanded, brushing tears from her face.

"Can we go outside with Elegante?"

🔲🔲🔲

The panga cruised the south side of the Boca Laguna dock. From the water, Clay, Layla, and Pedro could see the lights of the lodge flickering, waiting for the fiesta to begin.

"Pedro," Layla began. "The last cottage. See it?"

She pointed to the end of the chain of round stucco bungalows. Many were lit, but the one she pointed at was totally dark.

"Yes, Layla."

"If things don't go as planned, you'll have to find us here."

"Okay," Pedro said.

"Me and Clay will get out now. You have your phone? I'm hoping you hear from us in a couple of hours, but I can't make any promises."

"Layla's right. We have no idea on time. We'll be in touch once things have stabilized."

"Can you pull up onto the shore?" Layla asked.

He did her bidding. Layla grabbed her pack and steadied herself before she stepped from the panga, carefully straddling the seats. Clay followed.

"Gracias, Pedro. I'll call you when we know something."

"Suerte. I hope you find the girl."

They traipsed up the small hill towards cottage eighteen, both determined to put the puzzle of a missing Silvia to rest. It was time to call Gabriella. Let the games begin.

CHAPTER 35

With great difficulty, the two henchmen carried Silvia, kicking and screaming, to the SUV. Too late they realized her blindfold should never have been removed when they brought her into the house.

After henchman number two had beat the shit out of Francisco, he was so bloody they'd had to roll him in bedding and a blanket before lying him in the car wayback. He kept popping in and out of consciousness, moaning loudly.

"Should we give the girl something?" henchman one asked. "This is crazy town."

"Maybe. It's not going to get any better."

"What time is it?"

"Almost seven. Better get a move on. She'll need to be cleaned up."

"How?"

"Who knows?"

"Get the stuff."

Henchman two reached into a leather satchel and pulled out a syringe and the paraphernalia needed for a fix. "This will take a minute. Should have done it inside."

"Chinga! You're a big boy. Do it."

The second henchman went to work and in short time was ready to give Silvia a hit to quiet her down. The first of the evening—not the last.

She'd calmed down from her initial outburst but when he came close to inject her, she went wild, lying on the Escalade's back seat, hands tied.

"See, this is why you need it, chica. This will calm you."

Henchman two got out of the car to assist. He stood too close to her untied feet and she kicked him in the arm, narrowly missing his face.

"Puta!" he shouted. "Calm down or you'll make it worse."

Silvia kept kicking.

"I mean it, bitch. You better listen if you don't want more bad things to happen."

Her eyes went wild and she strained harder still. Her efforts were useless against his massive frame, and eventually the two men restrained her enough to tie off her arm and inject her. The drug swiftly took effect and in moments, her body stopped its futile attempt at resistance.

"Good, now we can drive without a hurricane in the back."

While Silvia lay motionless, the Escalade lurched ahead on the dusty road.

🜍🜍🜍

Gabriella walked back to the main lobby, only to find it empty. No sign of Dzib or Torres. She went down the hall into the manager's minuscule office to kill time while she waited for the guests to arrive. It was after seven and some might show up early. One thing that didn't sit right was that the businessmen had been calling in since the previous day, asking for the location. Why wouldn't they know it was at Boca Laguna Lodge?

After checking emails, which came through sporadically due to a poor internet connection, Gabriella found herself with a few moments of calm. She began idly opening drawers in a distracted manner, snooping around for lack of anything better to do. Finding nothing of interest, she stood, stretched, and walked over to a free-standing cabinet. It was locked, but she thought she had seen a key for it in the desk drawer she'd just rifled through. If it was a match, she'd check out the cabinet's interior. She jiggled the key and the lock gave way.

The cabinet resembled an arsenal, but one filled with office products not weapons, including stacks of invoices, rolls of register tape, copy paper, and an unorganized jumble of pens, paperclips, and rubber bands. On the bottom shelf lay a box covered in black satin that seemed out of place with the office miscellany. It took up the entire shelf. Curious, she got on her knees for a closer look. It was a fancy piece of work, nothing fitting to the low-tech world of a fishing lodge. Ignoring her mother's words which raced through her mind, "Idle hands are the devil's workshop," she was too intrigued by its presence to step away.

Once she lifted the box's intriguing cover, its contents confounded her—masks. Masks for a masquerade? They were full face, finely crafted in black velvet in the form of foxes, horned devils, pagan goats, and black rabbits. They stared up at her, each positioned with sheets of tissue placed carefully in between.

She sat mesmerized, and pulled several out for inspection. Her reverie was interrupted by a man's voice. She tried to place the cover on the box and push it back into the once-locked cupboard, but not fast enough. The mayor had entered the office and was staring down at her from over the desk.

"What are you doing?" he asked.

His voice had an unfamiliar edge, a tone he'd never displayed before.

"Oh, looking for a time card for the cook. She said she didn't get one this week and I told her I'd take a look in the office."

Dzib gave her a skeptical stare. By this time, she had pushed the mysterious box back into the cupboard and stood up, firmly closing the door. She brushed her hands off on her skirt where some of the masks' glitter had fallen and casually pushed back her hair.

"What were you looking at?" Dzib asked.

"I have no idea. Masks. Maybe for Dia de Los Muertos celebrations or something."

She began to move towards the door of the tiny office, but Dzib stood in the middle of the threshold, blocking her way.

"People shouldn't snoop where they're not supposed to." His voice had a threatening tone. "It could get them in trouble."

She waited for him to get his shapeless frame out of the way, but he stood firm. The only way to escape the situation was to push through. Their bodies would touch. She paused for a moment and stood by the desk, pretending to be straightening out the top drawer while she idly dropped the cabinet key back into it.

She changed tack, and stalling for time, said the first thing that popped into her head. "Why didn't the guests know ahead of time they were coming to Boca Laguna Lodge?"

His eyes bulged and became round as saucers. "What do you mean?"

"Well, Señor Chavez, for starters, had no idea yesterday where the meeting was taking place. That happened again with Señor Guzman from Cancun Bank today, as well as Señor Ferragamo."

"Of course they knew!" he said, his tone bordering on hostility.

Dzib was usually a docile simpleton. She had never seen him so emphatic.

"Well, duty calls. I must be off to check on the arrangements in the dining room and let the cook know she'll have to ask Bernardo for her time cards. I had no luck," she said with a false brightness. "Also, the drapes you ordered for the ballroom windows need arranging."

She began to inch forward, but Dzib made no sign of moving. She'd have to resort to pushing. Though a gruesome thought, the idea of being enclosed in a windowless office stuck behind a desk with Dzib blocking the door and her a hostage on the other side held even less appeal.

She breathed in and turned her backside to him so she could inch by, her butt grazing his belly. It was a dismal prospect, but better than chest to chest. His eyes lit up as her body approached and he gave her a once-over. She ignored thoughts of his moral decay and began to shove through, but not without repercussions. In her escape attempt, he slid his pudgy fingers along both sides of her waist, feeling her up under her ribcage, groping for, and narrowly missing, her breasts.

"Señor Dzib!" she barked in an uppity tone. "Don't touch me!" She forced his hands from her sides, sharply bending back his middle finger.

"Ouch!" he wailed, and immediately dropped his hand from her midriff.

In spite of the repugnant situation, she felt a flash of satisfaction knowing his pain level was that of a five-year-old girl. Trained well in the skills of retaliation by older, stronger brothers, she stamped on his foot, putting her entire weight into it, using that leverage to muscle her way through the nightmare. She was enraged.

"Ouch!" he squealed again, like a piglet.

"Careful!" she warned. "No toca! Didn't your mama ever tell you that?"

She was safely on the opposite side of the desk, a smug look on her face, and a foot out the door. She made an effort to stomp loudly as she exited, throwing shade at him over her shoulder.

🀫🀫🀫

After Gabriella left the manager's office, Dzib made a beeline for the locked cabinet to check on how much the girl had seen. All the masks for the members of his secret sex club with a rotating mystery location were there. He'd kept the group at a dozen, which made it manageable, especially when having to deal with the girls. Those who were sex workers were familiar with the routine. The rest were unfortunates whose souls had been sold—by boyfriends or neighbors or ruffians—and needed to be drugged to perform the tasks at hand. The working girls knew these nights could yield big bucks; with them, anything went. Dzib was always titillated as the evening unfolded, seeing them in full regalia, or lack thereof, breasts perky, most wearing only teeny thongs and pasties.

He was determined to deal with Gabriella when he got back to Tulum. Though far from pretty, she had a virginal appeal. He'd sabotage her back on home turf and if a struggle ensued, he would deal with the fallout later.

Since the cupboard with the masks was open and Gabriella knew about them, he decided to move them to his cottage so they wouldn't be discovered again. Of course, other than Gabriella, Bernardo, the cook, and her assistant, no other employees were on the premises. The accountant had left hours ago. Once Torres' cartel thugs arrived with the goods, he'd send them on their way, too. Their crass manners made him nervous, but due to the level of larceny he and Torres were dealing with, muscle had been a necessity.

At present, Dzib's job was to check in the members and see that all was prepped in the ballroom. He'd make sure the drapes he'd ordered covered the windows. Drapes would add a seductive effect, and candles—he'd ordered dozens to be lit by Bernardo before he left—would give the room a seductive glow. He'd asked management to pull chaise lounges from the cottages and to also hang a few hammocks. The games would be a challenge for some of the men, but the women, in their teens, would have no problem getting in and out of position, no matter what was required of them.

He checked his watch—half past seven. Festivities would begin in the dining room with an open bar and light supper, and afterwards, all would move into the ballroom where the women would be seductively lying around. Soon afterwards, the auction would begin, and the prize of the evening would be the little hussy.

Everyone underestimated Dzib, but he had snitches and channels everywhere. He'd heard early on about Francisco's meeting with the Panama bank official and the FATF. Before finding the wire on Francisco, they had planned to simply threaten him with a pounding, but things changed once his plan to expose their laundering scheme surfaced.

The goons had kept him apprised of the kidnapping situation and assured Dzib the banker would no longer pose a problem. As for the girl, her future would be decided at the end of the evening. Catch and release? Time would tell.

CHAPTER 36

For Clay and Layla, the dark evening was a gift—the Boca Laguna premises were void of everything save the sound of water lapping on the shore, the occasional coo-cooing of a late night bird, or a chirping gecko in search of a mate. They climbed the slight incline up the broad embankment as their eyes adjusted from the dark water, where the moon's glow had offered illumination, to the land, which was darker still.

"What time is it?" Layla asked.

"Eight thirty. The guests will be arriving," Clay said.

"We best get set up."

"Maybe we should be near the parking lot, in case the goons are there with Silvia. And the banker."

"If he's still alive," Layla said.

"Let's go to the cottage first."

🔲🔲🔲

Erwina drove slowly but with purpose up roads she had come to know, though driving them at night was a first. Elegante provided protection, and after Hector had led her to Julietta's grave and before leaving the villa, she'd placed the machete in the trunk. Even though her nine-millimeter rode in the passenger seat next to her, she had no idea what to expect once she arrived at the lodge.

Erwina worried that she could face perilous enemies, those who'd murdered Julietta. She also feared for her brother's life, and prayed he wasn't in a compromised position. He hadn't answered his phone in hours.

After the discovery of the body, she'd called the governor's mansion and had spoken with her brother's first lieutenant. She explained that a murder of an employee had occurred at his compound in the reserve. She demanded a dispatch of a criminal investigation unit and military attaché to Casa Paraiso, pronto. She told them her gardener, who had discovered the body, would assist.

She wiped a tear from her eye. Darling Julietta. Erwina had no idea who the killers were, but she prayed vengeance would come.

༄ ༄ ༄

Gabriella watched a navy BMW sedan pull into the parking lot while she chatted with the assistant manager. She pulled herself up to her full height, checked her watch, eight thirty, and prepared to greet the attendees.

As she approached the door, she noticed a black Escalade parked in the lot near the road, the only spot unprotected by motion sensors. Attendees would know to park close to the lobby, especially with luggage they themselves had to carry. She kept an eye on the car for a moment, but was soon caught up in greeting a foursome of men who were already in party mode.

"Señor Balcalla," she said, looking at his cédula identification, "how nice to see you. You have your valise with you, perfect. Bernardo will assist with your room location. Aah, Señor Muñoz. How glad you could come. Please follow Señor Balcalla to the desk."

She repeated her courtesy announcement and pointed the businessmen towards the counter. Four down, eight more to go. As she checked her watch, another car pulled into the lot, this one a black Mercedes. The evening would be one of quartets—four here, four there, four everywhere.

Bernardo checked IDs and registered the guests on a separate list supplied to him by Torres who had explained the costs would be picked up by his construction company, not the attendees. He'd already made arrangements for billing with the Boca accountant. Bernardo handed each man a map of the property.

The first group, already with a buzz on, appeared to be destined for a fiesta.

"There's a welcome gift in your rooms."

"I hope it's liquid!" one of the revelers said loudly. His fellow partygoers laughed.

Bernardo nodded, pointed the group towards the rear doors and said, "Rooms nine and under are to the left of the terrace, rooms ten and up are on the right."

The first group was approaching the back doors when the second bunch piled in. Gabriella did her preliminary welcome and ushered them towards Bernardo; she saw a third vehicle pull into the lot near the front lobby. If it was four more attendees, her job would be over and she could depart before another Dzib sighting. She peeked around the idling white Lexus SUV to get a better view of the Escalade. If it wasn't so far away she might have checked on it, but with the last group of attendees wandering into the lobby, she had work to do. She addressed them and pointed towards Bernardo who was taking names. To assist, she moved towards the center of the lobby, offering a smiling presence to the men who, in spite of a last minute meeting, were in elevated spirits. Gabriella went a step further and waited at the back doors, pointing the guests either left or right. Once finished with the stragglers, she walked over to Bernardo at the desk.

"Looks like that's it, right?" she asked.

"An even dozen. Our work is done. Now it's up to Torres and Dzib and the poor cook and her attendant."

"I talked to the cook," Gabriella said. "She's all prepared and said thank heavens for an open bar. Dzib agreed to be bartender, so she's off the hook. Let me tell you, I have never before seen so many types of tequila.

"Maybe they'll be drinking their supper," she continued, as she let out a low whistle. "There're a couple cases along with loads of beer in the refrigerators. The tables are set and they'll wheel out tray dollies full of ceviche on ice, shrimp, salbutos, empanadas, chiles, and tortillas. All someone has to do when it's over is close the tops and the clean-up crew will handle it later. I better sign off with Torres. He's in room one, right?"

"Oh, the governor showed up when you were in the manager's office, and Torres said to send him back. They want no disturbances," Bernardo said.

A huge smile graced Gabriella's face giving her a glow well beyond her natural level of attraction. "I'm free!"

"Me, too. Should I walk you out?" Bernardo asked.

"No, no. You go ahead. You've had a longer day. If you want to hand me those papers," she said pointing at the check-in sheets the businessmen had filled out, "I'll put them on the manager's desk so Torres can tally everything tomorrow. I'll text him."

"Well, have a good night," Bernardo said, handing them over. "I'm outta here."

🜹🜹🜹

Under cover of the arriving dignitaries, Torres' goons had pulled into the Boca lot far from where any activity was taking place. Silvia had faded quickly after her first injection and the banker's moans had subsided.

"Fucking great!" Goon Two said, looking at the cars in the lodge lot. "What the hell? You drive us right into the center of the party? You loco?"

"No, pendejo, it's cover. Don't you see? They got a reduced staff and don't have time to run to this end of the lot and check on an Escalade. This gives us time to get rid of our packages."

The other guy checked the back seat. Silvia's comatose body looked content in spite of tape over her mouth and plastic wrist straps to assure she wouldn't be punching anyone out.

"Now what?"

"Torres said he was in room number one. It's at the north end. I say we take the squealer right to his door, whether he's there or not."

"What, drop him?"

"He's in a blanket."

"Will Torres be pissed?"

"How would I know? As far as I'm concerned, we did our job. Maybe more than our job. I doubt he's still breathing. Dead men tell no tales. He won't be blabbing to the feds too soon. Even if he's alive, I doubt he has any brains left."

Goon Two let out a sharp laugh. "Well, wearing a wire never got anyone very far."

"Yeah, especially when you're caught."

They both laughed. "What about Lolita?"

"Wanna take a spin? That what ya mean, cabrón?"

"Hell, no! I want to get paid. If she's damaged goods, Torres will know. Not worth it. I've seen better than her."

"Yeah, in your barrio, right? A dolled-up puta. Give me a break."

"No, I'm serious. These fancy chicks. Half of it's hair and make-up. The rest is clothes."

"Who are you now? That fag from TV, RuPaul? You a maricón, carnal?"

"Oh, fuck off," he said stormily.

"Let's start with the rat," Goon Two said, gazing into the back seat. "The little princess is having a siesta."

Both doors opened and the goons met at the back of the Escalade to get the banker. They stared carefully at the lobby, brimming with activity, before opening the car's rear door.

Gabriella watched the last of the meeting-goers pass through the French doors onto the back terrace, a fait accompli. She decided to peek in the kitchen to make sure the food dollies were prepped. Her final task would be dropping off all sign-in paperwork in the office.

Satisfied after viewing the enticing display the cook had prepared, she headed for the office. Once there, she noticed the closed door and jiggled the handle, relieved to find it empty. As she glanced at the sheaf of papers, a thought struck her: It might be prudent to photograph the registration sheets. She entered the office, closed the door, retrieved her phone from her pocket, and started snapping.

元回回

The henchmen had trouble hefting Francisco's comatose body from the car.

"Chinga, are you a little girl now?"

"Fuck you, too!" the other said. "The damn blanket is slippery."

"Blood, carnal."

"Jesús y Maria! Not all over my Escalade."

"There's plastic. You saw it. I'm not stupid. Even though it's not *my* car."

"Shut up—move it."

They tugged, got a grip on the body, and started walking towards the rear of the lodge. "Do you know what room Torres is in?"

"Number one, dummy. As in, he's number one."

"Save it. For someone who gives a shit."

The black night offered cover; they glided close to the empty dining room where lights were on, and past the ballroom with floor-to-ceiling drapes. As they rounded the bend, a person came into view.

"Fuck, who's that?"

Henchman two stopped abruptly, shifting the dead weight of Francisco's motionless body. "The mayor?"

"Where's he staying?"

"Think Torres said two. Yup, it's the mayor."

They shut their traps and waited as they watched Dzib approach the cottages. Once he neared the door of his destination, they continued on with their job. "The light's on."

"Good, we'll make a sales call," the goon said, his voice dripping with sarcasm.

᠊᠊᠊᠊᠊᠊

Layla and Clay entered the cottage after searching in the dark for the key. They stepped inside and checked that the blinds were pulled down tight before Clay flipped on his flashlight.

"We're here. Now what?" he asked.

"What time is it?"

"About eight forty-five."

"Guess we should get the Glock and go out for a night-time stroll, check out the perimeters, the parking lot. See who's here. Oh, and I'll give Gabriella a call," Layla said.

"Jaime, too?" Clay asked.

Layla nodded, looked for a chair, and took a seat. She pulled her phone from her pocket. Gabriella picked up on the first ring.

"Where are you?" Layla asked.

"I'm in the manager's office. Alone. Dropping off the check-in sheets from, get this, the members."

"Members?" Layla asked.

"Yeah, Torres called them members today. Something's fishy, Layla. Bernardo left about ten minutes ago, right after all twelve showed up. They were in fine form, pretty toasted. They'll have drinks and supper before meeting in the ballroom.

"Bernardo asked them to sign in, but said they didn't need to pay. Torres made arrangements to pick up the tab."

"Is that weird?" Layla asked.

"I don't know. I haven't worked for him very long, but it seems strange, and Bernardo said it wasn't typical, but he did as he was told. His last words before he left were that he hoped there would be no girls. Now get this. I'm in the manager's office, dropping off the paperwork, and I took photos of everything."

"Why would you do that?"

"The more I've seen today, the more I know something's not right. Bernardo was squirrelly about the women coming. That pendejo Dzib tried to corner me in the office …"

"No!" Layla said.

"Yes, but I showed him. Now he's starting to act strange, too. Oh, and the governor's here."

"Well, you were expecting him, right?"

"Yeah. I was going to drop by cottage one and tell Torres I was leaving with his car," she said. "But Bernardo said that when I was in the manager's office, the governor showed up and they didn't want to be disturbed."

"Well, I don't think you can indict anyone on that."

"No, but I've been watching this operation all day. Listen, I think I should scoot out of here. My job is done. The cook leaves soon," Gabriella said.

"It will be Torres, Dzib, and the governor. No one else? No bartender?"

"Oh, Dzib will be tending bar. There's something going on. They're really playing this quiet. And I forgot to tell you …"

"What?"

"Wait, wait, I hear something," Gabriella said.

The phone went silent. Layla looked at Clay, who was totally in the dark.

"What, what?" he asked.

She shook her head and put up a finger. "Wait."

"I'm back. It was nothing but I got scared. Thought it might be the mayor, and I didn't want him to see me. Oh, when he found me in the office, I'd just opened this cabinet and there was a box of black velvet masks, one of a kind, of goats, and cats and devils, god-like masks. Beautiful. When he saw me looking at them, that's when he freaked out and tried to corner me."

"This is sounding weird, Gabriella. I think the best thing is for you to leave. Now."

"Oh, I almost forgot the most important thing! A black Escalade's in the parking lot!"

"Black Escalade?" Layla said, horrified.

Clay grabbed Layla's arm. "An Escalade?"

Gabriella could hear Clay through the phone line. "Si."

"Is it one of the businessmen?"

"I don't think so. They parked up close to the lobby. The Escalade's down at the bottom of the lot, where it's dark."

"Clay, they're here. The goons."

"What did you say?" Gabriella asked, frightened. "Should I be scared?"

"No, but listen closely. Take Torres' car, talk to no one, and leave, Gabriella. Me and Clay are here and Jaime's on his way down. We'll take care of everything, you hear me?"

"Yes, Layla." Her voice had become as demure as a kitten's purr.

"It's good you took photos. Send them to me tomorrow. That was quick thinking, but I want you to get on the road. Go to Playamar. Find Isabel and have a drink and a pizza and wait until she's off work. You two go home together. Promise me?"

"Layla, you're scaring me."

"Gabriella, I am taking no chances. I want you with someone tonight, got it?"

"Yes."

"Okay, goodbye and drive safe, and I'll let Jaime know you'll be staying with Isabel. Text me the address."

"Okay, ciao, Layla."

Layla pocketed her phone. "The governor is in cottage one with Torres. The black Escalade's at the bottom of the parking lot where there are no lights."

"For how long?" Clay asked.

"Not sure," she said.

"What's up?"

"It's our job to find out. Got the piece from the bathroom?"

"Yep. Call Jaime," Clay said.

He picked up on the first ring. "Jaime, where are you?" Layla asked.

"On the road, making time towards the lodge. What's up?"

"Let me know when you get to the kitchen alcove. It's murky—not sure what's happening, but the black Escalade is here."

"I'll text you when I get there," Jaime said.

"Oh, and Gabriella is heading north in Torres' car. We wanted her outta here."

"Good planning, boss."

She closed her phone. "He's en route. When we figure it out, we'll call him."

"So?" Clay asked.

"Let's get to work."

CHAPTER 37

The henchmen rounded the bend at the north end of the lodge with their package.

"Give me a second," said henchman two. "I gotta shift hands."

They were close to Torres' cottage where the lights were on, though the blinds were shut.

"Do we knock first?"

"Of course, pinhead. You don't traipse in on the jefe."

"Just asking!"

"Who taught you manners?"

"Like you're the Queen of England? Don't matter in this job, carnal."

They straightened their spines and walked up the stairs to the door. They heard voices.

"Knock."

After leaning the package on the terraza, henchman two knocked on the door. The voices stopped. He knocked again.

"Who's there?"

"Uh, it's Ramón. I have something for you."

The door opened and they stared directly at Torres. His face contorted before he sucked in a deep breath—two cartel thugs with something body-sized wrapped in a blanket stood on the doorstep.

"What the hell are you doing here?" He pointed at the blanket. "What's that?"

"The banker," Ramón said, sheepishly.

"Chinga! Why's he in a blanket?"

"We worked him over. He was wearing a wire."

"What?"

Another voice came from the shadows. It was the governor of Quintana Roo, Enrique Hernandez.

"What did you say?" he asked, pushing Torres aside. Both men stared at the blanket leaning against the cottage.

"We got that banker here. He may not make it."

"Good God! Get the hell in here!"

Ramón and his fellow lame-brain hurriedly pushed inside, body in tow. "Where do we put him?"

"Oh, Jesús y Maria," the governor moaned. "How could this happen?"

"Why did you say he's in a blanket?" Torres asked again.

"He's bleeding bad and I didn't want his blood all over the car."

"What happened?"

"Well, you told us to keep him at the casa, with the girl," Ramón said.

"Where is she?" Torres asked.

"In the car."

"Is she okay?"

"We had to give her an injection," the henchman admitted.

"Why?"

"She saw what we did to her boyfriend when we found the wire," the thug said.

"A wire! Where is it?" Torres asked.

"At the house."

"The caretaker will find it, cabrón!" Torres said.

"Um, no."

"What do you mean no?"

"She's dead."

"Who's dead? Julietta?" Enrique Hernandez shouted. "Julietta?"

"Is she the caretaker? I mean, was she?" Ramón asked.

"Fuck, yes!"

"Dead." The other henchman shook his head sorrowfully as though he was next of kin.

"What the fuck happened?"

"She saw Ramón beat up the banker. She freaked and ran out of the house, so he followed her and shot her."

"Chinga! Why'd you have to shoot her?" the governor demanded, turning to stare at Ramón.

"I got scared, I guess."

Enrique started to shake his head back and forth before he spoke loudly, "No. No! Oh, Christ, this cannot have happened. The girl was entirely innocent! Did you fucking know that?"

"Well, she was at the house when we got there with the banker and his girl. We had to keep her inside so she wouldn't tell anyone."

"You had three hostages when you were supposed to have one?" Torres asked.

"The girl was with the banker at Azul. We had to pick them both up or he would've guessed something was wrong."

"Is the girl fucked-up?" demanded the governor.

"High."

"No overdose? We don't need another dead body," Torres said.

"No. Just enough so she'd stop making a fuss. She saw what we did to her boyfriend and went crazy, and she may have heard the gunshots."

"Gunshots?"

"Yeah," said the second henchman. "Ramón shot the caretaker. In the back."

By this time the governor's face had turned bright red. He turned to Ramon. "In the back? You shot her in the back?"

Ramon nodded.

Enrique looked at the slug in front of him, finally grasping the lunacy of the day's events. He stepped close to the henchman and punched him in the jaw. "Fuck you!"

Ramón staggered backwards, but did not retaliate.

Torres recovered more quickly than the governor. He took care of details. "Where's the body?"

"We buried her," the henchman said.

"Where?" Torres asked.

"On the property. In the palm grove in front of the house."

"Oh great," the governor said. "Just great." He walked over to the chair and sank into it, his unattractive face taking on the pallor of a turnip. He stared at the motionless blanket lying on the bed. "You better find out if the banker's still alive. Where's the recorder?"

Ramón stood a little taller before saying, "We took care of it. Tore it to shreds. It's at the casa."

"Chinga! You left it there?" Enrique demanded.

"It's unrecognizable. In pieces."

"Feds or forensics could make something of it," the governor said.

Ramón smirked, still on top of the world. "Tulum police?"

"Hijole! Did you forget who I am, you scum-sucking ass? I'm the governor of this state. There'll be an investigation. A real investigation. It happened at my beach villa. People will want details. Her family and friends will want to know why a twenty-year-old girl was shot on my property. Do you know what kind of news this will generate?"

Torres jumped on. "You morons! When did this happen?"

Things had gone sour. Ramón looked down, suppressing a grimace. "This afternoon."

"Oh no," the governor moaned. "That's why I've had ten calls from my sister. Did anyone see you? Was the gardener there?"

"No one." The henchmen looked at each other.

"Listen, now we gotta deal with this guy. You," Torres pointed at Goon Two. "What's your name?"

"Bruno."

"Unwrap him and put him on that back bed. Now."

They assembled into triage mode. Torres ordered Ramón to find towels, and they started to clean up Francisco.

"Is the girl in the car?"

"Yeah."

"Go get her and put her in cottage two. It's Dzib's. I'll let him know. Were there people in the lobby when you walked by?"

"No, empty."

"Any cars in the parking lot?"

"A few."

"They probably belong to the members. What time is it?"

"Eight forty-five."

"Hijole. I have to change and get to the dining room. Enrique, can you finish up? Gotta find out when Karina is getting here with the girls. She's always late," Torres said.

"Who'll watch the drugged girl? Who is she?" Enrique asked.

"I have no idea. Girlfriend of the banker."

"How did she become part of this?" demanded the governor.

"Like he said," Torres motioned with his chin at Ramón, "she was with him the night he was kidnapped. He had the goods on us."

"Couldn't they just have warned him? Look at this mess!"

"That was the plan, but he was wearing a wire. He flipped."

"Oh, Christ. A dead girl. A near-dead banker. The feds will want to know everything."

Torres grabbed the governor by the arm and spun him around. "Hold it." Torres' voice came out as a snarl. "Who the fuck do you think you're dealing with? Some imbecile? How far back do we go? Have you ever known me to get you in trouble?"

"But the dead girl. She was innocent. She did nothing. My sister—"

"Fuck your sister!"

"What?"

"Fuck your sister!" Torres repeated with emphasis. "This is way beyond her hissy-fits. We'll say it was a burglary gone wrong. We're not dealing with Mexico City police or the feds—not yet. It's not even Tulum. Chinga, we're closer to Punta Allen."

Enrique's face was sullen. "I don't like you talking about my sister like that."

"Enrique," Torres began, taking it down a notch. "Listen, sorry. You know I respect Erwina. I just got rattled, but we're going to have to figure out a story and stick with it." He turned to the goons. "Get the girl, put her in Dzib's cabin. What state is she in?"

"Hands tied, mouth taped."

"Can she walk?"

"We dosed her pretty good. Probably not."

"Is she a working girl?" Torres asked.

"No, don't think so."

"If she has a purse, bring it to me. I want to know who she is, if he picked her up in Tulum, or from somewhere else. Well, don't stand there! Move! I'm going to call Dzib to let him know he'll be having company."

CHAPTER 38

Layla inched open the door on cottage eighteen, prepared to step into the darkness when she saw movement at the other end of the cottage chain. Something was happening in cottage one. She closed the door until it was open a mere smidgen. She couldn't believe her eyes—the henchmen from Casa Paraiso—and they were flying out the door.

"Clay, it's the Escalade crew."

"Man. What's happening?"

"They left Torres' cottage."

"Maybe we should follow them."

"They gotta be heading for the car. Gabriella said it's in the parking lot. We can come in from this side and see what they're doing from the other end of the lodge."

"Good idea."

Again Layla opened the door and they stepped into the moonless night. "What could be happening? Do they have Silvia?"

Clay shrugged. "We're gonna find out. No talking."

They moved in silence. Once they rounded the bend at the bottom of the lodge perimeter, Clay and Layla watched the goons approach the Escalade. The men moved towards the rear door that faced away from the lodge and manhandled something in the back seat.

Layla's heart fluttered. "I think they have Silvia!" she said excitedly.

"Calm down. We don't know," Clay said.

They stopped and waited. In minutes their question was answered. The goons were moving a very unmanageable woman whose legs were like rubber. She was so unresponsive they had to drag her the first few steps. To amend the problem, one held her while the other cut loose what Layla assumed were wrist straps. They each took an arm over a shoulder and dragged her between them, skirting the building, lugging the immobile body.

"It's Silvia!" Layla said. "Why else would they have her wrists strapped?"

"Yeah …"

"You heard them! They said three hostages and one was the banker, so of course it's Silvia," she said.

"The third?" Clay asked.

"The poor caretaker, for all of half a minute," Layla said, getting angry again at the senseless killing.

While the henchmen moved out of the picture, they shifted focus to the well-lit dining room. From their dark perch, Clay and Layla could see men beginning to gather around the bar where Dzib played bartender. During a pour, the mayor placed the bottle on the counter and picked up his phone, multi-tasking and chatting. Even from afar, it was apparent from his gestures that the phone call had surprised him.

He spoke to one of the men at the bar. Within moments they had traded places and Dzib was heading towards the lobby. Arriving at the lodge entrance, he looked both ways before exiting, then moved towards the north end of the building and disappeared.

"Something's happening. Maybe the hand-off?" Layla asked.

"Could be. Follow him."

As they slid into the shadows to pursue Dzib and the henchmen to figure where they were going with the girl, Gabriella walked out the lobby doors.

"This is like one big reunion," Layla said. "Do we talk to her?"

"No. You gave her instructions," Clay said. "Let her get out of this hellhole."

Layla's sentiments exactly. She nodded in the darkness and muttered, "The sooner the better."

🔒🔒🔒

Dzib arrived at his cottage at the exact moment the henchmen brought Silvia to his doorstep. "Gentlemen, allow me," he said in mock seriousness, eyeing the prize.

"Torres said to bring her here. She's pretty fucked-up."

The mayor merely smiled.

"We undid her hands. Should we re-tie her?"

He checked out the merchandise: unresponsive body, rubbery legs, head tilted precariously to the side. "I can handle this for now. Put her inside, on the bed," he said, as he unlocked the door. "I have to get back to the dining room. Let Torres know she's here."

"We brought her purse, Torres asked for it," Ramón said.

"Why?"

"Beats me."

"Give it to him and tell him the girl's at my cottage. Are you leaving?" Dzib asked.

"Once Torres says so, yeah," Ramón said.

"And the banker?"

"He's in Torres' cottage, and not very happy about it." That was an understatement.

"Why?"

"The guy was wearing a wire and we let him have it," Ramón explained.

A shadow crossed Dzib's face. "I don't have time to hear more. Torres will keep me informed. I'm sure he's made arrangements with you."

"Yeah. We'll leave the girl and let him know."

꒰꒱꒰

With Silvia's purse in hand, Ramón knocked timidly on Torres' door. The contractor answered abruptly. He looked like a man in a hurry, his svelte body now dressed in dinner attire.

"Get in here, both of you. What do you have for me?"

"The girl's purse," Ramón said.

"Is she in cottage two?" Torres asked.

"Yeah, asleep."

"Then, ándale. I'll be in touch when I get things straightened out."

"'Dios."

"Yeah, right, adios." Torres' comment was snippy.

Barely closing the door he looked at the expensive purse. "She's no working girl," he said to the governor, "or she's one with excellent taste."

He opened the clasp and discovered a lipstick, comb, and the cédula identity card carried by every Mexican. "Oh my God!"

"What? What?" asked Enrique.

"Do you know who we just kidnapped?" Torres asked, aghast.

"Who?"

"Fucking Silvia Ortega Castillo from Cuernavaca. The daughter of one of the Pemex 'flaco' boys. We just kidnapped Mexican royalty. We are so screwed!"

CHAPTER 39

Clay and Layla, still in the shadows, watched the henchmen rush out of Dzib's cottage for a second time. They were in as close to a state of panic as two seasoned goons could be.

"What's the problem?" Clay asked.

"They dropped Silvia off at Dzib's. Oh man, I hope he doesn't rape her."

"Layla, he doesn't have time for it. He's gotta get back to the bar. Plus, the others should be leaving any minute. It's almost nine."

"You're in Mexico, Clay," Layla said. "Timing's different here."

"This group is revved up for action, and I don't think they'll take kindly to a late date."

"We watch and wait?" Layla asked.

"Let's see what Dzib does. He should be outta there in a minute and so should Torres and the governor. Where are the girls?"

"Hmm, good question."

They quietly waited. Night wind blowing through the palms obscured any sound of party activity coming from the lodge itself.

Layla heard a distinct noise in the distance. "What is that?"

"A car?" Clay asked.

"Turning into the parking lot?"

They were too far away to move closer to the front of the lodge, plus having spotted who they assumed was Silvia, leaving their lookout was not an option. They were perfectly positioned to move on Dzib's cottage and grab the girl.

A squeal of brakes and series of car doors opening and slamming shut confirmed Layla's hunch—visitors. A husky voice came through in the darkness, "Take it easy, we're here to work. So, get ready, hear?"

Dzib's madame was rallying the girls. Layla was relieved Gabriella was on her way to Tulum, away from the craziness.

Another car rolled into the parking lot and again, more chattering and further commotion as car doors opened and closed. From their vantage point they heard more doors, but now from cottages, not cars. At the lodge's north end, Torres and Enrique Hernandez were departing cottage one. Party time. Dzib's cottage remained quiet.

"What happened to the goons?" Layla asked.

"I think they're splitting," Clay said.

"So, no weapons?"

"Not sure. We don't know if Dzib is carrying or not," Clay said. He adjusted Jaime's Glock that was firmly positioned in the waistband of his shorts.

"I don't think the governor would be, but you never know," Layla said.

"Where's the banker? Did the goons leave him?"

"Think they dropped him in Torres' cottage."

"Wonder what shape he's in," Clay said.

"Probably not good."

Voices carry, especially a gaggle of chattering babes. With a little verbal prodding, they made their way to the lodge. Layla heard another cottage door.

"The mayor's on the move," Clay said.

"He has to get the girls set up while the men are having supper. Bernardo told Gabriella the ballroom is where the party will take place. What that means, no one seems sure of, but both Torres and Dzib opted for long drapes."

"We'll never see inside," Clay said.

Another car started. "Is that the goons?" Layla asked.

"Has to be. Adios, boys," Clay said.

"I'm just glad Gabriella is gone," Layla said, under her breath.

"One safe, one to be saved," Clay said. He grabbed her hand and gave it a squeeze.

"Ojalá."

🔳🔳🔳

Gabriella was on the road with a ten minute start on the Boca activities. Two lumbering vans came towards her, hogging the road. A woman drove the first; the second was driven by a man. She felt relieved to be out of the Boca Laguna madness and away from Dzib, Torres, and the governor. She'd never met the governor and had no thoughts about him, either way. But even she, in her youthful naiveté, reasoned any and every politico in Mexico would have slime on them. One didn't rise to any office in the land without a tarnished past, present—and without a doubt—future. Not in Mexico.

CHAPTER 40

Dzib had the goons place Silvia on his bed, half projection, half wishful thinking. There was little time to daydream, however; duty awaited him in the dining room. Meanwhile, he cooled his heels. The madame, though always late, could be forgiven her shortcomings because she handled the hottest girls in Cancun, and the youngest.

He took a last look at Sleeping Beauty. Though pregame fun with one of the madame's girls was surely on his dance card, Silvia was the evening's goal.

🪕🪕🪕

The madame had been told by Dzib to steer clear of the lobby, head to the right side of the lodge, and enter through the back door next to the kitchen. Karina ran on pure adrenaline and was known for a mane of crazy dark hair and a surly attitude. Though slight of frame, she feared no one. At one time she may have been considered attractive, but life had stepped in. She motioned to her bodyguard while she shouted, "Girls!"

That was the only way to get their attention. Their chattering sounded like a flock of jabbering parrots. "This way, around the back. Get them in line, Manuel!" she ordered.

She pointed to the path and watched the older girls, that would make them twenty, start to lead the way, with the younger ones, mere teens, following up the rear. Little ducklings, not parrots at all. She fidgeted with her car keys as they fell in line. They dutifully passed before her, while she stood with hand on hip, mentally rating each. Nice breasts. Skinny ass. Too tall. Good legs. Doll face. Bad hair day. Now they weren't ducklings, but pieces of meat.

"Quiet, keep it quiet, and hurry. We're late. Manuel, make them move along!"

Manuel was her mother's youngest cousin, and though not known for his intellect, a muscled body weighing in at two hundred and forty pounds gave him all the advantage that was needed.

Moving the girls was like herding cats. "Keep going, keep going," he said, as Karina shot an unpleasant scowl his way.

Dzib had told Karina the cook's quarters could be used as a changing room where there was also a bathroom. The girls carried cheap Walmart duffel bags with their costumes and g-strings, bras or pasties, make-up, lotions, tissues and towels.

Finally, the last of them approached the back door. Karina had remained at the rear, ready to lock up as instructed. Manuel positioned himself like a sentry at the front of the line, watching the girls shuffle and shift from foot to foot. It would soon be showtime. After these events, painful looks were the norm while they waited in line for the bathroom after having sex with men three times their age. The occasional looker, under thirty, was the exception.

He'd have been invited by a business associate. But the good-looking young guys didn't need to pay for it; for them it was a diversion. For the old ones, a necessity—that and Viagra.

"Keep moving," she commanded. "Inside you go."

🪻🪻🪻

Gabriella liked the sleek lines of Torres' gray Porsche, so sporty and expensive. She drove a little too fast for the dark night and the rutted road. She wanted to get to Playamar, see Isabel's smiling, irreverent face, and order a margarita. Though she hadn't driven for a while, she quickly got the feel of the car and the manual transmission.

Tooling along, she began to replay in her mind all that had transpired in the past twenty-four hours. She could write a book about the goings on at the lodge, with her apparently corrupt boss and the mayor who had killed a man.

A shudder went through her, like a ghost walking over her grave. She stayed in the middle of the road, wishing the night wasn't so black. She recalled the turn that brought the road close to the ocean was up ahead.

The moonless night momentarily took on a different tenor—she thought she saw headlights behind. No. Nothing. With windows rolled down she could hear the ocean, but for a brief moment, lights did appear. No one could drive too fast on the Punta Allen road and only a maniac would try to pass.

She began to worry that the mayor could be tailing her. Reality sank in as she reminded herself he had a job to do.

The vehicle moved closer, going too fast for the road. She considered straddling the side of the road so they could pass, but berms didn't even exist on real roads in Quintana Roo, much less on this makeshift beach lane.

The vehicle had gained and was five car lengths behind. Her nerves kicked in and she clutched the wheel. She gasped when the car appeared directly in her rearview mirror. With a quick glance it looked like an SUV with two people. They *were* tailing her. If she pulled over, that still wouldn't allow room to pass.

She punched the gas; the car behind picked up speed, too. She was moving at a fast clip, and then came the turn by the ocean. She had forgotten all about it.

๑๑๑

Moments later, a rattled Gabriella pulled herself out of Torres' Porsche and looked into the faces of two imposing men. Their car's brights shone directly at her. She placed a hand above her brow to shield her eyes and tried to get a look at the car. Black Escalade!

"Who are you?" she demanded as she struggled to straighten her skirt after an awkward exit from the Porsche. "My car's off the road thanks to you. What am I going to do?"

One of them smirked and the other laughed outright. He had a high-pitched hyena laugh, unbecoming for a man of his girth. "We could help you."

"Well, how?" She sized them up. They could probably lift Torres' car from the ditch onto the road. "Why are you driving so fast? I would have moved over."

"Yeah, right, little lady."

286

"I've got to see if there's any damage to my boss's car," Gabriella said.

She steadied herself, feeling less off balance after stepping onto the flat road and out of the lopsided car. She walked to the front of the vehicle, her eyes adjusting between the night's darkness and the Escalade's high beams. "Oh, no. The right front fender. Hijole!"

"Who's your boss?" the smirky one asked.

"Oh, you wouldn't know him. He's from Maya Reál in Tulum. Señor Torres."

"Torres!" the other one spat out.

His voice made a chill run down her back. Even though her expression would be lost in the darkness, she put on her most matter-of-fact face in an attempt to center herself.

"Tone it down, Ramón," one of the goons said.

"I'm Señor Torres' secretary. Heading back to the office with paperwork on a land deal that needs to be handled pronto, while he's away."

"That why you're out alone?"

"Yeah. Maybe you could lift the car for me," Gabriella said.

"How strong do you think we are?"

She moderated her response. Not too tart, not too sweet. A fine balance. "Hmm. Not sure but looks like you're in a hurry. Maybe we can help each other out."

"Maybe. What's in it for us?"

"What? You forced me off the road," she said.

"Don't get snippy. We're here to help." Again came that weirdly girlish laugh.

"Yeah, help ourselves. We've had a long day. Need a release."

287

"Well, a friendly hand to help me move the car might be a good release," she said.

"Helping hands don't work like that." Ramón, the smirky one, moved closer to Gabriella.

Sensing trouble, she stepped away and moved in front of the off-road vehicle. "Please, help me get this car straightened out, okay?"

She was good at stalling.

"Hey," Bruno said to Ramón. "Let's take care of business or we're not going anywhere. Get it?"

"Yeah, yeah. Okay."

They both moved towards the sports car. "Give me the keys," Ramón said to Gabriella.

She handed them over. "Please be careful."

He frowned. "Stand back, and Bruno, I need you to push once I put it in first."

The operation barely took five minutes. They positioned the car off the side of the road so the SUV could slide by. Gabriella walked to the car. "Well, thanks. My keys and I'll be off. You first."

"Wait a minute. We helped you. Now you help us, right?"

"Sure, I'll go first but I don't drive fast enough. You guys really move."

She matter-of-factly held her hand out for the keys. Ramón grabbed it. "Into the car, chica. You don't think we work for nothing, do ya?"

His rapid movement caught her off guard. "Let go of me! Let me go!" she screamed.

"You can yell all you want. No one's gonna hear you."

He gripped both arms, pushing her backwards towards the SUV. "Bruno, the door."

Bruno complied and moved quickly to the vehicle, opening wide the door. Screaming loudly, Gabriella struggled against Ramón.

"You want me to hit you, puta?"

"Help! Someone! Help me! Take your hands off me!" Gabriella yelled.

He squeezed her arms tighter before picking up her struggling body. "Big girl," he said, laughing; there it was, that stupid laugh. "Time for a diet."

"Stop it! Stop it!" she screamed again.

He dropped her on the back seat. "Get over here, Bruno. I'm first, you guard."

Gabriella's screams shattered the night sky, but they were lost in the wilds of the biosphere, swallowed by ocean tides and the night wind rustling through jungles of palm trees.

CHAPTER 41

J aime was making good time on the Punta Allen road.
He'd long since left behind the arch, the defining mark
where Tulum left off and Si'an Ka'an Reserve began. Not
one to think too deeply on any subject, he found solace in
music. Country music. Not sissy stuff from Garth Brooks
or Randy Travis and their wannabe's, and no women
singers. Jaime was into country oldies and goldies—Hank
Williams, Bob Wills and the Texas Playboys, Chet Atkins,
Charley Pride. These boys were the heart of country. No
newbie singer could compete with "Hey, Good Lookin'" or
"I'm So Lonesome I Could Cry." He'd listened to Cash
and the Carters, but the truth of the matter, he was a sucker
for Hank and Texas swing.

He missed the ranchera music of his boyhood in
Guadalajara—Vicente Fernández and Pedro Infantes, even
Antonio Aguilar— but after doing a stint for El Patrón in
Brownsville, Texas, several years back, he'd fallen hard for
country. That's when he realized the Rio Grande divided
not only countries, but also musical tastes.

He had set the music on his mobile app, turned up the
volume, and settled in for the drive. For starters, he'd
decided on Charley Pride's "All I Have to Offer You is Me."

Since working with Layla the past few days he'd been living on the beach road. He remembered each dip, turn, and every angle of the peninsula. After driving thirty minutes, he saw lights in the distance. A long way off, but lights. He took out his earbuds and turned off the music. Time to pay attention.

🁢🁢🁢

"Get going!" Bruno yelled as Ramón strong-armed Gabriella into submission by laying his massive body on top of hers. "Get the job done! A car's coming!"

"Chinga! Can't get my zipper down. She's twisting like a snake!"

"Hurry!"

The headlights moved steadily towards the Escalade that held two men and an unfortunate woman who had been thrown into the back seat like a sack of flour.

"Shut up. Get your Glock out and if they don't like what they see, use it," Ramón said, still struggling to subdue a violent, arm-thrashing Gabriella.

"Help me! Help me!" she screamed, hearing the goons' conversation.

In moments, a Toyota sedan pulled four car lengths in front and stopped.

"Who the fuck is it?" Ramon shouted, doing his best to subdue a struggling Gabriella. "Cálmate, cálmate. This won't be so bad. Lay still."

"Probably a tourist."

"Get the hell up there and tell them to look the other way or take a piece of action from your Glock."

Bruno marched towards the car while his buddy struggled to both constrain Gabriella and muffle her screams. Approaching the car, he drew the Glock from behind his back.

"Hands on the wheel," he ordered, aiming the gun at the driver's window. "You alone?"

"Yes," a timid voice said. "What's the problem? Please, don't shoot me."

"Some woman had an accident—must have lost her mind. We're trying to get her into our car and take her to a hospital in Playa. Move along. She hit her head when her car went off the road and she's having a screaming fit."

"That car?" Jaime had maneuvered out of his Toyota, and pointed at Torres' Porsche.

"Back in the car, back in the car!" Bruno said, waving his Glock.

"Oh, okay, sorry," a cowed Jaime said, preparing to re-enter the Toyota.

Satisfied with the exchange, Bruno turned to walk back to the Escalade. With gun in hand, Jaime made his move. He whacked the guy on the side of the head, a devastating pummel to the temple.

"Aaah!" Bruno lurched to the side and fell on the sand like a cut tree.

His partner's howl momentarily distracted Ramón from trying to pull off Gabriella's skirt. He peered out the open car door. Seeing his friend on the ground stopped him cold. Ramón, whose pants were now unzipped, reached behind his waistband to pull out his own piece. Jaime took aim, shouting, "If you got a gun, put it down, cabrón!"

Ramon, disoriented, struggled out of the car, pulling out his gun and turning, but not fast enough. Jamie shot the gun from the goon's hand.

"Oww! Oww!" he screamed in pain.

"That's for starters. This here, this second one's for finishing up."

Jaime took aim and shot Ramón in the knee. The goon's leg buckled and he was on the sand in a second. Even on a moonless night, the stain of blood on the light-colored sascab was unmistakable. Jaime ran over, grabbed the gun, kicked him three times in the face, stepped on his hand, and waited for more screams. He gave an extra kick to the knee.

"That's for even touching her, you lowlife," Jaime said.

Ramón, former bully, was reduced to a pile of collapsed muscle and wet tears, lying in a fetal position on a sandy road in the middle of nowhere.

"If you put one hand up her skirt, and she'll tell me if you did, you're a dead man.

"Gabriella? It's Jaime. You okay?" Jaime shouted, his gun still trained on the goon.

"Yes, yes," a sobbing voice came from the car's back seat. "Oh, gracias á Dios, you're here."

"You know her?" a stunned Ramón managed to gasp.

"Shut the fuck up," Jaime said as he took aim at the front left tire of the Escalade and shot. The sound reverberated through the still night. He walked around to the right front tire and fired off another round. He walked to the back of the car and performed the same sequence of events two more times. He'd come full circle and was again in front of Ramón.

"Are you decent, Gabriella?" he asked. "Can you come out?"

"Yes, Jaime, give me a minute."

"Okay. I'm gonna check his pal." He trained his eye on Ramón. "No stupid moves."

He walked back to Bruno, lying in the road next to his Toyota.

"Still breathing," he muttered as he checked the man's pulse. "For now."

Back at the SUV, he said, "Okay, I'm gonna find a cloth and tie off your fucking leg and hand, stop the bleeding. I'll tie up you and your pal, if he's alive. He might not make it through the night but that's your tough luck, for trying to assault a girl, you pieces of shit."

He walked to the back of the Escalade, opened the rear and found a bloodied towel. "Who'd this belong to?"

No answer from Ramón.

"Hey, lover boy! Where'd this blood come from? Huh?"

"Don't know."

"Sure you do. From that little chica you murdered at the fancy villa, was it?"

Ramón's head jerked up. Even in his damaged condition, Jaime's comment got the goon's attention. "How'd you know about that?"

"I'm Harry Houdini, you louse. Chinga, you think it matters? I shouldn't even bother to tie off your bleeding limbs, pendejo. What? Were ya gonna kill this one, too?"

A muffled sob came from the SUV's back seat. "Did he kill Silvia?"

"No, at least I don't think so. Did you kill that Mexico City beauty with the banker?"

"No, just the girl."

"Just the fucking girl?" Jaime went nuts and hit him in the face with his gun. "Just the fucking girl? Like she's a big zero? Chinga! I'd kill you right here if a lady wasn't present."

Gabriella, sitting in the back seat of the Escalade, started to sob as she watched Ramón's face swivel sharply to the right. "Oh, please, no killing."

"I won't, Gabriella. Now listen. We gotta get a move on. You okay? Come out of the car. Let me look at you. No bruises?"

"Maybe one on my arm, but mostly he laid on me and couldn't get a hold on."

"Good girl. Listen, I'm gonna tie these two up. I have tape and straps in my car. Stand away from him, or sit in the car. I'll be right back."

Jaime returned in a few minutes and began to bind Ramón. The humbled bully gave a low moan but was docile. Finishing up, Jaime told him to sit against the car. He walked to Bruno—still out cold—and did the same. Jaime dragged him to the side of the road, taped his mouth, and placed him face up. He searched his pants for a phone and pocketed it.

"You'll get a nice tan in the morning, if you're still alive."

Walking back to the SUV and Ramón's propped-up body, Jaime got on one knee and stared directly into the eyes of the killer. "Hey, listen up. If I ever see you again, you're a dead man."

Seeing no sign of insolence, he pulled Ramón's hair back in a rough manner, placed the duct tape between his own teeth, and bit off a piece to cover the goon's mouth.

"It's just you and your thoughts until the sun comes up, buddy. Ciao."

His deed done, he walked to Gabriella, who was again sitting in the back of the car, head drooping over her chest. "Niña, how ya doing?"

Still shaky but gaining strength, she gave a feeble smile.

"Okay. Here's the plan. I'm going to walk you to the car. Got your keys?"

For a second she panicked. "The keys! Where are they? Oh, he … he …" she began, pointing at Ramón. "His pocket."

Jaime walked back to Ramón, shifted the thug's body, got his phone and the keys, pushed himself up, and gave the keys to Gabriella.

"Walk with me. You need help?"

She shook her head. "I'm okay."

At the car, he looked it over, then opened the door. "Did they run you off the road?"

"Yes. There was nothing I could do about it."

"It happens. Shit, I mean. I gotta go down to the lodge. You already know that. We think we know Silvia's there, and she's okay," he lied. "You get up to Playamar and stay there with Isabel until it closes. Tonight you sleep at her house."

The girl nodded. She put her hand on the car door and sunk slowly into the plush leather seat of her boss's car.

"Start the engine. I wanna hear this baby purr." She did as instructed. "Those Germans? Know how to build 'em."

"Jaime," she began. "I just want to say—"

"Forget about it, kid. We're all just doing our job, right?"

He closed the door firmly, and put his hand on the sill of the rolled-down window. "Now, get out of here, and text me or Layla when you get to Playamar."

Again she nodded. "Bye, Jaime, and thank you."

He gave a wave as she shifted from first to second and rolled onto the soft sand of Punta Allen road and into the darkness.

CHAPTER 42

The lodge was a flurry of activity, and Layla and Clay watched as a stream of girls made their way down and around to the back. It was now half past nine, the supper was in full swing, and the mayor had made his second appearance. He worked the crowd and continued to pour drinks until Karina arrived.

"You're late," he scolded.

"We got here. What's your beef?" She gave him a cold stare, daring him to respond. When he fell in line, she continued, "When do the festivities begin?"

He looked at his watch. "Twenty minutes. Time to move them to the ballroom. I'll show you the way. I had the clerk string up hammocks and put in several chaise lounges. There's other furniture, too, chairs and tables. Lots of rugs and blankets, candles and copal incense. It looks like a Maya sweat lodge, with a touch of rural Yucatán thrown in."

She gave him a sideways look. "Hijole, Dzib! Those men don't give a damn about that shit. They only have one thing on their mind. Well, maybe two," she deadpanned. "Sex, number one, and two— praying they can get it up."

He laughed. "Well, get them in there. The men are winding it up in the bar. What's your driver's name?"

"Manuel," she said.

"Send him to the ballroom in fifteen minutes to bartend. Oh, but first I need your help. I have an extra girl, a real beauty. She's been doped up, bad behavior. I was hoping you could make her presentable."

Karina's look went right through him. "Where'd she come from?"

"Uh, Mexico City. They couldn't handle her, but she's got what it takes. Even though she's a handful, we thought we'd make her the star," Dzib said.

"You didn't kidnap her, did you?"

"Karina," he said with a short laugh. "I don't have to kidnap anyone. You know that."

"Mayor, that's exactly why I'm asking. After tonight, you sending her back to where she came from?" the madame asked.

Dzib was quick to notice her interest. "If anyone could handle her, it'd be you, Karina."

"Anyone looking for her?" the madame asked, ignoring his attempt to stroke her ego.

"Finders keepers," the mayor said.

"We'd have to talk price," countered Karina.

"This one's high-end. Why don't you have a look? Help get her ready for the show. She's tonight's prize. She's in cottage two, and looks like she's in need of some fixing. You in?"

"Okay, okay. Number two? I'll get my makeup bags. I have an extra change of costumes, too. I'll send the girls into the ballroom, let them get into their lounge love act positions. First, though, meet with Manuel and explain how to handle the bar, where the ice machine is, the refrigerators."

"All right. Cottage two. I'll be there in ten minutes."

᠊᠊᠊᠊

"Clay, I think they're moving girls around," said Layla. "Maybe now's the time to grab Silvia. Dzib's out and so are Torres and the governor."

Clay hesitated. "Not sure. Let's get to the back side and see what's happening first."

They crept to the far side of the lodge where only a few cottage lights had been left on. Number one and two were dark, though they knew that Torres and Dzib had dibs on them.

Layla's phone buzzed in her pocket. "Damn!" She picked up. "Jaime, que tal?"

"Layla, I'm heading down."

"I thought you'd be here."

"Complications. Gabriella met up with the goons on the way to Tulum. They ran her off the road and tried to assault her."

"Hijole! Is she okay?"

"Lucky timing. I came on it right as they were ready to make a move. I hit one with my Glock pretty good. Could be permanent lights out."

"The other?"

"That would be the killer, Ramón. I shot his hand and took out his knee. He won't be moving around much either. I bound them, shot out their tires, and told the pendejo I better never see him again."

"Where's Gabriella? How is she?"

"She's shaken but she'll be fine. I'll be there soon. Same plan?"

"Yeah, behind the kitchen. Park, and we'll call if we need you." She shook her head and hung up.

"Layla, what?" Clay asked.

As she was telling him what Jaime had said, he touched her elbow. "Man, lucky. But listen, there's movement. Someone's heading towards the cottages."

They stopped talking and watched a slender figure dart into the night.

"The madame?" Clay asked.

"Yeah, I think so. Where's she going?" Layla wondered out loud.

"To Dzib's cottage? She's carrying … a bag?"

"Of course," Layla said. "Silvia's gonna be a mess. Probably hasn't showered for days in this heat. They can't set her up as the high price spread if she looks like a flower girl from TJ."

"Sure, the madame will clean her up. She knows how to deal with someone under the influence."

"More waiting," Layla sighed. "Did we blow it? We were so close."

"We still *are* close," Clay said.

CHAPTER 43

Karina raised her hand to knock before entering Dzib's cottage and remembered the girl would be out of it. Precedent didn't matter, or manners. This was a business transaction. Plain and simple, the girl was collateral damage. Hers to use as needed—another worker bee, sex slave, unfortunate sharing in life's misery. But for some, the misery was more dismal. If it hadn't been for owning the best set of knockers in all Mexico and that one pimp who'd had a thing for her, she'd still be turning ten to fifteen tricks a day. At this stage of the game, it wouldn't be any high-end place. She'd be servicing filthy farm hands in Chihuahua to keep them coming back to the fields, or low-level cartel boys—dangerous and the worst—in Colima, or some other cartel stronghold.

She opened the door and searched for the light switch. Lying on the bed, face down, was a dark-haired woman. Karina walked closer, checking out her body before flipping her over—nice legs, good clothes and sandals, and tiny jewels in her hair clasp that looked real.

Though her mouth was messy from run-off saliva, the woman on the bed was a beauty. Mascara had smeared all over her face and her cheeks were blotchy from crying, but this one had potential. Karina checked her watch.

"Niña," she began. She gave Silvia a shake, lying like dead meat on Dzib's bed. "Niña."

Silvia stirred, sat straight up, and began screaming. Loud. "Where am I?"

"What the hell!" Karina shouted. "Shut up!"

She clasped her hand over Silvia's mouth to stifle the screams. "You listen and listen good. You're in a lodge and you'll do what I say. Shut up. Hear me?"

She grasped Silvia so tightly by the arm a red blotch appeared. The girl's face went white. She became docile, like a lamb, or more appropriately, a cold fish. She collapsed back on the bed. Karina went to her purse and pulled out a pill box for a couple uppers.

"Chiquita, I'm sorry about grabbing you so hard. I'll get water and give you something that'll make you feel better."

Silvia started to sit up, and began to shake her head. "No, no more. Please, no more."

"Just sit there, like a good girl," Karina said.

"No more! No more!"

"Listen. You're doing this my way or I'll tie your hands and feet and push it down your throat. If that doesn't work, I'll bring the needle."

Again, Silvia slumped onto the bed, this time with her face towards the wall.

"Honey. Honey? Okay, we'll do it my way then."

Silvia shot straight up. "All right."

The madame, on the way to her bag, smiled and continued with her movements. Rummaging in her purse she found a couple of neo-percodans. After the uppers, a downer or two would make the girl more manageable. She was back soon with bottled water and pills.

Silvia looked at them, then at the hardened, uncompromising face of the madame, put all thoughts of resistance aside, and took her medicine.

🔲🔲🔲

The girls had entered the ballroom and made themselves comfortable on the lounges, in the hammocks, and at the tables where they were having refrescos. Madame Karina allowed no drinking when they were on the floor. She ran a tight ship and to stray would invoke her wrath. Occasionally they pushed or pulled on the tiny bits of cloth that temporarily covered their firm, young bodies. If they'd not yet attended one of Dzib's members-only parties, they'd heard rumors from girls who had. The men, older businessmen for the most part, would show up tanked and wearing masks. The girls could wear masks, too, if they chose to—and most did. Until the men undressed—not all of them did—they could pretend these relics weren't part of the over the hill gang. With clothes and masks on, it could all be considered a grand masquerade ball and they could pretend the man behind the mask was actually a prince in disguise. If only.

Many were whisked back to their quarters where the real action began. Some men made a show of romancing their chosen ones in the middle of the ballroom or salon or wherever the event took place. That was why most of the girls chose to wear masks. Not all were exhibitionists, and most were too embarrassed to have open sex in front of a crowd. To the more mature girls it was a plain old sex orgy, and to the younger, less experienced ones, it would be a painful rite of passage.

While waiting for the evening to get rolling, many chatted in small groups; a few sat alone. The night would be long and the lucky ones would be picked by someone who had an open bottle in their room so they could get shit-faced. They tried to pep themselves up by making silly jokes. Manuel had brought out the box of masks and placed them on one of the tables. The girls gathered around, making their decision on which to wear, some flirting with Manuel, the youngest man in a fifty kilometer radius. It was the beginning of a very long night to come.

⌐⌐⌐

Karina put some effort into making Silvia look good. To better manage the situation, she dropped her madame persona and became a girlfriend. "What's your name?"

No answer.

"Sorry, what?"

A grudging Silvia answered, "Didn't they tell you?"

Karina checked her response. "Oh, that silly mayor. He's so forgetful. No."

"Silvia."

"Your dress is pretty. I fluffed it up a bit. It'll work fine."

"What's going to happen?" Silvia asked.

"We're going to a party in the lodge ballroom soon. The mayor will come and get us."

"I'm tired. Can I take a nap?" Silvia asked.

"Good idea. It will be a long evening. Take your dress off. Don't want it wrinkled."

⌐⌐⌐

While Clay and Layla watched Dzib's room where Silvia was being held, now with the madame as jailer, Dzib had re-emerged at the lodge to shepherd the men into the ballroom. Most had already grabbed their masks. They entered slowly at first, then, as though it was Christmas morning, they made a rush on it, fueled by alcohol and the sight of a bevy of fresh beauties with fine young bodies wearing velvet masks and little else.

Torres and the governor, still fuming after realizing they'd accidentally kidnapped an important someone, also donned masks and followed their associates inside. When Dzib encountered them, Torres spoke his piece. "You know who you've got in your room?"

"A beautiful chica who will go to top bidder," Dzib answered smugly.

"Wrong," Torres said. "You've kidnapped one of Mexico City's society darlings. She's the daughter of one of the Pemex 'flacos'. Good work, pendejo."

Dzib's head swung around like he'd experienced an exorcism. He stared first at the governor, whose mask hid his true emotions; neither could he read Torres.

"Well, it's only a one night stand," Dzib demurred.

"Good God, man!" Torres boomed, then lowered his voice. "How stupid are you?"

"She won't know who we are," Dzib answered glumly.

"*You* are beyond a fool," Torres snarled. "I have no idea how we're going to avoid huge problems with this fuck-up on your part."

"You wanted the banker kidnapped."

"I wanted him scared, not nearly dead. We don't know if he'll make it through the night."

"You needed someone to teach him a lesson," Dzib insisted.

"I think you should cancel the prize," the governor interrupted, the voice of reason prevailing over a tumultuous sea. "This is unconscionable."

"No, no, we can't do that," the mayor said, pushing back.

Torres chimed in. "Yeah. We gotta get her out of here. Pray she can't remember tonight. Did they drug her?"

"Yes." Dzib went silent. "Well, I can't do it on my own. She's wobbly on her feet. Can someone help me?"

"Hell! It's like babysitting being around you! Enrique, go with him. I'll handle the men."

Still the obedient servant, Enrique nodded behind his mask. "Let's go."

🌀🌀🌀

Erwina made good time in spite of night driving and the rotten road. Even with bumps and ruts, her Mercedes delivered a solid performance. Soon the lights of the lodge appeared. Despite numerous attempts to reach Enrique, all calls had gone unanswered.

When she got to the parking lot, she looked for her brother's car and spotted it close to the lobby. No one seemed to be around, even though the lodge was lit up like a Christmas tree. Rather than announce herself by parking near the entry, she decided to stay close to the road. She made a wide turn in the lot and backed in.

Elegante let out a low whine. "Big boy, Elegante," she said. "Momentito, amor."

Her car parked, she climbed out of the driver's seat, grabbing Elegante's leash from the floorboard before opening the door. He jumped from his back seat perch to the ground, nose immediately in the air, sniffing the breeze. Erwina grabbed his leather collar, speaking to him softly while she clasped it to the leash. "You're my boy."

She led him to the edge of the parking lot in case he needed to relieve himself. "We'll find you water, Elegante."

🔲🔲🔲

Clay had noticed headlights coming into the parking lot moments earlier, about the time they'd seen the governor and Dzib come out the front entrance and wind their way towards the northern cottages.

"Where are they going?" Layla asked. "Number two?"

"Looks like it. Why both of them?"

"Silvia's probably messed up and the madame can't get her to the lodge alone," Layla said.

"Whose headlights are those? Someone pulled into the lot, then lights out."

"Hijole, are the goons back? Oh, no, just remembered, Jaime took care of them," Layla said. "They're out of commission up the road."

"Then who?" Clay asked.

"Policia?"

"I don't think they'd be coming in all secretive. Let's hold our position," Clay said.

There were no other options. The whole evening was proving to be one tiresome waiting game.

🔲🔲🔲

Erwina first considered going to the lobby to ask what room her brother was in, but with Julietta's macabre death fresh in her memory, she changed direction. She decided to snoop around the grounds, with Elegante for security. He led the way, sniffing the path and bushes as they walked.

"Clay!" Layla nudged him and whispered, "Heads up!"

He looked where she pointed. There stood a woman with a big dog. "Who is it?"

"Not sure," Layla said. "Wait, is that the governor's sister?"

Clay stared hard into the darkness as another newcomer ambled onto a scene that was becoming increasingly more crowded by the minute. "I think so. What's with the dog?"

"Protection?" Layla surmised.

"What's she doing here?"

"Looking for the governor? How would she know he was here? Wonder if she knows about the caretaker," Layla said.

"Did someone tell her Dzib and the governor are in that cottage?" Clay asked.

They'd just witnessed the two knock and disappear inside, leaving the door ajar, allowing a sliver of light to escape. Erwina and Elegante seemed drawn to it. The dog trotted a step ahead of his mistress, pulling lightly on the leash.

"I think we should follow them," Layla said. "We have to know what's up with Silvia."

Clay grabbed her hand and they crept stealthily towards cottage two.

CHAPTER 44

When the governor and Dzib entered the cottage where Silvia was being held, the mayor was first to speak. "Karina, there's been a change of plans. Torres discovered Silvia has a family. A prominent family."

"What? How would that affect tonight? We can't call this off." The madame not only provided the entertainment, she also received a cut of the prize money.

Dzib looked at the sleeping girl, lying on his bed clad only in bra and panties, snoring softly.

The governor piped up. "She's related to Slim's Pemex 'flacos.' Not one to be trifled with."

Rather than subdue the madame, the information bolstered her. "A kidnap victim?" She stared at Dzib and gave a practiced shrug. "She's worth big money."

He winced under her stare.

"I'll have you know, I'm governor of this state, and kidnapping is a crime, señora. I won't have it. Dzib, give me a hand with her clothes." Enrique pointed to the dress lying at the foot of the bed.

Begrudgingly, Dzib retrieved the dress. He held it up, fondling the soft fabric between his fingers, sniffing at the lingering scent of Silvia's perfume. "Well, let's get her in it, Karina."

The madame shook her head, throwing the mayor major shade. "You're on your own."

"Don't be a puta," Dzib said flippantly.

Karina may have been slender but she was one hundred percent muscle. Many a night she'd carried drunken girls up stairs and held off tiresome suitors.

"You puta de Madre!" she swore, fists clenched, white knuckles showing. "You're lucky I'm not gonna whoop your sorry ass. Help yourself." She stalked away, heading towards the baño, grabbing her purse in the process and slamming the door behind.

"Hold her up!" Enrique commanded, unruffled by the bickering. "Hand me her dress."

The two of them pushed and pulled the girl to a halfway sitting position against the wall. She slumped back down, like a spineless rag doll. After two more unsuccessful attempts, they finally managed to prop up her wobbly head. Enrique was trying to force the dress over it when the door swung open and the governor's sister walked into the room, followed by a very large dog.

"Enrique!" she screamed, as she watched her brother fumble with a flimsy dress over an unclothed woman lying on a bed. "What are you doing to that girl? How dare you undress a sleeping woman! And you! You …you …mayor!"

Her brother shrank back, unprepared to see his sister at the Boca Laguna, where a weekend sex party with under age girls would soon be in full swing three hundred meters away.

Erwina glared at the mayor. "Did you kill my poor Julietta?"

311

"Shut your trap, puta!" Dzib spat out the words. "That was Torres. He was being blackmailed." With fists clenched, poster boy for emasculated men after the madame's sharp rebuke, he took a menacing step towards Erwina.

Elegante let out a low but powerful growl, then went for the closest thing at eye level, the mayor's huevos. In an attempt to step backwards, Dzib stumbled against the bed. He screamed as the dog attacked him, snarling and pulling at the crotch of his pants. He tried to push the dog off, using his hands for cover, in a desperate struggle to protect the family jewels from Elegante's gnashing teeth. With that move, the dog went for an arm, tugging so hard he pulled Dzib off balance. His next leap brought the mayor to the floor. The governor and Erwina watched in horror as dog and mayor writhed in locked combat, Dzib's mangled, bleeding hands now shielding his neck. Elegante continued to grapple with the victim, aggressively moving towards the mayor's throat.

"Elegante!" Erwina screamed, to no avail. The mayor was a moving target. A blood curdling scream came from Dzib's mouth but only for a brief second.

"Elegante! No!" Erwina screamed again. Blood splattered everywhere.

"Enrique, pull him off!"

"He's your dog, Erwina! He only listens to you!"

"Elegante!"

Hearing the outcry, Clay ran up the cottage steps, Glock in hand, with Layla behind. The bloody scene was straight out of a horror flick. Undeterred by the chaos, Clay passed the gun to Layla and lunged for the girl, scooping her up in his arms. "Out! Out!" he shouted. "I got her!"

The screams brought the madame from the bathroom, towel in one hand and a small revolver in the other. Unfazed by the gun, the governor tore away the towel, and ran to the side of the fallen mayor to try to stop the bleeding. Erwina had called off Elegante, now sitting on his haunches, watching. Erwina ran to the bathroom and came back with more towels; she threw them next to the mayor. When she looked up, she saw the couple from Casa Paraiso. He held the girl in his arms.

Before an astonished Erwina could mouth a word, Karina sprung the question. "Who are you? What are you doing?" she demanded, ignoring the mayor's body jolting from loss of blood not a meter away. She pointed the gun at Clay; one miscalculation and the girl would be lost in the crossfire.

"Leave her—she's mine," Karina said, training the revolver on Clay.

Layla pushed Clay away to avoid him looking down a gun barrel. His task was singular: to whisk Silvia out the door. She looked back and saw Karina's deadly stare. "Hurry," she pleaded. "Hurry!"

Silvia's body, drugs fully ingested, was dead weight. When Clay swung the girl around, her legs knocked against the door, hindering his attempt to exit.

"Where do you think you're going?" the madame said with contempt. "Hold it!"

Layla couldn't take her eyes off the gun clasped in the the madame's hand. To go for it would be suicide.

"Run! Run!" Layla said.

Finally, Silvia's legs undone from the bang-up at the door, with girl in arms, Clay dashed outside and began running towards the cottage. Without another look at the bloody scene, Layla followed.

"Call Pedro and Jaime!" Clay yelled.

"She has a gun. Can't do both!" Layla shouted back.

A shot whizzed by her head. "Chinga! She's following us!" Layla shouted, realizing the madame was in pursuit, gun at the ready. Another shot rang out.

Clay continued to race towards the cottage, carrying Silvia's unwieldy body. The sound of another shot pierced the night.

"Gotta handle this." Layla stopped, her eyes having adjusted to the darkness. Judging by the trajectory of Karina's shots, the madame's had not. Layla stepped to the side of the path, using a hibiscus bush as cover. The madame ran like a crazy person, the gun swinging wildly from left to right, trying to catch up with Clay, who, even though carrying a body, ran like an Olympian. Though unfamiliar with the Glock, Layla took aim. The first shot surprised Karina but missed the mark.

"Puta!" she screamed, looking about, unsure where her assailant was hidden. "I'll get you!"

The madame darted down the same path Layla had traveled, gun aimed level with Layla's head by sheer coincidence, coming very near her cover.

Layla's move was genius in its simplicity—she stuck out her leg. The madame stumbled and Layla rushed in, pushing hard against the woman's body, accelerating the fall. Karina started to flail, first dropping onto one knee, losing her balance. She rolled down the embankment, unable to control the increasing speed of her fall. The gun fired, there was a scream, followed by a shriek.

"Puta! You puta!"

Layla didn't plan to check on the madame's wounds. She could see Clay carrying Silvia up ahead, just before he rounded the last cottage.

Layla jogged—winded—towards cottage eighteen, pulling the phone from her front pocket, trying to focus and run at the same time. She rounded the second-to-last cottage, stood against it—breathless—peering behind to see if anyone had followed. She saw no sign of the madame.

At the cottage, the door was slightly ajar. Clay had gone inside but no lights were on. Layla could make out Silvia's silhouette lying on the bed. Clay emerged from the bathroom. "Can we put this towel around her?" he asked.

"Give me a minute. Calling Jaime."

"Jaime, the mayor's dead. The madame who was guarding Silvia fell on her gun. She's lying on the path by the cottages, wounded if not dead."

"Boss, I couldn't stay in the car when I heard the first shots," Jaime said. "I'm close to the lobby, outside. I see some woman and a dog run up the stairs. I stopped dead in my tracks. The woman looks pissed off. She's carrying a gun and starts screaming for Torres at the top of her lungs. He comes out, with this weird mask on top of his head. She sees him and by this time all these girls come out, too. They're practically naked and they're gaping at what's going on.

"She looks at them, at him, and she freaks out, starts waving the gun and screaming, 'Who are these girls? What have you done? You killed Julietta!'

"This huge dog pulling a leash is watching her. Then he finds a corner, lies down and starts licking his paws. Torres is a deer in the headlights. There're all these guys dressed in fancy suits wearing masks, and everyone's yelling.

315

A real scene. The men stream out of the ballroom, running for their cars. The girls have moved back inside, looking for a place to take cover. Some guy's yelling at them, trying to round 'em up but they're everywhere. It's a circus.

"She screams again, 'Torres! Torres! You scum! You and that mayor ruined my brother!' He doesn't answer. He's in this zone, staring at her. Then he pulls out a gun and says like he's asking a waiter for a glass of water, real calm like, 'Put it down, Erwina. Don't be stupid.' She goes ape-shit—she's got a gun in her hand and it's pointed right at him. She yells, 'Stupid? Stupid?' She fucking aims and shoots him! He collapses. Looked like he got it in the chest. The girls scream, freak out, they're jumping up and down now. You must have heard them."

"Torres is dead? The mayor got it, too. Are the businessmen gone?" Layla asked.

"Yeah, it was a mass exodus. Wait a minute. The governor's going into the ballroom now. He's looking at the woman and they're talking, she's still holding the gun. She's walking over to a table and putting it down. She's motioning to the girls, and asking the young guy something."

"Listen, we need help to get Silvia to your car."

"So, you got the girl?" Jaime asked.

"Yes," Layla said.

"What about the boat?"

"Car's faster. It sounds like the governor's the last man standing, " Layla said.

"The governor just left the ballroom. The girls are crying. Man, it's a floor show!"

"We gotta get outta here with Silvia. Bring the car to the cottage."

"Sure. How is she?" Jaime asked.

"Drugged but fine. She'll be better when she's in the car, and so will we."

"Ojalá," Jaime said. "What about the boat guy?"

"I'll let him know we got a ride and he can take the panga back to Muyil," Layla said.

"I'll be right there, boss."

CHAPTER 45

"Find Enrique, Elegante, go, go!" Erwina told the German Shepherd. He stood, looked at his mistress, and cocked his head to the side. "Find Enrique, big boy."

The dog dashed out of the lobby into the darkness. Erwina walked over to Torres' body. She looked down at his face, head rolled to one side; blood was beginning to pool beneath his torso from the shot to the chest. A few girls had gathered around, both nosy and panicked by the night's cataclysmic events. Some averted their eyes, others couldn't look away. Erwina knelt and gingerly checked for a pulse. She pushed herself up and looked at the girls staring at her. Some were whimpering. Manuel came to ask if she needed help.

"Find towels, I guess, and something to cover him."

He was back in moments with towels and a tablecloth. Erwina watched as he draped it over the body. He placed the armful of bar towels on the floor where the blood had pooled.

"What's going on here?" she asked, coming to her senses. "What are you girls doing? You have no clothes on!"

A few started to cry. Erwina took another look at the cloth that draped Torres and moved away. Her attention shifted to a near-naked girl who stood beside her. "How old are you?"

"Fourteen."

"Why aren't you dressed?" Erwina asked.

The girl dropped her head, embarrassed, and covered her breasts with an arm. She turned around and pointed at Manuel, who was trying to make himself invisible. "He knows."

With keys in hand, Manuel looked ready to make an exit.

"Young man, young man. Come back here. What's your name?"

Losing his usual saunter, he walked over to Erwina. "Manuel, señora."

"Your full name."

He told her before she continued her questions. "Why are these girls nearly naked? What's going on?"

"Karina could tell you," he said.

"The woman in the cottage, with the girl?"

"Yes."

"I don't know where she is, so you tell me."

"It was a party for businessmen," he said.

"What kind of party? These girls—these children—aren't clothed. Tell me why."

He had the shame to drop his head. "It was a sex party. The mayor sponsored them."

"Oh my God! What Olivia Cache wrote about in *Por Esto*. The Cancun pedophile ring. I thought it was over. Are these girls sex slaves?"

A few started to whimper, and in moments many were crying their eyes out. "Yes!" one shouted. "We were kidnapped and sold to Karina."

"Sold? Like cattle? Who's Karina?"

"The madame," one of the older ones said. "Tonight was for Cancun businessmen."

"How often are these?" Erwina asked.

"Every couple months."

"Who runs them?"

"The mayor, but Torres gave him the contact list. It was for favors," a girl explained.

"Manuel, did you know all this?"

Again, he hung his head. "Yes, señora, but I couldn't do anything. I was told if I didn't work for the madame, they'd kill me and my family."

Footsteps from behind made her turn. It was Enrique. "Torres is dead," she said, stating the obvious. "He had a gun and I shot him." She pointed to the weapon that had fallen near the dead man's body and looked down at the still-warm gun, heavy now, in her own hand. "Enrique, tell me you weren't a part of this."

The outline of the body of his lifelong friend lay under a restaurant tablecloth, feet protruding at one end. He said, "Put down the gun, Erwina. Over there." He motioned to a table.

"What about these girls?" Erwina demanded. "You're better than this." She laid the gun on a table filled with plates of food, empty glasses, crumpled napkins.

"Where's the madame?" Erwina asked.

"Shot dead, out on the grounds. Must have been the couple. They rescued the kidnapped girl."

"We should let these girls go," Erwina said. "Have the driver take them to Tulum, get the madame's phone so they can call their parents. From a safe place. Who was the girl?"

"Someone important from Mexico City. She and her boyfriend, the banker, were kidnapped by Torres and Dzib's henchmen. Torres was co-opted by the cartel and then along came the banker, piling on more. Torres got it from both sides and was in a dangerous position. He tried to pull me in."

"Where's the banker?" Erwina asked.

"Oh. Gotta see if he's still alive. After the kidnapping, they beat him to a pulp. He's in Torres' cottage. He wore a wire to frame MBC's CEO for laundering, and Torres suspected the DEA had flipped him in exchange for witness protection. But Torres—he was a marked man either way."

"These girls have to go before we call Tulum police, Enrique, but state federales will be here soon. When I found Julietta"—her voice broke at the mention of the girl's name—"I called and told them where to find her body. I drove here to tell you because I couldn't reach you."

"I know. I'm sorry, Erwina."

"Manuel," she called the driver to the table. "Can I trust you to take these girls to a safe place in Tulum, let them call their families?"

"There's too many for one van," he said.

"I can drive," one of the older girls said, eavesdropping.

"That will work," she said, nodding at her before turning towards her brother. "Enrique, find the madame's purse and look through Torres' cottage for cash so I can give the girls whatever we can find before the police come. They've been through living hell. And Manuel, if you don't call me from Tulum, I'll send the police for you, understand? Enrique, what about the mayor?"

"It's a mess in there. I covered his body."

"Oh, God. What a scene," she said, shaking her head and glancing at Elegante, back in the corner, licking his paws. "We'll call *Por Esto* from Chetumal. I want to talk to the reporter myself."

"I'll be back with whatever money I find and the driver can get the girls out of here."

"But Enrique, one thing," Erwina said, her faculties kicking in before he left the ballroom. "You were never here."

"I'm here, Erwina, all the girls see me."

"Listen, you only came after I called you and told you about Julietta. That's when you came. Did you know that banker well?"

"No. That was left to Torres. I wasn't in the loop."

"Torres, Dzib, the madame. Dead. And the banker, if he lives—he can't associate you with any wrongdoing. Believe me, there's plenty of blame to spread around—you don't have to be part of it.

"Check on the banker, Enrique, and when you return, we'll make the calls—police, ambulance, and the federales. We'll let these girls go. They've had enough trouble. Get them back to their families. Hurry," she said.

CHAPTER 46

Jaime brought the car around to the bottom of the parking lot where Clay and Layla waited, Silvia cradled in Clay's arms. Layla had called Pedro, releasing him from his duties, promising that Gloria would have the rest of his money the next day.

Layla had stripped one of the beds in the cottage, grabbing a sheet and bedspread to wrap around the girl. Even though the night was warm, Silvia occasionally shivered once she lay stretched out across Layla's lap in Jaime's back seat.

When they were a half hour from Tulum, Silvia began to whimper. The night was still dark, but the moon had shifted position, as had the girl. She struggled to get her arms free from the bedspread. Layla assisted, pulling it down so she could better move her upper torso. She placed an arm around the girl's shoulder.

"Silvia, Silvia," she said. "Can you hear me? I'm a friend of your tia, Alma. My name is Layla. We saved you from the men in the Escalade."

"Where am I?" she protested loudly, crying out. "Where am I?"

Jaime stared straight ahead and Clay glanced discreetly backwards.

"Don't worry. You're safe," Layla said. "Do you remember anything?"

"That scary lady. She was going to get me dressed, but gave me drugs first."

"She's gone. You'll never see her again," Layla promised.

"And those awful men kidnapped us. Francisco ..." her voice broke when she said his name. "Where's Francisco?"

"He's at Boca Laguna Lodge."

"Where? Where are we?"

"We're in the biosphere, Si'an Ka'an. Far away from the people who kidnapped you."

"Is Francisco okay?"

"I'm not sure, Silvia."

A sob escaped. "Oh, God, I remember what those men did to him."

"Yes, we know. Your aunt sent me to find you. I had help from Jaime, who's driving, and your friend Gabriella, and Clay," she nodded towards the Canadian in the front seat.

"Where are we going?"

"In fifteen minutes we'll be in Tulum at my hotel. I'll call Alma from there, and Gabriella, to let them know you're safe."

"When will we find out about Francisco?"

"Soon," Layla stalled. "But right now, let's take care of you. Lie back and get some rest."

༚༚༚

By the time they arrived at Analisa y José's, Silvia was sitting up in the back seat. At the hotel room, Layla checked her phone before phoning Alma. She saw a message from Martín and accessed it, then she made the call to Alma and put it on speakerphone.

"Tia," Silvia said, her voice still shaky. "I was so scared. I thought I'd been kidnapped for ransom."

"No, mi amor. It was more complicated than that. I don't think they figured out who you were. Gracias á Dios," Alma said.

"What was Francisco involved in?" Silvia asked.

"He was laundering money for his bank and various partners. Two of them are dead, confirmed by the police," Alma said.

"How is he?"

"He's in intensive care in Cancun."

"Oh, Tia …" She began to sob.

"Silvia, we'll keep close watch on him. He managed to alert the authorities about the corruption by the governor and the banks and others."

"He wore a wire for the DEA," Silvia said.

"Yes, he did, and he taped conversations about money laundering with the Quintana Roo governor before you were both kidnapped. That'll lead to indictments of Enrique Hernandez while he's still in office."

"If Francisco lives, will he go to prison?"

"I don't know," Alma said, "but because of this kidnapping mess, a sex ring using underage girls and run by Cancun businessmen was uncovered. Apparently those three, the Tulum mayor, Torres, and the governor, were deep into a number of illegal dealings. The only one still alive is the governor, who has denied any wrongdoing, but they will demand a scapegoat. All his corrupt activities will be exposed. He stole thousands of hectares of land in Quintana Roo worth millions, then sold it off and banked the money in Panama. They'll throw the book at him. As will I, in the newspaper."

Silvia began to cry softly. Layla gave her a gentle hug. "Alma, I'm going to tuck Silvia in for the night. It's late."

"I'll see you tomorrow at the airport," Alma said. "You have my arrival time. Will we see you in Mexico City?"

Layla glanced at Clay, who had wandered onto the deck and was slouching back in his chair, legs outstretched, eyes closed, as worn out as she.

"Not right away. I got a call. Business calls me back to Guadalajara, but on my next pass through, I'll make arrangements."

"Layla, how can I thank you?" Alma asked.

"I'm just glad it worked out. Did they find out any more about the girls that the governor's sister reported?"

"No. After discovering her caretaker's body at the villa, she drove to the lodge to find her brother and tell him, but said he wasn't there. She saw men running from the building and naked girls in the lobby. She told them to leave and they drove off before the authorities arrived," Alma said. "She saved them—they were sex slaves."

"Gabriella took photos of the attendees' sign-in sheets. That'll corroborate the sister's story," Layla said. "I saw the girls myself—it was a sex party, plain and simple. These young girls, what I've seen here and elsewhere, what they've been put through. Stolen from their barrios, used and abused for sex … there should be a law to … to hold these culprits accountable."

"There is a law, Layla. It's rarely enforced, though."

"Listen, Alma, I'm going to make sure Silvia's comfortable. We'll see you tomorrow at the airport, okay? Ciao."

Clay drifted in from the deck and peeked into Layla's bedroom where Silvia had gone to lie down. He closed the door and turned to look at Layla. "Guadalajara? Fact or fiction?"

Layla raised an eyebrow. She gave Clay a meaningful look and reached for his hand, pulling him in for a tender hug. She turned her face up to his. "Work," she said.

"Layla, Layla," Clay said, gently brushing back her hair as he gazed into her eyes. "You know I'm going to miss you."

Their kiss was so passionate, it left her breathless. "We have tonight," she said, getting comfortable in his arms, "and every chance we get after that."

THE END

Spanish Glossary

Adelante: Enter/come in/move it
Almendrón: Almond tree
Ándale: Onward/moving forward
Antojitos: Appetizers
Aqui: Here

Baño: Bathroom
Barrio: Neighborhood
Basta: Enough!
Bienvenidos: Welcome
Boca Paila: Area in Si'an Ka'an Reserve known for fishing, bridge
Bodega: Warehouse/store room
Bueno: Hello/used when answering phone – or good
Buenas tardes: Good afternoon
Buenos dias: Good morning
Buenos noches: Good evening

CDMX: Ciudad de Mexico, short for Mexico City
Cabrón: Dumbass

Café negro: Black coffee

Calle: Street

Cálmate: Calm down

Carga: Cost or price

Casa: House

Cédula: Mexican identity card

Cenote: Natural freshwater sinkhole common in Yucatán

Cerveza: Beer

Ceviche: Seafood marinated in lime

Chacá: Type of tree used for fences

Chetumal: Capital of Quintana Roo, bordering Belize

Chiapas: Mexico's southernmost state with large indigenous population

Chica: Sweetie, honey

Chinga!: Disparaging exclamation

Chit: Tree used for making palapas

Chunyaxche: Maya pyramid site also known as Muyil, south of Tulum

Ciao: Bye (Italian but frequently used in Mexico)

Claro: Certainly

Cocina: Kitchen

Cojones: Part of a man's anatomy

Como esta?: How are you?

Como no?: Why not?

Como siempre: Like always

Cuernavaca: City 1-1/2 hours north of Mexico City

Cuidado: Be careful

Culiacan: City, Sinaloa state, on Mexican west coast, head of cartel ops

DF: Slang for Mexico City
Dia de los Muertos: Day of the Dead
Dónde: Where

Ejido: Land grant, gifted to citizens by Mexican government
El centro: Center
El jefe: The bos
Esta aqui?: Are you here, is it here
El Viejo: The old one
Escarcega: Town 300 miles east of Chetumal in Campeche

Federales: Mexican federal police (similar to state troopers)
Fel. Carillo Puerto: City 60 miles south of Tulum
Fincas: Farms
Flacos: Youngsters

Gracias: Thank you
Gracias á Dios: Thanks be to God
Guapo: Handsome

Hacienda: Large villa
Hasta mañana: Until tomorrow (good bye)
Hectare: 2.5 acres of land
Hermana: Sister
Hermano: Brother
Hijole!: Good grief (or stronger)

Hola: Hi
Hoy: Today
Huevos: Slang for a man's lower anatomy
Huipiles: Maya woman's cultural dress

Ja ja ja: Yeah yeah yeah
Jefe: Boss

Ladrón: Thief
Listo: Ready, or one can be listo, as in very "together"
Lo siento: Sorry
Loco: Crazy
Los malos: Slang for cartels
Los pistolas: The guns
Los politicos: Politicians

MBC: Mexico Bank Corporation (fictitious)
Manaña: Tomorrow
Mangalar: Mangrove swamps
Maricón: Homosexual
Merida: Colonial city of one million in Yucatán
Mi amor: My love
Milpa: Maya cornfield
Momento: One moment, please
Mucho gusto: The pleasure is mine
Muerto: Dead
Municipio: Municipality
Muyil: Pueblo south of Tulum, access to Si'an Ka'an lagoons

NAFTA: North American Free Trade Agreement

Nada: Nothing

Nada mas: Nothing more

Narca: Female drug dealer

Negocios: Business

Niña: Little girl

No toca: Don't touch

OXXO: Mexican 7-11 style corner grocery store

Ojalá!: By the grace of God

Palapa: Roof or structure made from palm leaves

Panga: Mexican fishing boat

Pareo: Women's sarong like wrap

Patrón: Person in charge, undisputed leader

Pemex: Mexico's nationalized gas and oil company

Pendejo: Dumbass

Pequeña: Small

Perro: Dog

Pibil: Maya chicken recipe

Pinche: Used as pejorative adjective

Playa del Carmen: Riviera Maya city 50 miles south of Cancun

Plaza: Town square, or in cartel language, territory

Policia: Police

Por favor: Please

Por fin: At last

Por supuesto: Of course

Presta nombre: Signature on a land title that disguises true owner of record

Pronto: Right away

Pueblo: Town

Punta Allen: Pueblo at tip of Si'an Ka'an Reserve road, 30 miles from Tulum

Puta: Disparaging comment on women

Puta de Madre: Disparaging remark

Que bueno: How great

Que paso?: What's happening?

Que tal?: What's happening?

Quien esta?: Who is it or who is there

Q. Roo: Abbreviation for Quintana Roo, state where Cancun is located

Ranchera: Mexican music genre

Refrescos: Soft drinks

Rojo: Red

Sala: Living room

Salbute: Small tortilla of shredded turkey, cabbage, pickled onions

Salud: To your health (usually as a toast)

Sascab: Sand used on streets in Yucatan

Selva: Jungle

Si'an Ka'an Reserve: One million hectare biosphere reserve, UNESCO site

Sinaloa, Mexico: Stronghold of Culiacan Cartel activity, state on west coast

Soy: I am

Suave: Smooth/also smoothed concrete, typical in Mexico buildings

Telenovela: Mexican TV series

Terraza: Terrace

Tienda: Small store

Tinaco: Water/rain catch on roof

Tia: Aunt

Tio: Uncle

Tipos: Guys

TJ: Short for Tijuana, border city between Mexico and US

Todo bien: All is well

Tulum: Pyramid site and popular resort town 65 miles south of Cancun

UNAM: National Autonomous University of Mexico

Verdád: True

Yo comprendo: I understand

Yo no se: I do not know

Zapóte: Exotic Mexican hardwood

Zócalo: Town square or plaza

ACKNOWLEDGMENTS

My sincere gratitude to my editor, Jennifer Silva Redmond. Special thanks to Jill Wyatt Logan of Todos Santos, Baja, Mexico, for the use of her remarkable artwork, *Palm Boat with Blue Shadows,* and thanks to the team at Damonza for their cover graphic talents. Thanks to Kevin Berry for his input and advice.

Thanks to Carmen Amato for her encouragement and support, and also thank you to Nicholas Kitchel for his digital mastery and assistance.

Grateful thanks to Paul Zappella whose patience and support helped me, as always, to keep on keeping on.

ABOUT THE AUTHOR

Jeanine Kitchel's love of Mexico led her to a fishing village on the Mexican Caribbean coast where she bought land, built a house, and opened a bookstore. A former journalist, she wrote travel articles for newspapers and Mexico websites before branching into fiction. Look for her travel memoir, *Where the Sky is Born: Living in the Land of the Maya*, and *Maya 2012 Revealed: Demystifying the Prophecy*, a journalistic view of the Maya 2012 calendar phenomenon.

Book one, *Wheels Up—A Novel of Drugs, Cartels and Survival,* began Layla's struggle. Stay tuned for book three in the trilogy by contacting the author and sign in for updates through her website at *www.jeaninekitchel.com.*

If you enjoyed *Tulum Takedown: A Wheels Up Yucatán Thriller*, please leave a review on Amazon.

Reviews provide helpful insights to others and help them find new authors. No matter how short, a review will be greatly appreciated.

Thank you in advance.

Made in the USA
Middletown, DE
20 September 2021